MONSTER MAKERS, INC.

MONSTER MAKERS, INC.

by
Laurence Yep

ARBOR HOUSE
New York

To Gabriel,
A new beginning

Manufactured in the United States of America

10 9 8 7 6 5 4 3 2 1

Library of Congress Cataloging-in-Publication Data

Yep, Laurence.
  Monster Makers, Inc.

  I. Title.
PS3575.E6M6   1986   813'.54   86-14042
ISBN: 0-87795-831-9

·1·

When the com buzzed, I slapped the plate and answered, "Hello, Monster Makers, Incorporated. Yes, Virginia, there is a Godzilla."

The com screen cleared to display a tourist in her twenties. She was wearing an orange feathered vest and had peacock-blue swirls painted on her head in a clumsy imitation of the local women. "Do you really have Godzilla on your island?"

I must have talked to a thousand tourists, and not one of them had come up with a new question. But Dad had concocted the menagerie for the publicity. He thought we'd get a few investors that way, but so far we hadn't even had a nibble. "Yes, ma'am. We have a number of the classic monsters in miniature."

"Oh." Her voice fell in disappointment. "You mean he's not full size?" They always seem surprised to find that he isn't thirty stories high.

I counted to ten quickly. After all, the "full-size" Godzilla had been a human actor in a suit. "No, ma'am. None of our fabricants is over one meter high. What if they got loose? You wouldn't want them trashing New Benua."

She wrinkled her forehead. "Can't you build them bigger?"

"We can't change scientific laws, ma'am. Increase the size of a Godzilla and you increase the stress on the bones geometrically."

She blinked. "Come again?"

I sighed. "Say we double the size of our Godzilla. Then the stress on his bones is four times what it is on the bones of our current model."

She fluffed her vest. "Why don't you just build one with bigger bones, then?"

Dad's assistant, Singh, leaned on the top of the com screen. "No, no, dear boy. You simply cannot teach genetic engineering to someone who still thinks the stork brings babies."

"What did you say?" the woman demanded.

Before I could stop him, Singh had come around the desk and butted in between me and the screen. The tips of his big handlebar mustache twisted up when he saw how cute she was. "Madam, can I count on your discretion? We must build them small to keep the feed bills low."

I could hear the satisfaction in the woman's voice. This was something she could understand. "Oh. Why didn't you say so in the first place?"

"My associate here is overzealous about guarding secrets." Singh went on smoothly. "Visiting hours are every Wednesday from two to four. You just missed the tour this week."

"Are those Terran standard hours?" the woman asked busily as if she were writing down the information.

"No, madam, local. Carefree only has a twenty-hour day." Singh's dark face split into a Pan-like leer so I knew he meant business. "I do hope you'll come next week."

There was a nervous giggle. "If there's time."

"I shall be devastated if you do not visit us." Singh pressed his fingers against the com plate and turned it off. "This job is simply wasted on you, dear boy."

I kicked back in my chair and rested my heels on the desk. "Smooth, real smooth with the ladies. I can see why you're busy every weekend."

Singh turned around. He hadn't had time to freshen up his body paint. "Sometimes on the week nights too."

I clicked my tongue. "Tsk, tsk. It's a wonder you find time for work."

Singh chucked me under the chin. "My work consists mainly of correcting your mistakes."

Singh's pet urya plopped its enthusiastic hundred kilos onto my lap. It was about a meter and a third long and covered with long golden hair like a collie—except this collie had sensor pods on eye stalks that grew from the sides of its head. Its sharp blue muzzle parted and the long purple tongue lapped at my face.

"Ugh, this thing's got the worst breath in ten light-years." I tried to shove it away, but the urya caught my wrist in its small blue paws. Originating on Monsotl about two light-years away, they're all the rage as pets in the Rim worlds, though I've never particularly liked them. They remind me of hairy waist-high rats that have specialized in obsequiousness.

"Now, now." Singh wagged a finger at me. "Ladadog likes you."

I gave a yelp as Ladadog's opposable thumb pressed a nerve. Lately, he always seemed to do some such annoying thing whenever he was showing affection. I forced the little beast to let go of my wrist. "Well, I don't like him. I thought you sent him to obedience school."

"I did." Singh scratched underneath Ladadog's chin. "He's been like a new animal ever since he attended Madam Ilsa's Academy."

"You could have fooled me." I grabbed Singh's precious pet by his identification collar and dumped him from my lap.

Screeching, the urya ran and clung to Singh's waist. "Just because you prefer that vicious weasel to genuine affection—"

"You know Sam is a unique design," I snapped. "She could be a big help on a world like Carefree. It's ninety percent ocean."

"The ability to swim isn't as important as the ability to love." He calmed Ladadog with several pats of his hand. "Sam tried to bite Ladadog just now."

I jerked my head at the shaggy barricade. "Well, he's always throwing things at her."

"He hasn't hit her, has he?"

"No, but it isn't for lack of trying."

He slapped my feet off the desk. "Well, despite your bad taste in pets, your dad sent me to spell you. He wants to see you."

I scratched behind my ear unhappily. He almost never wanted to see me during the day. "What voice was he using, Dr. Jekyll or Mr. Hyde?"

Singh was studying his reflection in a window. "Definitely Mr. Hyde. Best put on your armor, dear boy."

I got up slowly, trying to remember what I might have done wrong. "Just my luck. It's still at the cleaner's."

Singh plopped down into the chair. "Then you should be ready to duck." Ladadog leaped into his arms and cuddled against him.

I had no sooner stepped outside than my legs were knocked out from underneath me and I was lying flat on my back, staring into Sam's otter-ish old-woman's face. A meter long, she was fifty kilos of muscle and curiosity wrapped up in ginger-colored fur. She wriggled tufted eyebrows that were ten centimeters long—almost as long as her whiskers.

"No, girl," I scolded her, "you had your breakfast."

In some ways, I could see why Singh would protest about Sam. She was mischief cubed—and contrary to boot. But she had been Mom's special design and her own particular pet. After Mom died, everyone—including Sam—assumed she was mine. But as a pet she ranked down there with Cygnan raptors, tax collectors, and other nosy pests.

Sam defiantly twisted her lean, slender body around, and a webbed forepaw hooked the pocket of my shorts so she could reach inside with her other forepaw.

I aimed a finger at her. "Cut that out, or you lose those paws."

Sam paid about as much attention to me as she would have to a chigger buzzing around her head. She just went sniffing all around. "See? You're too suspicious." She had an ID collar similar to Ladadog's. I grabbed hold of it now and pulled her off me.

A snort told me what she thought of that. In a well-run world, she would have found choco-bars in every pocket.

Still, Sam didn't hold a grudge. She padded right along beside me in that funny, humping walk of hers. She had to haul herself along mainly on her forepaws, arching her back so that her rear legs, designed more for powerful swimming strokes than for strolling, could tiptoe along.

Though it was only morning, the heat was already rising from our barren little island. The sharp volcanic rocks looked like fangs, so that it almost seemed as if the island itself were breathing on the whitewashed dome of the com room. Beyond the com room to the south the dock floated, with the slider tied to it like a peaceful floating milkaroo.

A hundred meters to the north I could see the blue-tinted air that marked the force field around the "critter" pen. A chigger buzzed into the field and disappeared with a flash, though a bigger creature would have just gotten a little shock. None of our critters had collars because Dad had designed them without the ability to swim. Even if they got loose, they could not escape from the island.

Behind the field an Aldebaran chomper wallowed in a pan of dirt. Dad had fabricated a large demo to break down stone and coral, aerate the soil, and provide protein for pioneer farmers, but like a lot of his designs it had never caught on. No one wanted to find a giant worm poking its multiple mouths out of the potato patch.

People hadn't gone for his line of prehistoric pets either. The baby ankylosaurs with their clubbed tails were hell on furniture, and the mini-mastodon, Sheila, shed all over. As a result, we just lumped them in there because they fit with the monsters.

And there, perched on a rock, his face turned up to the sun, sat the prize of the menagerie: Godzilla. A third of a meter high, he was bigger than most of the fabricants who bumped, stumped, and slouched around him. When he saw me, he jumped off his rock and stomped over, tail swinging, paws clawing at the air—looking ready to trample down whole cities.

When a little duck-billed dinosaur blocked his path, he rocked up on his feet menacingly and raised his paws. The dinosaur just stood there. Godzilla reared his head back and opened a mouth full of sharp triangular teeth, but the dinosaur still held its ground. Taking a deep breath, Godzilla put his whole soul into an angry, earth-shaking *Fwee-ee-eep*.

Dad swears it wasn't a design flaw. He says that something—perhaps an allergy—was affecting Godzilla's vocal cords. Whatever was wrong, the duck-billed dinosaur wasn't the least bit impressed and simply shoved Godzilla out of the way. Godzilla's fierceness was all show.

Godzilla indignantly waddled up to the fence and gave a little whine. His brown eyes stared at me painfully.

"What's the matter, boy. Too much gas?" I asked.

Godzilla belched and breathed out a thin ribbon of fire, accidentally toasting another chigger.

"Sorry, boy. I'll have to check you out later." Another hundred meters on and I had to skirt Mom's garden, which filled the air with the smell of rotting kelp. She had built the rock wall herself with volcanic slabs and then built up the soil with pulverized rock and kelp. Since Mom had died five years ago, Dad had given up on the vegetables and encouraged only the flowers. They were mostly small red blooms growing on rubbery pink-and-green stems.

I called Sam away from the garden wall. "You know better than to nose around there. Dad would skin you alive." I added, "And me too."

Another hundred meters and I was at Pandemonium. That was what Mom had nicknamed Dad's lab. It was a prefab surplus bubble some hundred meters in diameter and set to float so just the top was above the surface; we could sink it when one of the frequent typhoons swept through and ride out the storm safely under the waves.

Dad was outside. He was a big man who kept fit by swimming and riding me like a drill sergeant. The heat made the steam rise from his wet shorts and top, though he'd pulled on his old marine cap to protect his balding head from the suns. I tried to put on an easygoing show for Singh, but I didn't like the idea of going through one of Dad's lectures.

It's funny, but I can't remember ever his having hit me, much less raise a hand to me. He just had this way of talking and looking at me as if I was one of his genetic experiments—a failing one.

He had pulled off one of the pads that kept the globe from hitting against the rock and was squatting down, inspecting the gauges on the flotation tanks. I stepped up to him and cleared my throat. "Singh said you wanted me."

Dad went on fussing with the gauge before be finally tapped the plate. "What does this gauge read?"

Dad knew the answer perfectly well. He just wanted to prolong the agony. I leaned forward and looked at the gauge. "Ten kilos per square centimeter." I straightened up in surprise. "It should be thirty."

Dad rested an arm on top of his knee. "Right, sport. Any ideas what happened?"

"I checked the tanks just last week, Dad. They were fine."

Dad shot to his feet like a starship kicking in its boosters. "Fine? The valve's so rusty it's almost falling apart. We're lucky it's just leaking and that it didn't explode."

I knelt and looked at the valve. It was orange-red with rust, all right. "I don't understand. I just greased and cleaned them."

Dad jabbed a finger at it. "Does that look like it's been cleaned?"

"No, sir, but I—"

Dad's hand chopped at the air. "Sport, you're eighteen now. When I was your age, I was going to school and working in a factory part-time to pay the bills."

I picked up a smooth, flat stone and skipped it over the water. I was pretty good at it since that was about the only thing to do on this miserable island. "Yes, sir. I've read your bios."

Dad stuffed his hands in his shorts and rocked up and down on the balls of his feet. One corner of his mouth twisted up. Suddenly he was more like the old, calmer dad that I remembered before we came here. "Am I that bad?"

I shrugged, but I knew better than to say anything.

Dad sighed. "Last week you didn't tie up the slider. The week before that there was the fire in the com room. I'm not asking a lot, sport." He trotted out his old cliché once again. "Anything worth doing is worth doing well."

I gripped the rusty valve. "Dad, I don't understand how all these accidents have been happening."

Dad seemed to consider several replies, but from the twitching of his eyebrows I could tell he was trying to hold back his temper. "Sport," he finally said, "there are a lot of people who would be happier if we were closed down. They're just looking for an excuse. They'd love it if they could accuse us of negligence and make it stick."

"But the accidents weren't my fault."

Dad rolled his eyes wearily. "It's always someone else's fault, isn't it? When are you going to learn to accept some responsibility?"

I didn't look at him. "Too bad you can't isolate a responsibility gene. "

Dad squatted down beside me. "I just don't understand you."

I looked at the ball of my thumb. It was now covered with rust. "Child raising is an art, not a science."

Dad laid his elbows across his knees. "I'm just asking you to help out, that's all. People out here are still leery of genetic engineering. But once we show them it's safe, we'll be rich. Then we can take it easy."

"You'll never take it easy." Sam, who was something of a copycat, began to swipe at the valve. I shoved her forepaw aside.

Dad's eyes fell on Sam. "All right. What about your other chore?"

Sam butted her head against my hand so I began to stroke her hard little skull. "Her training is coming along fine, Dad."

Dad folded his arms skeptically. "Show me."

I was afraid of that. "Don't you want me to take care of the valve?"

"I'll do that myself." Dad strode over to the little pen we had set up beside Pandemonium. It measured some ten meters on each side and contained about a dozen fish—the kind called guzzlers that are covered all over with spines so Sam wouldn't be tempted to eat them. A ring floated off to one corner. The object was to teach Sam to herd the fish through the ring.

I patted Sam on the back. "All right, girl. Remember everything I taught you." Rising, I raised my hand over my shoulder. Sam's head bobbed up intently as she watched. "Go get them, girl." I brought my hand down and pointed at the fish. Sam loped along and dove into the pen with a big splash.

I said a silent prayer and then circled my hand. "Round them up, girl."

As clumsy as she might be on the land, on the blue canvas of the water, Sam was a furry, red arrow—a little auburn paintbrush, darted now here and now there. Dad just tapped his foot impatiently as Sam swam around the pen. Give Dad an individual cell and he could read its DNA the way someone else would read an address book. But he only cared about the technical aspects of his engineering—not the aesthetic.

Curling her body in swift graceful turns, Sam made ever-tightening circles around the fish. Gradually, they were forced together into a compact clump. I began to think that this time, maybe this time, she would finally do it.

Dad was standing still, intensely interested now. Of all our fabricants, Sam had the most financial promise—and so far had been the biggest disappointment.

When she had the fish bunched together, I pointed at the ring. "Come on, girl. Through here now."

But she just left the fish behind as she darted through the ring herself. As always, she wound up clowning around—this time, biting and swinging back and forth through the ring while her spiny charges simply drifted away in different directions. With a sigh, I tapped my hand against the rock to recall her.

Dad threw up his hands in disgust. "She still thinks it's a game."

Sam pulled herself out of the water, and I patted her wet, bullet-slick head. "But she's doing more."

"Her training is taking too long." Dad looked down at Sam, who was rolling on her back, begging for a scratch. "The agreement was train her to herd fish or sell her to some rich tourist as a pet."

"It's not like there's a set routine to train her." I figured that Sam had done her best. Her legs wriggled ecstatically as I leaned over and scratched her belly.

Dad was determined to make his point. "She costs too much."

"She catches almost everything she eats," I protested.

"I was talking about her snooping and her mischief." Dad jerked a thumb back toward Pandemonium. "Last week she wrecked a rack of tubes. And the week before that she bit a tourist."

"In the purse."

Dad tugged exasperatedly at the peak of his cap. "We still had to buy her a new one."

Dad was backing me into a very tight and uncomfortable corner. "She used to be just as bad when Mom was alive. You didn't say anything then."

Dad's hand chopped the air. "That was different."

I rolled Sam back and forth as she nipped playfully at my hand. I wasn't just arguing to protect Sam. I was trying to preserve this last little bit of Mom that was left in my life. "She was Mom's pet then."

"Sport, I don't like playing the villain. And I don't like losing her anymore than you do." Dad held his thumb and index finger a centimeter apart. "But we're just this far away from bankruptcy. We need money."

Dad looked serious. More serious than I had ever seen. "Sell one of the critters then," I argued desperately.

"The critters draw in tourists. They're my demos." Dad pointed an accusing finger at Sam. "She's the only creature that is useless."

"Except for me," I said sullenly.

Dad regarded me levelly. "I didn't say that. Look, you admit yourself she's a nuisance."

Whenever the value of Sam came up, I had the feeling that we were like two wounded fencers dueling. "Sure," I agreed, "but it's like Mom's garden for you. You never used to like plants. Now you're always taking care of them."

It was even harder for Dad to talk about his feelings than it was for me. "Your mom . . . well, she brought a special quality into my life, and the garden is what's left of that quality."

My hand rested on Mom's pet. "That's what Sam does for me, Dad."

Before Dad could say anything, we heard a sizzling sound like bacon frying in a pan. I twisted around to see sparks of light flying up from the pen.

"It's the fence," Dad shouted. "I told you to check it before the menagerie could get out."

"I did." I jumped to my feet, but Dad was already racing for the pen.

◆ 2 ◆

*T*he mastodon stared at me with beady little red eyes and shook her head. I eyed the sharp points on her curving tusks and found myself wishing that Dad hadn't been quite that accurate—or cheap. Dad wouldn't let us use the trank guns because he said it would use up too much trank juice.

"You little lingam!" I heard Singh swear from somewhere on the island. It didn't sound like he was having better luck than me.

The mastodon raised her trunk and trumpeted in answer—a strange sound like a bass kazoo. *Bw-wat!*

If ever there was a time for Sam to prove her worth, it was now. She had helped me work Sheila, the mastodon, among the rocks so that Sheila was trapped. But now Sam's head had begun bobbing and she was glancing elsewhere. I knew the signs well enough to know she was getting bored.

I thought if I could tell how Sam had helped me, I might get her name erased from Dad's list of disappointments—even if my name was written there in permanent ink. "Come on now, girl." I waved Sam in. "Drive her out to me."

But she hung back and eyed me like some customs officer expecting a bribe; when there wasn't any forthcoming, she simply sniffed and trotted away.

"Come back here, you little weasel," I shouted, but Sam's only answer was to shake her arched rump at me.

The yelling only made Sheila more nervous. *Phumph,* she snorted. *Bw-wa-wat!* She looked ready to charge now.

"Easy now, Sheila," I coaxed. "Easy." I edged away from the crabbing net that lay in front of me. We'd had to improvise equipment to catch the fabricants. Step by step I shuffled sideways toward my left. With each step, I let the rope to the crabbing net slip through my palms. The mastodon still watched me, but she lowered her trunk. Apparently, she didn't see me as a threat anymore.

"Come here this instant," Singh shouted to some unknown fabricant, "or I shall put you into an enormous stewpot."

The mastodon suddenly scooted for freedom, but I was ready. Just as her fat, stumpy legs brought her into the center of the circular crabbing net, I jerked at the rope so that the net rose around her.

The first problem in monster hunting is catching the monster. The second problem in monster hunting is: What do you do once you've caught it? Sheila didn't seem to mind in the least that she was in the middle of a net. She just went on—and I went with her.

I said the first thing that popped into my head, which was, "Whoa, Sheila, whoa." But if Sheila heard, she paid no attention. She just went charging on like a shaggy little tank—dragging me along like I was a butterfly. As we passed a startled Sam, I yelled, "Thanks a lot!"

I had to hop over a big rock in the middle of my path and then do a kind of jig as I got swept along a bed of gravel. Suddenly a huge rock spire loomed in front of me. I managed to angle to my right. The taut rope hit the rock with a loud *twang*. Quickly I looped the loose end over the top of the rock and tied a quick knot.

Bw-wa-at! Sheila trumpeted angrily behind me. I danced back as she circled, watching with satisfaction as she kept going round and round the rock, annoyed that the rope kept shortening as she did so.

"Help, aid, assistance, succor," Singh shrilled. I left Sheila playing ring-around-the-rosy and followed the shouting to Singh. He was standing precariously on top of a pedestal-like column of rock while underneath him a half-dozen fabricants snapped, growled, and salivated. A huge net covered both Singh and the monsters.

I cupped my hands in the shape of a megaphone around my mouth. "How did you ever get into a mess like that?"

He spread out his arms awkwardly. "Do not stand there. I have caught them."

"It looks like the other way around to me." I went back to Pandemonium and got the holocam. I didn't exactly hurry, though—more like sauntered.

When I got back, Singh was doing a little flamenco on his pedestal as he tried to keep the monsters from reaching him. "You were a trifle slow."

"I couldn't find the holocam right away." I calmly raised it and snapped several shots.

"Here now." Singh waved a net-covered hand at me. "Stop that this instant."

"I thought some of your girls would like a souvenir of you." I put the holocam safely under lock and key back in the lab and then got a trank gun. I'd had my fill of doing things the hard way. We'd already wasted the whole morning trying to chase down the fabricants. Returning to Singh, I sedated the fabricants one by one until they were all snoring peacefully at Singh's feet.

Glowering at me, he eased down from the pedestal and then made his way under the net. "I pray that one day I can repay your kindness."

"It might be more constructive to get the anti-grav sled." I reloaded the trank gun and went back to Sheila, who had managed to wind herself so thoroughly against the rock her cheek was pressed against it.

It took all her breath to give out a tiny *bw-w-at* of defiance.

"You and me both," I said, tranquilizing her.

I just wish I could have used the gun on Dad. All the time that Singh and I were carting the animals back into the pen, he was repairing the fence with this angry scowl on his face.

When we had dumped the last of our catch on the rocks, Singh steered the sled over the boundary of the fence. "Next load coming up."

"I rigged up a cattle prod." Dad pointed to a stick that lay at his feet. At one end of the stick was an electrode jury-rigged to a battery pack on a belt.

"This looks like a most proper tool." Singh eagerly belted on the pack.

"Ready?" Dad asked.

"Wait!" But it was like Dad didn't hear me. I had to jump to clear the pen before Dad switched on the force field again. As it was, my backside got a good jolt that made me jump as the field sputtered into life.

"Hey!" I protested.

"Sorry." Only he didn't look very apologetic.

I got ready for another lecture. The only real trouble I had was figuring out whether I was going to have to weather a class-one storm or just a class-ten squall. I should have had more faith in Dad. It was a class-one storm.

"The cover was loose on the control box," Dad said. "The morning mist condensed on the box and shorted out the wiring."

I fussed with the cattle prod. "Well, it wasn't my fault. That lid was down and locked."

From the way Dad straightened, you would've thought I'd used the cattle prod on him. "I certainly didn't touch it. Did you, Singh?"

Singh paused in mid-thrust as he used the cattle prod to fence with invisible enemies. "Not I."

I winced. "Which leaves only me. Only I didn't do it."

I thought Dad would really blow up then, but he was too tired and disgusted. "What am I going to do with you, sport?"

I was feeling pretty tired and disgusted too. "You could sell me with Sam."

It was the wrong thing to say, because that reminded Dad of his other major complaint. "Say, just where is Sam?"

I decided to tell half the truth. "She was helping me with the roundup."

That seemed to calm Dad down a little. "Really?" I could see his mind considering the commercial possibilities. "Show me."

But though we saw at least three monsters, there wasn't any sign of Sam until we reached Mom's garden. I shaded my eyes with my hand. "I can't understand what happened to her."

We both saw the fountain of dirt spurt up at the same time. As we ran to the wall, I was hoping that maybe it was one of the critters, but when we got to the wall, we could both see that it was Sam tearing up the garden.

Alarmed, I vaulted over the wall. "Sam, get out of there."

Sam looked up with a flower clutched between her teeth.

Dad climbed over the wall a little more deliberately. "You see? She's more trouble than she's worth."

Unfortunately, Sam thought this was some elaborate game of tag and darted all around while I chased her. "The storms have done more damage. We've always put it back to rights."

"Come here, you little pest!" Dad dove after her and wound up with his face in the dirt.

I stopped cold. "Dad. You OK?"

Dad slowly shoved himself up. His dirt-covered face had the same grim look it always has before he makes one of his important announcements. "That does it." He glared at Sam, who was busily tugging up a vine.

He was getting ready to get rid of Sam for good. I was desperately hunting for something to say when I heard the buzzing from the com room. Before we'd actually begun the hunt, I'd left the com loudspeakers on to signal across the island. "I'll get that," I said and jumped back over the wall. For once, Sam did something that I wanted without being told. She leaped after me and kept at my heels despite that funny run of hers. Maybe Dad would change his mind if she wasn't around.

"You've really done it this time," I said to her. "You're going to wind up in some rich person's kennel—or around somebody's neck as a furpiece." But Sam only loped along with that maddening and unrepentant indifference of hers.

Inside the com room, the board's lights were all blinking and it was buzzing like a hive full of wax stabbers. The first caller was a woman. "You're paying for this, Kincaid. I know it was one of your monsters that burned through my nets."

"What?" It was the first inkling that any of our beasts were off the island. "Who is this?" I asked, but the caller had signed off angrily. I supposed we'd get her name when she sent in her bill— a big bill, in all probability.

I snatched the flower from Sam's mouth. "Give me that." Sam butted her dirty head against my leg apologetically. It was as hard to stay mad at Sam as at a two-year-old kid. Sam might make a lot of trouble for me, but there wasn't a malicious bone in her body. "OK. I guess us outcasts have to stick together." And I began to stroke her head.

While I did that, I tried to figure out what had gone wrong. Dad had purposely made the menagerie demos without the ability to swim, and they'd never had any chance to learn that I'd known of.

The next caller was a man who claimed that one of our monsters had molested him while he'd been swimming. "Sir, it was purely friendly curiosity," I said. "Our creatures can't reproduce."

I could almost feel the frost rising from the com board. "Don't use your filthy mouth on me, young man." And he clicked off angrily.

So far I was really batting a thousand. I fielded another half-dozen complaints, trying to calm both the angry and the hysterical. By then, I knew that Dad had either slipped up on the design or Godzilla had been practicing paddling in the water trough. Either way, we were in big trouble. This was a public relations disaster of the first magnitude. As soon as we got all the beasts into the pen again, we had to round up Godzilla right away.

But the next call convinced me that we could not even wait that long. I found myself staring at a Kreech. His earflaps were already fanned out to show his agitation. I knew it was bad news the moment I saw him because there are only two types of Kreech: fussy and fussier.

"Hello," he said in a voice as polished as a brass doorknob.

"This is the manager of the Xanadu Arms." The Xanadu was a resort so posh that its number was unlisted. "May I speak to the Director of Public Relations?"

I didn't tell him that he was speaking not only to Director of Public Relations, but chief bottle washer and janitor too. All I said was, "Yes, sir. Speaking."

There was a pause as if he were surprised at how young I was. "I believe we have something of yours."

I had to grin at that. "That would be a good trick, considering that I've never been to your place."

"No," the manager said. "One of your beasts is on our premises. We would like him removed with all due dispatch."

I did some quick mathematics in my head. The Xanadu was over twenty kilometers away. Even if Godzilla could have swum that far, he couldn't have gone that fast. "That's impossible, sir." Then in the background, I heard shouts and screams and the crash of a tray of dishes.

The manager, however, remained unruffled. "Nonetheless, we have a small green scaly creature fricasseeing our peafowl."

"Does it have green scales and spikes on its spine?" I asked.

"I believe so." His voice faded toward the end as if he were looking up from his com. "Yes, it definitely does."

I groaned silently inside. That had to be our one and only Godzilla. He was never aggressive on our island, but even the most timid animal will change if you put it in unknown territory and scare it. "A team of our specialists will be right over," I promised. Local Dog Catcher was another one of my hats.

"Please hurry," the manager said. "We serve tea promptly at four."

I was going to suggest they hold a barbecue instead, but I didn't think the manager would be amused. "Right," I said. I made sure to keep Sam close to me while I went to find Dad. But I was sure this would take his mind off Sam herself.

Halfway to the lab, I found Singh poking around the rocks with his prod. "I have you now!" he declared in triumph.

"Another beastie?" I asked.

"Another rock shrimp." Singh smacked his lips. "We will feast tonight." He hefted the prod in his hand. "This would be most useful on a picnic." His free hand picked up a stunned rock shrimp by its tail. He added it to an already bulging bag strapped over his shoulder. Singh was certainly a good worker—especially where his stomach was involved.

I kept looking for Godzilla as I searched for Dad. But there wasn't any sign of the little monster. Dad, though, was at Pandemonium, taking out his anger on the faulty valve.

"Dad—" I began.

"Wait a moment." He grunted as he tried to loosen up the valve by pounding it with a wrench.

"It won't wait," I insisted.

Dad looked up angrily and then saw my face. "What's wrong now?"

"Can Godzilla swim?" I wondered.

"You know the answer yourself." He twisted the valve experimentally and it began to move. "Swimming isn't in the design."

"We've been getting complaints from all over," I said, "including the Xanadu Arms. I think it's Godzilla's doing."

Dad set the wrench down. "That's impossible."

I shrugged. "The manager's described a creature that's a dead ringer for Godzilla."

Dad looked away from me for a moment toward the lab. "Maybe I should have field-tested more."

"Nobody's perfect, Dad."

Dad pivoted in exasperation. "But the designs were perfect."

"No design's perfect for living creatures," I said. "Not for people or for monsters."

Dad was so busy thinking about his new problem that he missed my meaning entirely. "Well, better load the equipment into the slider." Shaking his head, he walked into the lab.

·3·

*T*he jets weren't working too well, so the slider rode low over the surface. Waves hissed and rose around the bow. Spray spattered against the windshield. Beside me, Sam gave a worried chirp.

I tried to reassure her. "It's OK, girl. Even if the jets went out, we'd float on top."

Dad had bought the slider as war surplus along with the globe that was Pandemonium. About fifty years ago when Carefree had first been settled, the Stellar Union had fought a war with the neighboring Xylk Empire. The history spools say that Xylk Empire is an elegant title the Xylk gave to their own solar system, so most folk are inclined to laugh at them. Or if the spools mention the fighting at all, they call it a border skirmish.

But it was taken seriously enough by the people on the Rim where the Stellar Union has its border. Carefree isn't the only frontier world with its share of crater holes and rusting relics. Even now, we were skirting a radioactive crater the size of our island. Little warning buoys beeped a signal to stay away.

Strange to say, we still didn't know what the enemy actually looked like. The Xylk sent out their cannon fodder—a massive species called the Rell—to fight their wars while they pulled the strings offstage. But if their slaves were anything to go by, the Xylk must have been twice as big and twice as mean.

"I wish you'd fix this old heap," Dad complained. He thumbed the com button for the dozenth time and tried to raise our island to find out how many other fabricants were still missing. He stared down at it, puzzled. "I still don't get any answer."

I left one hand on the wheel and draped my other arm over the back of my chair. "A lot of times the com can only receive, not send." I banged the top of the com more out of habit than in any hope that I could fix it that way.

Cher-er-rk? Sam gave the com a little curious pat.

"We could get in trouble with the HDF for not keeping this in running order." Just about everyone and every vehicle belonged to the HDF. The letters stood for the Home Defense Force, a fancy name for a combination posse, search and rescue force, and militia. When the Union Navy had pulled back after the Xylk War—excuse me, police action,—it had been cheaper to leave the surplus behind for the home folks. Most of the stuff was antique now, but the HDF was still good enough to give pirates a second thought.

"When can I work on this pile of junk?" I squirmed in the seat, trying to find a comfortable spot on the springy seat.

It was late afternoon by the time we reached the Xanadu Arms. A large orange marker buoy bobbed up and down in the water ahead of us. As soon as we neared it, the buoy began announcing in a sweet but firm female voice, "You are not giving the proper signal. This is a private area. Please leave."

"Interesting." Dad swiveled around in his seat to study the buoy as we passed. "It must react that way when metal enters its magnetic field."

The next buoy had the polite, frosty tones of a maître d' in a fancy restaurant who has just been undertipped. "Only guests of the Xanadu resort may be in this area. I recommend a speedy exit."

Dad was too preoccupied to worry about the message. "I wonder just how wide the magnetic field is."

I glanced at Dad. "Maybe we should wait here until some guard comes out to check."

"Nonsense." Dad shaded his eyes to see the distance between

the buoys of this second line. "The longer we wait, the more damage they might do to Godzilla."

I nervously eyed the buoys of the next line. "I'm more worried about the damage to us." But I kept on going. I wasn't going to start another argument with Dad.

The third buoy had a voice as deep and menacing as a bulldog's growl. "Trespassers will be shot."

I scratched Sam between her ears. "No doubt for the amusement of the guests."

An energy beam suddenly sizzled in front of our bow. Then it shut off. "That was a warning," the buoy warned. "The next shot will hit you."

"You made your point," I shouted to the buoy. I swung the slider around. It seemed to take forever.

"That's overreacting." Dad frowned.

I breathed a sigh of relief as we cleared the third line of buoys. "It's their property."

"But some kind of watch animal—say, an icthyosaur—would be a more effective deterrent." Dad was sitting up in his chair in excitement. There was nothing like a new idea to make him forget his troubles. "Who knows? This may have turned out to be a blessing in disguise now that they've seen a sample of my work."

"I wouldn't count my sales until they're—uh, hatched." I moved us back to a space between the second and third line of buoys and then killed the jets. We floated on the surface of the waves calmly.

A man came riding low on the waves on an armed skimmer. It wasn't much more than a disk-shaped water jet, but the noses of an automatic cannon and machine guns poked from the shield. He was in a skin-tight red uniform that proclaimed him to be a guard even before he called out, "You heard the warning. Get." The amplifier made his voice sound tinny even though it was loud.

"Your manager invited us," Dad shouted back.

"In that pile of junk?" The skeptical guard laughed and swung his skimmer to bring his cannon to bear on us.

I patted the side of the slider. "See the corporate logo? We're MMI. Monster Makers, Incorporated."

The skimmer was built for speed, not for idling, so the guard had to circle around to see the logo. "You mean that little monster is yours?"

"It's not a thing," Dad said indignantly. "It's the best genetic fabricant that money can buy."

"Yeah? Well, why didn't you call in?" the guard demanded. "You could have been blown out of the water."

"The com isn't working," I yelled.

"I gotta check." The guard circled us warily as he called in. The next moment he was beckoning to us. "OK. Follow me." The guard turned toward the resort and started for it. "But next time spend a little less money on your monsters and more on your com equipment."

I kicked in the slider's jets and we rose above the waves. "He doesn't seem too taken with Godzilla." I opened the throttles so that the slider would move as fast as it could after the skimmer, but the distance was already widening. Still, the guard must have sent out the proper recognition call because the buoys said nothing as we passed by.

It wasn't too long before the guard was a little black speck on the surface. He kept that distance, moving around us in a wide circle on his swift little skimmer.

Ahead of us lay the Xanadu Arms. Attached to a sea mount, the Xanadu Arms could submerge if a storm came up, but most of the time it floated in the sun as if some giant had thrown several long necklaces of pearls down on the sea. Each gleaming pearl was a huge pleasure globe that housed some new delight to ease the boredom of the rich. And underneath, on the sea mount, was a coral garden filled with strange creatures; Altairan narwhals, Carefree nautiluses, even Betelgeusean men-of-war (their venom removed) floated there like ghosts.

A scaly Simcan as big as a refrigerator started to walk toward the dock when he saw us. He was dressed in the same red outfit as the guard—though the uniform made the Simcan look like a beef tomato with legs. No one will ever accuse a Simcan of having an imagination. They never forgive and they never let up—which makes them ideal for security. He spoke now into a mike hanging on his lip and then marched down toward us warily.

The next moment, a hole appeared in the nearest globe and a little blue Kreech bustled out on three stumpy legs that protruded from under his kilt.

I cut off the jets and let the slider nose into the dock. In the distance I could hear more screams and the crash of glass. "It sounds like we came to the right place."

"I hope you've got a lot of insurance," the Simcan said in a deep gravelly voice.

"As a matter of fact, we don't," Dad said. "It was either feed our fabricants or pay the premiums. Your insurance company is going to have to cover it."

"They're still going to want you to compensate them." The Simcan growled as if his voice had switched into low gear. "You're going to be washing dishes for the next thousand years, and I and all my heirs are going to see that you do."

Dad stared up at the Simcan as I worked my way around to the slider's bow. "Just who are you?"

"M'cer, the captain of security." He put out his hand for the mooring cable. I think his pride was hurt that a pint-sized fabricant had penetrated his security, and he wanted to take it out on us.

But I just kept hold of the cable. "Well, M'cer, maybe we'll just leave."

Annoyed, the Kreech wriggled the fold that was his mouth. "Sir, I should think that you'd want to keep down the cost of damages?" I recognized his voice when he spoke. It was the manager.

Dad stood there for a moment and his lips moved silently as if he were trying to figure out the best argument. Then his shoulders started to sag like they did when he had worked for that company in the Core years ago. Dad was better with ideas than he was with people. Mom had always handled the business end of things. It looked like I was going to have to do her job now.

I spoke before Dad could. "You're gonna bankrupt us anyway. Like my dad always says: If a thing's worth doing, it's worth doing well." Sam was already starting to climb out over the slider. "Sam, get back in."

The Kreech stomped all three legs on the dock. "Sirs, we will have your heads. You two will be in prison so long you'll forget your names."

Dad was looking at me in astonishment, but I ignored him. "Fine," I said. "At least I know what we'll be doing. But what will *you* be doing once Godzilla finishes demolishing your fancy little playground?"

Suddenly the top of a globe in the center of the resort exploded and an anti-grav cart filled with desserts went floating up into the sky. All the desserts were on fire. The four of us watched the cart glide majestically through the air and out to sea for a sugary Viking funeral. "I hope," I said, "that your guests like their desserts flambé."

The manager sighed. "All right, sir. You win."

"No lawsuits?" I asked

"We can't—" M'cer started to protest.

But the grim-faced manager silenced him with his hand. "No lawsuits."

I looked over at Dad. He gave me the OK sign and—miracle of miracles—an approving smile. At least I'd done one thing right today.

"You got yourself a deal." I handed the cable up to M'cer and then climbed onto the dock along with Dad. While he was mooring the slider, I patted his shoulder. "And bring our gear like a good fellow." I was enjoying seeing how many shades of red M'cer could turn under his scales. "Come on, girl." I snapped my fingers at Sam, and fifty kilos of curiosity surged onto the dock.

"Sir, you are not bringing another monster into the Arms." The manager stared down doubtfully at the creature sniffing his legs.

"She's a pet," Dad said, "and a hunter."

He slapped Sam's paws as she tried to lift the hem of his kilt. "Well, sir, tell her to keep her paws to herself."

"You should be flattered. She doesn't go for just anyone." I started for the nearest globe.

◆ 4 ◆

You didn't need to be a bloodhound to sniff out Godzilla's trail. He'd left a path of destruction a month-old infant could follow. Saltwater from a broken wall aquarium ruined an expensive woven carpet while maids crawled around on their hands and knees, trying to collect all the flopping fish. Another fellow was lying on his stomach while a medico ministered to his singed behind. One shopkeeper was examining a rack of expensive silk kilts and wailing, "Look at the burn marks. They're ruined. Absolutely ruined!" Another was crying over a ton of broken ceramic ashtrays that had once proudly proclaimed they were souvenirs of the Xanadu Arms.

I glanced at Dad. "It could be worse. He could be full-size and this could be Tokyo."

The sight of all the damage made the manager move even more briskly until we were all practically trotting. The lobby looked like something from a war holo, with charred furniture and terrorized guests in jewelry and furs huddled together weeping like refugees.

"Sir, it will take years to recover from this," the manager moaned.

Dad looked around musingly. "I didn't think he had it in him."

"Maybe you ought to design for the military," I suggested.

Sam gave a loud chirrup and led us into the solarium. Potted ferns lay broken on the floor, and trees in their tubs lay on their sides among the overturned tables and chairs. The shattered china and crystal crunched under our feet as we entered.

"Did I say years? Make that centuries," the manager corrected himself mournfully.

In the middle of the solarium stood a girl about my age. If she had come out of Dad's design tanks, I think I would've given him an A plus. Her thigh-high boots were of some supple suede and emphasized long legs that ended in a pair of loose shorts over curving hips. A bolero jacket covered her neck-high blouse.

The girl was wrestling with a guard two heads taller than she was—and winning. "You are not going to shoot him." She was saying.

The guard was doing his best to keep hold of his remson carbine. "Ma'am, we have to stop him."

"But you're doing more damage than he is!" Hooking her foot behind the guard's leg, she pulled it out from underneath him. As he fell, he let go of his carbine, leaving the girl in sole possession.

"How dare you!" The manager raced over to the debris. I thought he was going to attack the girl, but instead he stood over the fallen guard. "How dare you assault Miss Shandi."

The guard pointed an accusing finger at the triumphant Shandi. "But she was doing all the assaulting."

What made her look old-fashioned, even exotic, was that she had let her black hair grow long and curly like a boy's instead of shaving her head and using head paint like most girls. Her hair framed an oval face that tapered sharply to her chin.

She rested the carbine against her hip. "Don't be such a toady. I did assault him, and I'd do it again." She didn't look the least bit apologetic, either—as if she always spoke her mind without worrying about whose feelings got hurt.

The manager licked his lips nervously as if he were now astride a tightrope. "Really, Miss Shandi. I'm sure that Huang was only doing his duty."

She waved her free hand around the solarium. "This idiot was shooting up the room."

The guard sat up. "That monster was scaring the guests."

She thumbed the catch and removed the hexagonal charge pack. "These old fossils could use a little excitement in their lives. It'll get their blood going and their hearts pumping."

"Well, *we're* here now." I tried to fake as much confidence as she felt when I strolled over toward her.

She pocketed the charge in her waist pouch and let the now useless gun plop back in the guard's lap. And then, even though we were the same height, she tilted back her head as if she wanted to look at me from a distance. "And just who are you?"

She had golden eyes that made me feel like a carpet that was being priced—and not very high. Most people would have had the manners at least to conceal that kind of cool examination.

"We're the people who created the fabricant," Dad explained.

"Really?" She seemed intrigued. "As a pet?"

"As a demonstration model." Dad produced one of his business cards. "MMI. The best in genetic engineering." He waved a hand toward Sam, who was investigating some object in another part of the room. "That's another one of my fabricants."

She ran a finger along the edge and watched the holographic display. When the card went dead, she pointed it at me. "What's he? Another demo?" I knew right then and there I wasn't going to like her.

Dad rubbed his chin. "After a fashion. He's my son."

There was a clanging and clanking of metal that sounded like a bell factory. The manager pressed his knuckles against his mouth. "Will this torment never end?" He went racing off.

Putting the card into her pouch, Shandi ran past us. "Come on. He's probably got more trigger-happy guards."

Dad looked at me. "There's definitely one young lady who knows her own mind."

"She acts like she owns everything."

Huang got up and began to dust himself off. "She *does* own practically everything. And what she doesn't own, she doesn't want. That's Shandi Tyr."

"The Tyrs?" I asked.

Huang looked as if I were unworthy to speak the name. "The same."

I let out a low whistle. If there was anything worth owning in the star sector, the Tyrs owned it—from ore-rich mines, to the factories converting the ore into different metals, to the plants using those metals in building ships. They had their hand in almost everything else, too, from communications to munitions to coffin makers. No wonder she had never learned any manners. She didn't have to.

Dad slapped my arm with the back of his hand. "And she likes my design." He grinned. He started to jog after her.

"Whatever you do," I warned Dad as I ran after him, "don't make her a life-size Godzilla." Fortunately, Sam was curious enough to come with us.

We found them in a globe full of huge rusty iron cylinders. The manager was standing in the middle of the wreckage and wringing his hands. "The Tschangé is a shambles, an absolute shambles."

I circled around one junky dented cylinder. "This looks like where old boilers come to die."

The manager drew himself up indignantly. "I'll have you know that this was once a mobile done by the great Tschangé himself."

"It was like a string of old tin cans," Shandi said. She was squatting over to the side.

The manager inclined his head stiffly. "Miss Shandi, I would expect a buffoon like this boy to react that way. However, I thought you of all people would understand aesthetics."

"I'm more interested in your ventilation." She raised a twisted metal grill to show us that the mesh had been melted. "I think you have a monster loose in your air ducts." She was leaning over close enough so that her voice echoed in the duct itself.

There was a faint smell of methane around the duct, so I knew she was right. Even so, I felt she shouldn't add to the mess. "Get back," I said. "You'll scare him even more."

She regarded me coldly. "I doubt if he could be more frightened than he already is." But she straightened up.

"You're not helping his disposition any." I ignored her and looked down the duct. It looked big enough for me. "Do you have blueprints?" I asked the manager.

"Yes"—the manager nodded his head slowly—"or I can have copies printed out for you."

As the manager left, Dad came over to me. "Are you thinking of driving him into an ambush?"

"Something like that." I dangled my legs into the duct.

Dad caught me under the arm. "Don't be stupid. He's frightened. He may not know you. I hate to think of his fire in an enclosed space."

"Do you know a better way?" I challenged him.

Dad thought for a moment and finally had to sigh. "I'll go."

"You might not fit in some places." I shook free. "Look. I won't get that close. Dad, we have to do something, or one of his goons"—I jerked my head toward the manager—"is going to shoot Godzilla."

"Send Sam first then." Dad turned and tapped the recall signal on a rusted hemisphere. Sam, who'd been investigating another part of Tschangé's masterpiece to see if it was edible, came loping over.

"Oh, isn't she just darling!" Shandi exclaimed.

My mom had put a whole year into Sam's design, and Shandi made Sam sound like a toy. I scowled. "She wouldn't make a good fur coat, if that's what you're thinking."

"I wouldn't hear of it." Shandi held out her arms, and to my surprise Sam went right to her. "Would I, girl?" She wrapped her arms around Sam and nuzzled cheeks and Sam began chirruping happily.

"We've got better things to do." I slapped Sam's treacherous little rump.

Dad looked at me funny. "If I didn't know any better, I'd say you were jealous."

The manager reappeared with an armload of blueprints. M'cer, towing an anti-grav sled, followed him into the room. M'cer had a scowl that would have done credit to Godzilla. The three of them went over the blueprints while I took the trank gun from the cart.

Shandi eyed me indignantly. "You're not really going to use a cannon on that poor little thing?"

I took a step backward before she could disarm me like she'd done the guard. "The dart will just put him to sleep."

"But he could suffocate or have a bad fall," she protested. "He'll calm down once he gets hungry."

I cracked the gun open and checked the CO_2 cylinder. "That's our business."

She planted a fist on her hip. "I wouldn't have brought him here if I thought everyone would be trying to shoot him."

She was not only mega-rich, she was mega-stupid. "You brought him here?" I asked.

She nodded unrepentantly. "I found him at sea, clinging to a board. He was whimpering just like a little lost puppy, so I took him in. He was fine for the first hour, so I left him in my room and went out for something. Then some stupid maid opened the door to the suite and he got out."

She was the first rich person I'd ever met, and I can't say I liked the breed much.

Dad looked up from the blueprints. "He was probably seasick for that first hour."

I glared at her as I loaded the gun. "You were lucky Godzilla was ill. Your money can't protect you all the time."

She blinked in surprise. "I don't expect it to."

I strapped a shiner on my wrist. "Right," I said skeptically.

She started to wag a finger at me. "Now see here—"

"Can it, lady," I growled. "That act may work with your servants, but not with me."

Shandi was just as unpredictable as she was rich. Instead of throwing a tantrum and demanding my scalp, she leaned her head to one side and seemed to—well, study me, the way Dad would check out some new and intriguing gene design. "What does work with you?" she wondered, more to herself than to me.

M'cer listened to a receiver in his ear. "My men say that there are noises in the ducts over in F-Eighteen."

The manager stabbed a finger at the blueprints. "That's here."

M'cer excitedly traced a line. "And that leads straight to the laundry room."

Dad tapped the paper. "But there are side ducts here and here. Can you block them?"

M'cer plucked his lower lip. "That would take time."

Dad rubbed his fingers together while he thought for a moment. "We could put some harmless but stinky gas into either duct."

"And have it carry through the whole resort?" The manager shook his head.

"He hates cats," I suggested. "A tourist brought her pet kitten to our island, and Godzilla nearly had conniptions."

M'cer curled his lip scornfully. "Cats?"

I shrugged defensively. "Maybe he's allergic."

"Impossible. It has to be environmental, not genetic." Suddenly Dad snapped his fingers. "I've got it. Have a guard meow into either side duct."

"I can't ask my guards to act like fools," M'cer objected.

"They'll look even more foolish if Godzilla tears this resort down around their ears."

M'cer sighed. "I'm right on it." He began speaking into the com. Apparently, his men were a little doubtful about his orders. "You heard me. Meow like a cat."

Dad lifted a bulletproof vest and a welder's helmet from the cart. "Here. Wear these."

"Too bulky." I knelt down and hugged Sam. "They'll slow me down."

"This is no time to play hero." Dad thrust the vest at me again.

But I was kneeling and whispering in one of Sam's ears. "This is your second chance, girl. Show Dad what you can do before you wind up as somebody's hat. Let's go find Godzilla." And Sam dove into the duct in a fluid motion of muscle and grace.

"Take this. I'll get another." M'cer handed me his com. I put the receiver in my ear and hooked the mike over my lower lip. The weight was so negligible I didn't even notice it.

"Now I don't want any arguments, young man," Dad said severely. "At least wear this." He tried to force the helmet on me.

I ducked away from him. "Neither do I," I said, and, snapping on the shiner, I dove into the duct after Sam.

"Wait for me," Shandi said and followed.

· 5 ·

I'd slid head first down the duct for about four meters before it leveled out. The next thing I knew, Shandi had landed against me. I felt her hands slap at the soles of my feet. "Oof. Get those stinky things out of my face."

"If you don't like them, you can just go back the way you came." But I edged forward a little.

She flicked a fingernail against my sole. "I can't climb back that way."

The last thing I intended to do was take along dead weight. "Then you can just wait here."

"And have you bungle everything?" she asked.

For a moment, I was half tempted to use the trank gun on her, but then I heard Sam chirp from somewhere ahead of me. "I'm right here, girl." Cradling the gun across my forearms, I began to crawl forward down the duct. "I don't have time to nursemaid you. Why don't you leave the hunting to the professionals?"

She followed right behind me, her palms hitting my heels. "Have you hunted the mountain worms of Orbos? Or the krag in the Sea of Peace?"

Money certainly provides a lot of answers. I tried to crawl faster to put more distance between myself and her. "Spare me the travelogue."

Shandi grabbed at my ankle so that my chin went forward against the gun. "I've never met anyone who carried a tree-size chip on his shoulder."

I kicked back at her irritably. "Why is it that everyone else has a problem and not you?"

I expected some indignant tirade. Instead there was only a pause. "I don't know," she finally admitted. "It's never come up before."

She said it so honestly that I almost felt like I'd just picked on a puppy whose curiosity had gotten it into trouble. "Look," I said more kindly, "not everyone has enough money to pay their way out of trouble."

She gave a tug at my ankle. "At least I don't envy what I can't buy."

I had to admit there was some justice to that. "We manage."

For a while, neither of us said anything as we moved forward on all fours, our hands and knees and feet making soft hissing noises on the metal.

Finally she asked, "You think I'm spoiled, don't you?"

"Aren't you?" I demanded.

"Thoroughly and shamelessly," she confessed. "And don't you wish you were too?"

Shandi wasn't just brutally honest about other people. She was honest about herself, too. Despite my original intentions, I was finding it hard to dislike her. "Well," I had to admit, "you can't be all bad if Sam likes you."

Before Shandi could say anything, a terrible cat imitation echoed down the duct from up ahead. The second guard kicked in with a sound that was more like a sick milkaroo than a cat.

The meowing had gotten progressively louder as we neared the side duct. "You receiving me?" M'cer asked over the receiver.

"Yeah," I said into the mike. "Your boys pick up anything?"

"Not in the side ducts," M'cer said. "Your pet seems to be moving on to the laundry room."

"Right. We're going on." I started to crawl forward.

It was funny down in the ducts. There were long stretches of dark metal painted a dull gray inside. Suddenly there'd be a louvered vent, which made a striped rectangular pool of light. It felt like we were crawling down the long, hard throat of some giant gilled worm. We could hear the weird meowing in the distance, and our own panting breaths, and the scratching of Sam's claws on the metal.

All of a sudden Sam began chattering nervously ahead of me. "What is it, girl?" Alarmed, I began to crawl as fast as I could.

"Hey, wait for me," Shandi called from behind me, but I didn't pay her any more attention than I did to M'cer. I was in such a rush that I bumped heads with Sam. No matter what Dad might have said, her skull is a lot harder than mine. I was still lying there stunned as a frantic Sam tried to claw her way right through my shoulder. I wish I'd trimmed her nails.

"Easy, girl, easy." I got hold of her neck. She became aware of my scent and calmed down a bit, though she was still shaking. I began to stroke her fur to check for damage, but I couldn't find any.

"Did she see something?" Shandi sounded a little short of breath.

"I'm not sure." My petting had soothed Sam. "I think she was more angry than scared."

"I don't blame her one bit." Shandi reached over my shoulder to pet clumsily at Sam.

"Something scared Sam," I informed M'cer. "I'm going to take the lead."

There was a pause as M'cer relayed the news. Then he came back on. "Your dad says to return. I think he's right. We'll let down a rope and draw you out."

"Sorry," I said into the receiver. "There's so much static that I can't hear you." And I jerked the receiver from my ear so it dangled by its wire from the mike.

There was a thump as Shandi rested on her elbows. "You're going to go on?"

I began to creep forward. "I haven't come this far just to stop now."

"You really care about your pets, don't you?" She sounded thoughtful.

There was a time when creatures like Sam and Godzilla had been my only friends. "They're more like family than pets," I said. "But you're welcome to head back."

Shandi was full of surprises. "This is one mess I intend to help clean up myself." I had to admit she might not be half bad if she weren't so spoiled.

I slid on past Sam. She pressed her wet muzzle against my face and chittered a protest, but I pushed her head away and went on. Sam tried to stop Shandi next; when she was equally unsuccessful, she trailed along behind us, chittering plaintively.

I was so busy looking down the duct that I almost didn't notice the whiff of swamp gas. "Hold it," I warned and sniffed the air. It had a warm, funny smell. Behind us, Sam was making alarmed, warning noises. There wasn't any sign of Godzilla himself, though. Carefully I slid my fingers forward. It was only when I'd stretched my arm out as far as I could that I felt the hot metal.

"The tricky little cuss has heated up the duct," I said. That must have been what had frightened Sam.

"How far?" Shandi wanted to know.

"I'm not sure." I rubbed my singed fingertips together. Unfortunately, the local outfit for Carefree leaves the legs and arms bare—if not more. I was trying to figure out what to do next when I heard a rustling behind me.

"I've got a jacket. You can use your vest," she suggested.

I turned sideways in the tunnel to look behind me. Shandi had flung her jacket in front of her. "What are you going to do about your knees?"

"I'm going to support my weight on my hands and keep my knees off the duct." She pushed herself up from the duct in illustration.

"How long can you keep that up?"

"I've scaled Mount U-Jit," she said smugly. Mount U-Jit was one of the tallest mountains in the star sector. "How about you?"

I jerked my vest off. "Me? I don't climb anything. I get queasy in a pair of boots if the soles are too thick."

"Poor baby. Do you have to put up with this all the time?" I realized that Shandi was talking to Sam and not to me.

Sam chittered anxiously. When I had put my vest down in front of me, I turned to see that Shandi had taken Sam on her back. "She seemed so upset at being left behind," Shandi explained.

"It's your back," I said.

I could feel a warmth through the cloth, but it wasn't bad. And about five meters on, the duct cooled off so we could move on our hands and knees again.

"For a skinny little thing, you've got some muscles on you," I had to allow as I slipped my vest back on.

"Daddy doesn't believe in my being idle," she said breezily.

We went on for about another thirty meters and had just headed into a bend when I heard this screeching noise all around me. At first, I thought it was Sam or Godzilla, but then I realized it was the duct itself. M'cer's voice immediately began buzzing in the dangling receiver like a giant chigger. I put it back in my ear in time to hear him demand. "—cell. Now tell me what's going on."

Almost at the same time, Shandi had grabbed hold of my ankle again. "What'd you do now?" she demanded as if it were all my fault.

Before I could tell either of them I didn't know, the joint suddenly gave way underneath me. I blinked my eyes in the sudden blinding light. I had time to see startled faces far below in the kitchen, and then I was falling toward them.

Just when I was trying to remember a prayer, any prayer, I jerked abruptly to a halt. "Gotcha!" Shandi cried. She had an iron grip on my ankles. "Oof. What did you have for lunch, rocks?"

As I swung back and forth in the air, I quickly made a decision. "I take back any cracks about you coming along."

"And . . . ?" she prompted playfully.

I don't do my best thinking when I'm hanging upside down. Maybe it has something to do with all that blood rushing to my head. At any rate, I babbled the first thing that came to my head. "I think you're taking unfair advantage of the situation."

"Humph," she said. "Seven meters looks like a long way to fall head first." Then, instead of going back, the two of us slowly began to slide out of the duct.

"Whoa," I yelled. Another section of duct fell with a clang right onto a table of salads, sending greenery and tomatoes every which way as if someone had just nuked a vegetable patch.

An angry chef waved a cleaver at me. "Cut that out," he said as if I wanted to drop another piece of duct on him.

"Believe me, I'd stop if I could," I shouted. Suddenly, the trank gun slipped out of my belt and fell past me. I made a swipe at it but missed. By then, I was almost out to my knees.

There was a loud clatter and a hiss like a large snake, and then the chef was staring down at the tranquilizer dart sticking out from his leg. The trank gun had gone off when it landed on the floor.

"Sorry," I called.

But the chef was already getting groggy. He sat down slowly onto the evening's dessert.

Shandi grunted. "Maybe if I spread my legs." I could hear her boots screeching on the metal sides of the duct.

I was studying the floor below, hoping to land on someone fat, when I was halted in mid-slide. "You did it!" I said to Shandi.

"Of course I did it," she said indignantly. I even began to move back upward into the duct.

She was now lying on top of my calves, and that was a momentary distraction. Though her breasts looked small, they were surprisingly soft. "Hmmm. Now, where were we?"

"You were pulling me up?" I suggested.

"Was that it?" she wondered out loud to herself. "No, I think you were about to apologize."

I should have been angry, or at least afraid, but Shandi was like Sam; everything was a game to her. "Well, I'm sorry about the budget deficits of the Stellar Union and polka-dot ties and snoring."

"What about my cleaning up my own messes?" she demanded. The words came out strained because I was hanging upside down. "You're being a big help right now. The biggest. Enough said?"

"Not on your life. I've got eight courses of crow planned for you." She hooked her hands into my shorts and gave a quick tug that almost pulled them off.

"Hey," I protested as I started to slide back out.

She clamped her body down on my legs and got a grip on my vest. "Why do boys have to have such skinny rumps anyway?"

Gradually she pulled me back enough so I could grab hold of the edge of the duct and shove myself in the rest of the way. Behind Shandi, I could hear Sam's curious chirping. She must have gotten off when Shandi grabbed me. "It's OK, girl," I called to her. "I'll be with you in a sec."

"That's easy for you to say," Shandi said.

Finally, we were lying side by side. I swallowed because what I had to say next came hard. "Thanks. You're really not as bad as I thought."

She tugged playfully at my scalp lock. "You're long on complaints and short on compliments, aren't you?"

I tugged my shorts cautiously back over my hips. "Compliments just aren't steady issue in my family."

"Apparently not." She slid backward to give me more room. "What's your name anyway?"

"Piper Kincaid."

"Well, Pipes, what happened? Was it our little darling's fault again?"

"Not unless Dad gave him a screwdriver claw. I think the Arms has a case against the contractor." M'cer's voice was an angry little buzzing from the still-dangling receiver. "This duct wasn't put together right and just wasn't ready to support all this weight."

"Speak for yourself." She sniffed.

I told M'cer what had happened—including the fact that none of the guests should expect any salads or dessert.

"I don't think they have much appetite anyway." M'cer sighed.

We both had to stretch some, but we made it over the hole into the next part of the duct. Shandi had to carry Sam on her back. Then our little safari was trekking on. There was the murmur of voices through the duct as we passed through the restaurant. I waited until we'd gone another fifty meters before I checked in with M'cer again. "I think the duct is widening, and I can feel a draft."

"You must be near the laundry room," he cautioned. "What're you going to do when you meet Godzilla?"

"Try to talk to him. He ought to recognize my voice and calm down."

"Be careful," M'cer said, as if I didn't know that already. I seemed to have gained the Simcan's grudging respect—either for going after Godzilla in the ducts or for handling the difficult Ms. Shandi.

I crept forward meter by meter. A turn brought us suddenly within sight of the vent. Light spilled through the grill to form a striped puddle of white on the duct floor. I could see that the vent ended in big fan blades covered by mesh. Steam and warm air blew in from the laundry room, but there wasn't any sign of Godzilla.

"He's not here," I said to M'cer.

"What do you mean, 'He's not here'? He has to be there," M'cer snapped.

"We're at a dead end and there's no sign of him. Dad didn't build any invisibility genes into him." I was feeling as frustrated as M'cer sounded. "Are you sure there aren't any more side ducts?"

M'cer sounded puzzled. "I don't understand it. There are only those two side ducts, and my men say that there wasn't any sign of Godzilla there."

Suddenly there was a loud clank as if some large object had

been dropped into the duct. Then there was a rumbling like a small tank trundling through.

I shoved Sam to the side, though she squawked in protest, and crawled over Shandi's legs and back along the duct. But this time I shone my shiner overhead and not on the duct itself. About five meters on, I saw the square hole where a section had been ripped off.

Godzilla had climbed out of the duct and hidden until we were past. Now he'd gotten around us.

Shandi came up behind me. "How did he do that without our hearing him?"

I shone the shiner down the duct, but Godzilla was out of sight. "Remember when I was hanging by my shorts?"

Shandi suppressed a giggle. "We were pretty occupied at the time."

"He could have shoved the plate up and we wouldn't have heard," I said. Then I gave the bad news to M'cer. "Sorry. Godzilla's on the loose again."

·6·

M'cer said he'd have a ladder brought to the open section of the duct in the kitchen so we could climb down. He and Dad would be there too to knock out Godzilla.

"I'd like to speak to my dad, please," I requested.

Dad spoke to me a few seconds later. "What is it, son?"

I squeezed past Shandi and Sam so I could be first again. "You got the other trank gun? I lost mine."

"I got it," Dad assured me, "but you'd better stay where you are."

I started to crawl forward. "I don't think he'd attack me. Just be there in the kitchen. M'cer's men might get trigger-happy."

"Right," Dad agreed.

I began to call to Godzilla. I hoped he'd hear my voice before he used that bad breath of his. My knees felt scraped raw, but that couldn't be helped.

Suddenly the duct began to vibrate like someone was pounding it with a sledgehammer. I got M'cer right away. "Any of your people trying to break into the duct?"

"No," a worried M'cer said. "Let me check."

I began to move as fast as I could even while the duct vibrated all around me. Shandi touched my ankle. "What's Godzilla doing now?"

"I don't know," I said, "but I don't think it's too good for the Arms."

From the number of excited voices and the distance we had gone, I figured we must be back over the restaurant. Suddenly, there was a screech of metal, and we could hear screams. The sounds roared down the metal duct all around us.

"Godzilla's getting into the restaurant," I told M'cer and then scrambled after our little monster. I heard an odd tinkling, clashing sound of crystal.

Shandi was panting. "What's that?"

"We'll soon find out." I bulled forward.

Godzilla had ripped a vent from a wall of the duct. I poked my head through the opening and saw that I'd been off a few meters. We were over the cocktail lounge, not the restaurant. It was a circular room some fifty meters in diameter. About two meters away, Godzilla was hanging from one of the many chandeliers that dotted the plastic ceiling. It was like looking at an upside-down forest of glittering trees.

"Hey, boy," I tried to call, but he couldn't hear me among all the screams.

The chandelier swung back and forth under his weight, sending a little prism down like a tear every now and then.

Shandi poked her head over my shoulder. "I don't think those chandeliers will hold our weight."

I studied the fixtures that held the chandelier to the ceiling, and reluctantly I had to admit that she was right. "Maybe he'll stay put."

But even as I watched, Godzilla launched himself onto the next chandelier. I held my breath while he swung through the air. He landed with a crash of glass, sending down a rain of prisms on the dancers and drinkers. The chandelier itself jerked out from the ceiling a few millimeters, but then it stopped.

Dad, M'cer, and two guards with a ladder stumbled into the bar and right into a panicky mob that was fighting to get out.

"Waiter, garçon," I called down to a waiter. He had trays of hors d'oeuvres on an anti-grav cart that he was bringing to replenish the buffet spread.

"Don't be so polite." Putting her fingers into her mouth, Shandi let out a piercing whistle. "Hey, you."

The waiter looked around in surpirse as if he couldn't place the voice.

Shandi gave another whistle. "Up here."

The waiter finally leaned his head back and saw us. It was hard to say what shocked him more: Godzilla or the sight of two people materializing from a wall.

"Take all that stuff off and send the cart up here," I ordered.

But the waiter just stared up at us dumbly as if I were speaking a foreign language. Dad, though, had gotten through the mob in the meantime, and he had heard me. He came running over with the trank gun in one hand and started to lift off a tray with his other hand.

The waiter caught Dad's arm. "Sir, you'll have to get a plate."

They struggled for a moment until Shandi shouted down, "Charge it all to Miss Tyr's room."

The magic name of Tyr made the waiter stop. Dad pulled free and swept the trays off the cart so that they crashed on the floor. Then he set the controls of the cart to high and it began to rise slowly in the air.

Underneath the vent, the guards were struggling to raise the ladder so Shandi could get down. In the meantime, Dad went running back across the floor to Godzilla.

"Shoot," M'cer urged Dad.

Dad raised his gun to his shoulder, but he didn't actually aim it. "I've got to wait for a better shot. A fall from this height might injure him. Have some men get the nets. I think we left them in the lobby."

M'cer barked a quick order into his mike even as the manager came running into the lounge. A large man followed him in a leisurely kind of waddle—like a goose on vacation. The little Kreech skidded to a halt and looked around the lounge. Chairs and tables were overturned. Everywhere there were puddles of spilled drinks and broken glass. His mouth dropped open and he clapped a hand to either side of his head. "And we just finished renovations in here."

A falling prism made the manager aware of the culprit once again. He glared up at the chandelier and the clinging green monster.

"Kill it."

"We're just waiting for the nets, sir," M'cer explained. "Then we can tranquilize the monster."

The little Kreech was quivering with rage. "This must stop at once. Shoot it."

"But, sir—" M'cer began to protest. He wasn't such a bad egg after all, I guess.

"That is a direct order." The manager's voice was almost a skriek. "If you don't kill it, I'll find someone who will." He pointed to one of the other guards. "You. How would you like to be the new head of security?"

The guard hesitated, looking at M'cer, but a second guard started opening up the flap of his holster. "Right away, sir," the second guard said.

By that time, the cart had risen up by our hole. Shandi looked down at it doubtfully. "That's not built for heavy weights. I thought you were going to coax Godzilla onto it."

"It only has to hold me for a short while." I eased a leg out. I bobbed like a little boat on a choppy ocean.

Shandi impulsively leaned forward and gave me a quick peck on the cheek. "Be careful. You're as ugly as your pets, but you grow on a person."

"Like a wart, right?" I slid down carefully onto the cart. It wobbled as it adjusted to my weight and suddenly swung down a hundred and eighty degrees.

"Get back here, you idiot." Shandi sounded just as scared as I felt. "It won't hold you even for a minute."

I clung to the top of the cart with all my strength, praying to about everyone I could ever remember, until the cart halted and then slowly, centimeter by centimeter, righted itself.

"Come on." An alarmed Shandi was holding out her hand to me.

Below me, the guard was raising his stinger. Dad rushed over. "No." Dad swung up his gun butt against the guard's chin, and the guard went heeling over backward. I wondered if Dad would have fought that hard to save me since my particular design wasn't at all that unique.

The guard's stinger skidded across the floor and the little Kreech went scrambling after it. I knew what was on his mind. "Give me a shove," I ordered Shandi.

"Listen to that thing." Shandi caught Sam before she could join me. "It's breaking down." Sure enough, the motor was starting to whine and little plumes of smoke began to rise.

"I'll do it with or without your help." I put a foot against the wall and kicked off. I used all my strength, but I only drifted over the lounge floor with agonizing slowness. Below me, the manager had gotten the gun.

"Dad!" I shouted.

Dad looked up and then turned in the direction I was pointing and saw the manager. He tried to rush over to stop him, but the second guard snagged Dad's ankle. I guess Dad hadn't hit him hard enough to knock him out for long. The next thing we knew, the guard had yanked Dad's leg out from underneath him and Dad was falling on top of the guard.

"Hey, boy, don't worry," I called to Godzilla.

Godzilla recognized me by now. He gave a terrified *fwee-ee-eep* and clung tighter to the chandelier.

My momentum was still carrying me forward even as the manager straightened up. The guards with the nets came into the lounge finally, but Dad was still struggling with the second guard. "Spread those nets," I heard Shandi call imperiously. She was halfway down the wobbly ladder with a squirming Sam under one arm.

"You heard Miss Tyr," M'cer called, and the guards hopped to obey. "You too." M'cer dragged the waiter along by his collar and sent him stumbling after the guards. The waiter just caught the edge of the net and helped spread it out while they ran into the room.

In the meantime, though, the man who had come in with the manager finally moved to stop the Kreech, but the manager snapped off a wild shot. The beam from the stinger played across the ceiling, raising a burn mark. By then the man had grabbed the manager's arm and pulled the gun from the manager's hand.

"No, boy!" I shouted.

But it was too late. The frightened Godzilla tried to swing to the next chandelier, but his perch gave way. The chandelier ripped from the ceiling with a groan and chunks of plastic.

Godzilla launched himself into the air, his claws reaching out for the next one. But he hadn't been able to get enough arc into his swing. He was going to fall short. With a terrified *fwee-ee-eep*, he fought to grab hold of the next chandelier.

Dad and his opponent managed to roll out of the way, and M'cer, the first guard, the manager, and his friend threw themselves to the side just as the chandelier crashed against the floor.

The guards with the net weren't going to be in time. I was just reaching for the controls to lower the cart when the motor sputtered. Sparks flew in every direction as it died, and then I was falling too.

◆ 7 ◆

*T*he fixtures on the wall whizzed past as I dropped through the air. I was too busy trying to think of how to explain this mess to Dad to be scared.

The cart stopped abruptly in the air and my chin struck the top. Then the cart crashed to the floor and tilted over, with me still holding onto it.

I lay there, stunned for a moment, and then Shandi's face hovered into view. "Let go, you idiot." The next second Sam was licking my face.

I managed to straighten out my fingers and then took a couple of experimental breaths. Nothing seemed to hurt. "I think I'm OK."

"Shut up. Think I'm going to take the word of a suicidal maniac?" She began expertly to feel my arms and legs. "Scream if anything hurts."

But nothing did so I crawled away from the cart. The men with the net hadn't made it as far as Godzilla, but the edge of the net had been underneath the cart, so the net had managed to break most of the fall. The men themselves were sitting around the edge of the net and staring with big eyes at something.

I turned to look in the same direction and saw Godzilla squatting on top of the little manager. They both looked equally dazed.

There was the hiss of a trank gun, and a dart suddenly quivered from Godzilla's thigh. He gave a frightened whine and tried to get up, but since he was on a strategic spot, the manager gave a pained yelp and wriggle—panicking Godzilla even more.

Shandi ran over to Godzilla and shook her finger. "You've been a very bad boy."

Despite the squirming manager, the sleepy Godzilla hung his head like a repentant child. *Fwee-ee-eep.*

"Yes, you have." Shandi threw her arms around Godzilla and gave him a hug. "But I forgive you."

Dad reloaded the trank gun as he came over to me. "You all right, sport?"

I sat up. "Nothing's broken. Just some bruises."

"Think of that the next time you try to solo on a hors d'oeuvres cart." Dad gave a relieved sigh.

"He's amazingly durable." Shandi was holding Godzilla so that he would remain quiet until the tranquilizer took effect.

"I designed the little monster that way." Dad reloaded the trank gun.

Shandi drew her eyebrows together disapprovingly. "I meant your son."

I eyed the newly reloaded gun. "What's that for?" I asked Dad.

"I may need it for the manager when he gets his senses back." Dad got up.

Even as Godzilla slumped forward in Shandi's arms, the manager started to bellow, "Get this monster off me."

We got the net out from underneath the cart and wrapped Godzilla in it. An army of waiters had already started to clean up, and they didn't seem to appreciate having a giant otter ruining their handiwork, so we collared Sam.

The manager took the large stranger on a tour of the wreckage in the room and finished by us. "You see the carnage? They can't be allowed to wreak havoc on the rest of society."

Dad and I lifted Godzilla onto an anti-grav cart. "If this is your lawyer," I warned, "it won't do you any good. You agreed not to sue. I've got witnesses."

"This," the manager said with wicked glee, "is Constable Shadbell of the Union Council. He's going to close you down as a public hazard."

M'cer looked over at us apologetically. "I want you to know, it's not my idea."

"Afternoon, Constable," Dad said.

I stared at Shadbell. I'd heard a lot about him though I'd never met him before. Dad had known Shadbell when they'd both been in the service. Shadbell had been a hero of sorts in one of those "police actions" that the Stellar Union was always fighting. Dad said he'd coasted through the rest of his life on the strength of his reputation. Mostly he'd gotten lazy in a job where the worst thing he had to handle was a noisy drunk on Saturday night.

"Afternoon, Doc. Your pet has done a lot of damage." Shadbell stuffed a hand into his pocket. I thought he was going to take out a badge or a gun, but he only held up a handful of candy.

"It won't happen again," Dad promised.

"I know it won't." Shadbell popped the candy in his mouth and began to crunch it noisily. "You are hereby ordered to cease and desist further operations."

"And that thing"—the manager pointed to Godzilla—"should be destroyed."

Dad raised the trank gun. "No one's touching that animal."

"You can't threaten anyone with that," the manager scoffed.

Dad swung the gun toward the manager. "Ever see a tranquilizer dart in a heart? I understand the Kreech heart is in the center of the chest."

"Now just hold on." M'cer was reaching his hand toward the gun in his holster. "I know you're upset and don't really mean that."

Dad kept the gun on the manager. "I don't want to hurt anyone."

"And I don't want to have to shoot you," M'cer warned, his hand still moving. "But it's my job to keep the peace here."

Shandi shoved in front of us. "Wait a moment. I was the one who brought him here."

The manager shrugged. "It could have easily been someone else."

Shandi drew herself up right then. Forget the fact that she was covered in dust and grease and looked like an old rag. She acted as regally as any queen. "I'll take responsibility for the damages." The manager shook his head. "That still doesn't solve the real issue." He was determined to shut MMI down.

Suddenly a big voice boomed inside the restaurant. "I knew it. All I had to do was look for the worst damage."

A regular bowling ball of a man rolled into the debris-filled lounge. He wore an expensive knee-length tunic of Vegan felt that ended in a hood and a long liripipe that trailed down his back as if it were a snake that had tried to swallow him and was now being worn as a decoration.

"Daddy!" Shandi went flying and threw herself into his arms.

He swung her around. "All right, lem. How much is it going to cost me this time?"

"Not as much as that time on Alvin." Shandi landed nimbly on her toes. "But you're late."

"I had to pound some sense into a Rigelian banker. That took a while because he has all those secondary brains. The secondary brains are supposed to control just the limbs, but I think they also sneak a vote in on other decisions. Talking to him was like talking to a committee." Mr. Tyr strode right up to Dad and M'cer. "Now what seems to be the problem?"

Shandi's long legs outpaced her father's. "They want to shoot that poor animal."

Mr. Tyr studied Godzilla. "So would I, just to put the poor beast out of its misery. I've never seen such a bad case of the uglies."

Shandi linked her arm through her father's. "But it's my fault. I found him floating in the water and brought him here."

Mr. Tyr pivoted slowly on his heel so he could face his daughter again. "How many times have I told you not to pick up every stray animal you see?"

Shandi frowned. "Oh, Daddy, if I listened to you I'd be bored to death."

Mr. Tyr sighed. "All right. I'll pay the bill again."

Shandi gave her father a big hug. "I already told them that."

The manager, though, was intent on having his revenge. "That's not the point. Kincaid's company has to be shut down and all his animals destroyed."

"Just look at them." Shandi held out her hand, and Sam immediately went and cuddled her head against Shandi's palm. "Have you ever seen anything this cute? The damage happened because Godzilla got scared."

The manager straightened up indignantly. "Ms. Tyr, it nearly barbecued my staff."

Shandi coaxed her father. "Think what a good watchdog he would make."

Mr. Tyr scratched the tip of his nose. "I was thinking he would make a better personnel manager."

Shandi wouldn't give up. "No one else has one. You're always saying that publicity is worth fifty percent of a deal."

"Well." Mr. Tyr's mind seemed to turn over possibilities. He glanced at Shadbell. "What would it take to let the company stay open?"

Shadbell gave a little cough. "There's been a complaint filed, Mr. Tyr. It's not that simple."

Tyr may have come on all folksy, but I could see where his daughter had gotten the tough, appraising look. The original looked twice as sharp and twice as cold. "What if the complaint was withdrawn and a list of precautions was written up?"

"We'd implement them," Dad assured Shadbell. "Even if my son has to sleep in the pen."

Shandi seemed to be waiting for me to correct Dad, but I couldn't shake the feeling that this whole disaster was my fault. Just like all the other times.

The manager looked at the constable indignantly. "Well, I refuse to withdraw my complaint."

Mr. Tyr looked down his long nose at the manager. "How'd you like me to buy this place just for the pleasure of demoting you to dishwasher?"

The manager adjusted his kilt. "Sir, I would quit before I would do that."

Mr. Tyr's smile tightened. I don't think I would have liked to have been on the receiving end of that. "Then you'd better quit eating too, because I'll see that you never work at anything again."

The manager's mouth formed a tight slit. "I am just trying to perform my duties."

"I don't know how many people I've fired for saying that." Mr. Tyr clapped an arm around the little Kreech. "But I'm not out to make trouble. Let's settle up for the damages and call it quits."

The Kreech sagged like a deflated balloon. He knew when he was beaten. "I'll add up the costs."

From her waist pouch, Shandi took out Dad's business card, now much folded and wrinkled, and handed it to her father. "He's ever so clever, Daddy."

Mr. Tyr barely nodded before he turned toward Dad. "Kincaid, Kincaid." You could see him mentally flipping through a file in his head. "The geneticist?"

"You've heard of me?" Dad grinned.

"I lost a bundle when you created that wheat blight on Procyon."

Dad winced. "I don't work in viral genetics anymore. I have designs—"

Mr. Tyr slapped Dad on the back. "Say, that's just the ticket! My little girl has been wanting a different sort of birthday party."

"Well, no, that's not—" Dad tried to say.

But Mr. Tyr was already swinging away, dragging his daughter along. "We'll come over tomorrow afternoon."

·8·

It didn't take long for news to spread even to the most isolated colonists. Our first visitor the next day wasn't Mr. Tyr but Frankie, who was homesteading a place some thirty kilometers up the coast. She was basically a good person, but a bit of a busybody the way Soltjans are. My ape ancestors might have been curious, but her marsupial ancestors were used to rooting around in marshland mud, and Soltjans just revel in gossip.

The sun had barely risen when she came out in a small two-person scoutship, slim as a dagger, nicknamed a skitter. Its rotors made a loud buzzing noise as she landed. I didn't give her a chance to get out but ran to her ship even before the rotors finished spinning.

She lifted up the cockpit canopy and lowered her headset so it could hang around her furry neck like a necklace. "I was at de post dwop and bwought yo' mail out." Her mouth was shaped like a duck's bill and composed of a material like human nails but more flexible. Frankie had trouble with consonants, but I could still understand her.

"Frankie, if you spent half as much time minding your farm as you did everyone else's business, you'd be one of the wealthiest people on the planet."

Frankie wasn't the least bit ashamed. "Whad's de use of good mud if you can't spwead it awound?"

I held up my hands before she could get out. "It depends on how much of the dirt is natural and how much is synthetic."

Frankie lowered a small sack of letters and packages. "Going to put on a weal thwee-wing ciwcus for the wich folk?"

"And we don't even have the tent up." I took the sack and waved good-bye to her as I stepped back.

Frankie looked all around to take in the scene, but there wasn't anything really special to see. "Need any help?"

"No, no, it's all under control." I waved good-bye more insistently.

With one last disappointed look around, Frankie put her headset back on and lowered the canopy. Even as she lifted off, I went back to the pen. There were a hundred things to do and so little time to do them in.

Singh didn't even wait for me to put down the sack of mail before he started in again. "Really, dear boy. You're being positively cruel. You must tell me what she looks like."

Singh had gotten on my nerves ever since we'd gotten back. Wishing Singh far away, I picked up the critter inventory list. "Who?"

Singh adjusted his vest for the dozenth time. "Our patron of science and the woman of my dreams."

"It sounds like you want an audit of her bank account, not a physical description."

"My interests are purely aesthetic," Singh said huffily.

I almost tripped over Ladadog. "She looks normal, if that's what you mean."

Singh pantomimed breasts. "And does she conform to the classical norms?"

"She's got all the standard-issue equipment." I stepped around both the master and the pet to check the pen.

Singh obstructed my view again. "I am seriously concerned about you, my friend."

I hipped him aside. "If you mean, is she attractive, I guess she is."

"You *guess* so?" Singh slapped his legs in frustration. "My dear boy, you are like a brother to me, so I worry about you. Sometimes I think your parents left something out of you."

I tried to concentrate on the count. Everyone was accounted for, including a subdued Godzilla. "I've got all the standard issue too."

Singh sighed. "Never send a boy to do a man's job."

Something just snapped me inside right then, and I reached up and grabbed the collar of his vest and pulled his face down to mine. "Speaking of jobs, why don't you do yours?"

Singh just eyeballed me for a moment, and I realized how precarious my situation was. Singh's ancestors come from that Punjab warrior caste who are used to stomping over any opponent foolhardy enough to try to fight them. Plus, he's close to two and three meters high and muscled accordingly. All in all, only a fool goes up against gene stock like that.

He put a hand to my fist and casually disengaged my fingers. Then he straightened and smoothed his vest collar. "The next time you do that," he said quietly, "you had better have a couple of thugs to help you."

I went back to my list. "Yeah, sorry. I guess I'm just nervous about the visit. There's a lot riding on it."

Singh grunted. "The acorn never falls far from the oak. Has your father slept at all, or has he been inspecting his designs and plans?"

"No, he's been rehearsing his sales pitch. He's got five different versions." I winced at the memory since I'd had to be his audience. "The same jokes, though."

Singh checked his scalp lock for the dozenth time. "There are a lot of things I admire about your father, but I fancy he wouldn't know a joke if he tripped over one."

"Not if it doesn't have DNA." I walked toward the dock. Everything checked.

Singh snapped his fingers, and his urya came to heel. "Fortunately we will be rich soon, and rich men do not need senses of humor. They hire joke writers."

It's funny how the mind works, but I was looking hard for some excuse to dislike Shandi. "You mean, they buy everyone."

Singh gazed down at me with a superior air. "Your trouble is that you do not know how to bargain."

"No one's going to own me."

"Money is not the only medium of exchange." Singh smiled enigmatically.

Dad was pacing nervously on the dock. He'd put on his best vest and kilt and done up his scalp lock with one of the few remaining flowers from Mom's garden. In the meantime, Sam must have picked up on his mood because she was padding up and down right beside him. Both Sam and he stopped, though, as we came down. "Things are all right?"

"A hundred and ten percent." I offered him the clipboard so he could check it himself, but he declined.

"What about you?" he demanded.

I hung the clipboard from a hook on the outside wall of the com room. "What about me?"

"Aren't you going to change?" Dad looked to Singh for support, and much to my indignation he nodded.

"Listen." I got hold of Sam's indentification collar because she had started to chatter angrily at Ladadog. At the same time, Singh took hold of his pet. "They're coming to see a working lab, not fashion plates."

Singh glanced at the chronometer hanging around his neck. "I don't think there's time for him to change anyway."

"At least I heard you take a shower this morning." Dad brushed something from my shoulder. "Well, who knows? Maybe some of our hard work is finally going to pay off."

"He's just buying her some birthday toys." Though not Sam. Not if I could help it. Even if she was a pest, she was my pest.

Dad rubbed his hands together. "But maybe some of his rich friends will see our animals and want them. It could start a fad among his group."

I looked down as Sam bucked against my hand and chirruped. "What is it, girl?"

But then we could hear the humming noise and see the distant speck on the horizon. It didn't take long for the powerful Tyr craft to swell into a huge pleasure slider.

"It's as big as a destroyer," Singh murmured in awe.

"And it's got some legs." Dad shaded his eyes. "Look how fast it's coming."

The slider was a big oval some fifty meters long that looked like a big tray with a lot of square boxes on it. It was built for comfort and safety rather than for speed. About a hundred meters out, the slider cut in its bow jets. The water foamed and churned to a white froth as its forward momentum slowed and then stopped. The captain certainly knew his or her business. The floater drifted into the dock as smooth and gentle as a baby carriage. It dwarfed our slider.

A sailor on the bow jumped onto the deck and deftly tied up while a bored woman in a white captain's cap sat on the aft deck. It was Shandi who poked her head out of the steering house. "Hello, darling."

Singh glanced at me, but Sam was the one who pulled free and leaped onto the slider. Shandi was already sliding down the steel pipes of the steering-house ladder. She was wearing a cuirass of leather strips over a pair of checkered tights. On her wrists were two long leather bracelets. I'd heard that the "Roman legion" look was all the rage in the Core worlds. "How's my sweetheart?" she wondered and gave a big hug to Sam.

Dad waited as the sailor shoved a metal gangplank down to the dock. He had an intent expression on his face as if he were selecting which speech to make to Mr. Tyr, but it was only Shandi who got off the floater.

"You call that standard equipment?" Singh muttered to me from the corner of his mouth. "Dear boy, you had better have your scanners junked and replaced. She's ravishing."

But I was paying more attention to the confident way she strolled onto the dock. She had looks, money, power—and knew it.

While Sam romped around her legs, she shook Dad's hand warmly. "Dr. Kincaid. Shall we get started?"

Dad hesitated. All his speeches had been designed for her father. "We were expecting Mr. Tyr too."

Her manner became a little brusque. "My father's still at the resort. There's been some trouble with his mines on Aldebaran Seven. He has to go there now."

"Oh." Dad tried to hide his disappointment. "Well, I'm glad you could pay a social call anyway."

"I'm quite capable of negotiating for him. I have before." I had to admire how easily Shandi asserted her authority.

Dad rubbed his chin. "Well, I suppose you know what animals you want for your birthday."

Shandi softened a little. "Let's leave that for later, shall we? Right now I'd like to see your island."

"Yes. Well, this way, Ms. Tyr."

"Shandi, please."

Singh forced the collar of the squirming Ladadog into my hand so that Singh could give a courtly bow and kiss her hand. "Your servant, Miss Tyr."

Shandi and Singh were two of a kind. "I have quite a few of those already."

Singh returned her stare. "I am quite sure of that."

Shandi's hand, which still lay in his, closed around his fingers. "What I could use are a few friends."

"For life," Singh promised fervently.

Shandi pulled her hand free and glanced over at me. "Hello, Piper. How's my monster hunter today?"

I would have liked to have done something equally as stylish as Singh, but I was busy trying to keep Ladadog away from Sam. "Fine." I remembered to jerk my head in greeting.

Singh moved in smoothly and blocked me from view. "This way, Miss. You'll be most amused." He held out his arm for her.

Shandi slid her arm breezily through his. "I'm sure I will be— one way or another."

Dad led the way while Sam bounced along on one side of Shandi and Singh hung on the other, leaving me to tug along his recalcitrant pet. I recognized Singh's Technique Number Fifty-one: the Attending Cavalier. Singh only trotted out that number for the heavies. I knew most of Singh's techniques, having watched him exercise them on various tourists—generally, the cuter and richer, the better. Shandi was the cutest and richest of them all.

When we reached the pen, Shandi greeted Godzilla merrily and he came right over to whine to her. Then, while Dad tried to go into his sales pitch and Singh tried to impress her with his cleverness, I let go of Ladadog. The last thing I saw of him, he went loping off into the rocks while I slipped into the pen and led the demos over one by one.

Shandi cooed and fussed and made the appropriate noises. Then she noticed the cardboard cutouts of various skyscrapers that had been stacked up off to the side. "What are those?"

Dad dismissed them with a wave of his hand. "They're just props for a little show that Piper puts on for the tourists."

"But I'm a tourist." Shandi turned around to look and saw me lingering in the background. "Aren't I, Piper?"

"It's corny." I shrugged in embarrassment. In fact, it was pure hokum, but the tourists seemed to eat it up. And the postcards they bought paid for the animals' feed.

"Why don't you let me be the judge of that?" She knew how to turn on the charm when she wanted. "I want the whole experience of the island."

Dad sighed as if he wished he'd never cooked up the idea of the floor show. "All right, Piper."

I set up the cardboard cutouts. I was going to look like enough of a clown without going into the regular spiel so I just called out. "Tokyo, boy. Tokyo."

Right on cue, Godzilla assumed his stance—kind of like a punch-drunk heavyweight who hasn't gotten much sleep. His paws feinted at the air.

It must have been Shandi's presence because Godzilla really hammed it up. He snorted and stomped along as if he were a hundred times his actual weight, his claws clacking on the rocks. Stopping abruptly, he swung his tail so that it knocked over the first cutout. Then he smashed and stomped on a few more cutouts, pausing every now and then to beat his chest.

Finally I pointed to the last one. "Tokyo, boy. Tokyo."

He paused for a moment, taking on an intense look as if he were constipated. His stomach rumbled and then he opened his mouth, exposing needle-sharp fangs. There was the sharp, pungent smell of methane vapor. And out came a column of fire that spread over the cutout so that the building disappeared in flame.

I stepped up to him and patted his head approvingly. My other hand slipped him a bit of choco-bar.

Shandi slipped inside the pen before anyone could stop her. "You trained him yourself?"

"Biggest mobile cigarette lighter in the Stellar Union." I tried to sound cool and indifferent.

"You're a person of many talents."

"The hardest part was to teach him to be quiet. His cheeping just doesn't go with the rest of the show."

"He'll have to have his voice dubbed." She started to hug Godzilla but wrinkled her nose. "What's happened to his breath?"

"It's methane from his digestive tract." I started to explain. "Like swamp gas. That's what makes the—"

But Shandi stopped me. "No. Don't disillusion me. There should be some mysteries in life."

Dad cleared his throat. "We also have some more commercial applications."

Shandi stroked Godzilla's head. "Then perhaps I could see some of them."

Dad nodded in the direction of Pandemonium. "We'll have to go to my lab. Singh, you'd better give the animals an early feeding." I don't think he wanted Singh distracting Shandi anymore.

Singh hesitated and then reluctantly disengaged himself from Shandi. Taking her hand, he kissed it again. "Till later."

Amused, Shandi studied him as if he were some big toy she was thinking of buying. "Perhaps."

We left the pen and went over toward Pandemonium. She paused, though, by the garden. There were still a few flowers left. "How lovely," she said, "and how unexpected."

"It was better in my wife's day."

Shandi seemed to be waiting for more and looked surprised when Dad just ushered her inside Pandemonium.

Once we were safely sealed in Dad's lab, Shandi became all business. "Now let's forget this birthday nonsense, shall we? Daddy is a dear, but he doesn't like people to know just how much I help him. In fact, sometimes he doesn't even know himself. So show me your designs, and I'll sell my father on the ones with the best commercial uses."

Dad paused by the computer console. "He'd listen to you?"

She poked a finger into Dad's side. "You take care of the designs and leave Daddy to me."

Dad plopped down in his chair. "Are you interested in anything special?"

Shandi sat down in a chair next to him. "I think Daddy would appreciate animals that can help our exploring teams."

"You name it, I can make it." Dad punched buttons on the keyboard, and the colored three-dimensional outlines of various animals flickered over the screen.

Shandi rested her left leg over her right knee. "Even for a vacuum?"

"Even that." Dad's fingers punched more keys, and the shape of the creature appeared on the screen.

Shandi leaned forward intently. "How do you keep the internal pressure from making it explode?"

Dad began a simplified discussion of biotechnics, and from the way Shandi nodded her head and asked intelligent questions, it was obvious she knew something about it. Delighted, Dad got more complicated. Shandi kept up with him even when I was having trouble.

I got out some quick-thaw lunches in the kitchen, and when I brought the tray back in, Shandi was sitting with Sam's head in her lap, stroking it thoughtfully. "But what about alien ecosystems? We don't want to introduce animals that might replace the native fauna."

Dad put some numbers on the screen. "We put in a gene that imprints the creature to something—the exploring team, a sound, even the shape of the spaceship. I can assure you my designs will be absolutely safe."

"No one and nothing is perfect," Shandi observed.

Sam reared up suddenly when she smelled food, and I bumped into her. Dad caught a glass of iced stim before it tipped over. He looked at me with a sigh. "I suppose so."

Shandi wagged her foot at Sam. "Let's deal in real cases for the moment. What could someone like Sam do for an exploring team?" I just stood there staring at her. She had to suspect how I felt about Sam.

In the meantime, though, the wheels began to work overtime in Dad's head as if he were trying to get rid of Sam. "Sam can stand fifty kilos pressure per square centimeter and hold her breath for several hours under water."

Shandi helped me set the tray down. "Pipes, from that scowl on your face, I would have thought you were modeling for a gargoyle spout."

I kept right on frowning. "Sam's not for sale. She's not cut out for exploring."

Dad sputtered over his stim. "Piper!"

Shandi, however, didn't seem the least bit offended. "No, it's refreshing to meet someone who says what he thinks."

Dad glared at me. "That's no excuse for behaving like Godzilla."

Shandi lifted her head and gave me the same open appraisal that she had the first time we had met—though this time, she'd marked the price tag up a bit. "You don't know how boring my life can be. Everyone is so polite to me because of our money. Piper is the first person I've ever met who speaks his mind."

"What little there is of it," Dad grumbled.

Shandi leaned down to rub her nose against Sam's. "I know. Sam's been raised as a pet. I was only speaking hypothetically."

She glanced up indignantly at me. "Just how heartless do you think I am?"

I fed some fish from my lunch to Sam. She chomped it down appreciatively. "You seem to think your money can buy everything—from solutions to friends."

"It's my father's style to buy friends." She took a bit of the fishcake.

Sam butted my leg so I fed her another tidbit. "And what's yours?"

She arched her eyebrows resignedly. "I don't know. His money casts a long shadow."

Her frankness was disarming. "It doesn't sound like you have many friends you can call your own."

"There are none," she declared flatly.

"How about one grouch?"

She ticked the items off on her fingers. "Who's also stubborn and quick-tempered." She lowered her hand and the corners of her mouth drew up hesitantly. "I'll take what I can get."

Funny, it was the first time I can remember seeing her smile; and it was such a shy, short-lived expression, here one moment, gone the next—like the sunlight caught on a curving wave—that it reminded me of someone far younger.

It was the first clue I had that maybe her self-assurance was just an act, even a kind of armor, that hid a shyer, more vulnerable Shandi—a hint that she was human after all.

"I guess we all do," I said.

Suddenly a little button by the collar of her cuirass began beeping, and she was all business again as she pressed a finger against it. "Yes?"

"Sorry to interrupt you, miss, but we've got three—um, little monsters trying to board us."

Dad stood up so quickly that his stool tipped over. "The pen must have shorted out again."

I was already starting for the door. "It's funny that Singh didn't tell us."

The air felt hot coming off the rocks. The fence around the pen was dead once again, and Singh's urya was yapping noisily. Sam snarled at him, and Ladadog returned the sentiment. Resignedly, I got hold of Sam's collar. The last thing we needed was another one of their brawls. "Easy, girl." I took Shandi's hand and guided it to the collar. "Hold her, will you?"

I reached a hand down for Ladadog's collar. I'd had my troubles with Ladadog, but he had never been vicious. Suddenly, though, Ladadog tried to bite me. I managed to get my right hand out of the way at the same time my left hand snagged his collar.

He still tried to bite me, but I tightened my hand on the collar, so that he gave a strangled yelp. "What's gotten into you, boy? Where's your master?"

But all he would do is give frantic yips and snap his fangs. "Well, if you're not going to help, you're not going to stop us either." I dragged the protesting Ladadog over the rocks and locked him in the com room. He threw himself against the door angrily like a small, hairy battering ram.

While Dad repaired the pen, Shandi and I got trank guns and darts from Pandemonium and then headed for the dock. In the meantime, Sam had been playing her usual games—refusing to help us but tagging along—when all of a sudden she began running back and forth nervously by a crevice.

"What is it, girl?" I knelt beside the crack in the rock. There was a body wedged between the sides. I looked at the face.

It was Singh.

·9·

"**Y**ou'd better go back to your ship," I said to Shandi.

"I've seen dead people before." She looked into the crevice and then glanced back at me. "He's been clawed and bitten pretty bad."

"Let's try to get him out." I lay down on the rocks so my hand could reach his wrist. His skin was still warm and I felt for a pulse. It was there but very feeble. "He's still alive."

Shandi got down beside me and reached into the crevice to feel Singh's neck. "Pull when I count three."

We both tried, but Singh was tightly wedged. "It's no use," I panted. "We need help."

Shandi nodded and stood up. "Let's get your dad. Then we can rescue my crew."

I wiped my hand on my shorts. "You're pretty matter-of-fact about murder."

Shandi looked at me levelly. "There are all kinds of corporate intrigues, from stock fights to assassinations."

I snapped off the shiner and set it down. "And you've seen an assassination?"

"I've been caught in three attempted ones." She started for Pandemonium. "The last time I was the one who killed the would-be assassin."

She spoke coolly, as if she were talking about nearly losing a wallet instead of her life. "Your dad was the target?"

She held up two fingers. "Twice. I was the target last time. There are plenty of people who would like to strike at Dad through me. And, like I told your dad, I do make business reports to him—and even make deals."

I tried to put myself in her shoes for a moment and just wound up shaking my head. "That must be hard, never knowing whether people like you or your money."

"It's harder never knowing who to trust."

Take away the money and take away Shandi's self-assured facade, and you would still have one amazingly strong, tough person. "If I'd had your kind of childhood, I think I would have locked myself up in a closet."

She gave me another one of her quick, fleeting smiles. "I think you would have managed better than that."

I appreciated the vote of confidence. "I'm surprised that you're here unarmed."

She gave a throaty chuckle. "What makes you think I'm un-armed?"

"Well, your wardrobe for one thing." I waved my hand vaguely at her cuirass. "There's not much there."

"The first rule of hiding something is misdirection. While people are looking elsewhere, I have this." She slid her hand across her stomach. It was an innocent enough gesture—almost as if she were rubbing herself; but a plate in the cuirass opened and the next moment a long, lethal blade appeared in her hand.

I eyed the wicked-looking point. "I bet you know how to use that thing too."

"Daddy believes in hiring only the best tutors. I had an ex-marine." Another flick of her wrist and the blade disappeared. "A corrupt governor hired him to murder me."

"That's some final exam." Shandi was like a kaleidoscope; every time I looked there was a different pattern to her.

She raised and lowered one shoulder. It was a little gesture, but it spoke of a whole lonely way of life that I would never know. "I passed. He flunked."

I slid an arm around her, and though she was wearing a cuirass, it was surprising how light and even fragile she felt. "Hearing about your life is like learning about a different species."

She put her arms around my waist stiffly—not because she rejected my touch but because she wasn't used to asking for or receiving help from someone. "Don't make me feel like a monster."

"I didn't mean to do that. It's just that all that money puts you in a world that's more savage than ours."

"Humans are still animals." She held on to me ever so lightly. "What's hard is controlling the fear all the time. Everyone wants to use me, right down to the servants. And there are a good many people who want me dead. There's only one person on whom I can count. That's me."

I inclined my head to the side. "The survivor."

She looked at me defiantly. "Yes."

I felt privileged in a way because I didn't think she exposed that fear to many people. Then, just as abruptly, she broke that brief contact and let go as if she had done something shameful. Feeling suddenly awkward, I stepped back too. "And money works better than any drug to bring out the beast."

After we had found Dad at the pen and told him what had happened, Shandi patted Dad's shoulder. "They'll close you for sure now."

To do Dad justice, that wasn't his main concern. "All I want is to catch the culprit and bring him back. He almost killed my friend. I can't let him stay on the loose. If I'm responsible, I'll face the consequences."

Together the three of us went to Shandi's floater. Our fabricants seemed annoyed that we were ending their fun for the second time, so they played a quick game of hide-and-seek, but we managed to sedate them. Shandi's crew didn't come out of the bridge until she assured them that it was all clear.

Then we went back and managed to drag Singh out of the crevice. Dad inspected the damage and shook his head. "I don't understand it. None of my demonstration animals is designed to kill."

"You could have fooled me," the captain muttered under her breath.

Shandi voiced my own feelings. "No, it's really not so hard to believe."

"Maybe everyone is right." Dad just scratched his head in puzzlement. "Maybe this operation is crazy and dangerous."

Dad was like a proud, tall tower toppling. I didn't know what to say so I was grateful to Shandi when she spoke up. "Let's wait and hear what he has to say first before we convict any of your animals. Like who stuffed him into the crevice?"

"He was trying to get away from whatever was after him," I suggested. "And then he passed out from loss of blood."

"But there's hardly any blood around outside the crevice. It's almost like he knew his attacker," Shandi argued and turned to Dad. "I bet he put up a struggle. Maybe you can find a tissue sample of his attacker under his nails."

Dad knelt and took one of Singh's hands. "That's a possibility." He dug a handkerchief out of a vest pocket. "I need something sharp, though."

"Here." Shandi produced her little steel toothpick and handed it to Dad hilt first.

Dad raised an eyebrow but he merely thanked her and quickly dug what he could from under the nails. Then Shandi motioned for her crew to put Singh on the makeshift stretcher. "Why don't you let my floater take Singh to the hospital. In the meantime we can round up your animals. Maybe we can prove they're all innocent."

I was starting to be glad she was there. "Well, if one of them didn't do it, who did?"

Shandi took back her knife from Dad and put it away. "First things first. Let's collect the animals and get tissue samples."

Dad carefully stowed the handkerchief in a vest pocket. "That's no problem. We've got tissue samples from every organism on this island."

I rubbed my arm. "He means it, too. You don't dare stand still for very long or Dad'll take a sample from you."

Shandi followed the stretcher toward the dock. "Did you yelp?"

"Not as loud as Ladadog. Did *he* ever put up a fuss." I gave a sad shake of my head, remembering how torn Singh had been between wanting to perform his scientific duty and not wanting to hurt his pet.

When we reached the dock, Dad turned off toward the com room. "I'll call the mainland to let them know your ship is coming in with Singh." As soon as he heard us, Ladadog immediately began to howl to be let out.

Dad bent slightly and caught the frantic bundle when he opened the door and held the animal off for a moment while he gave Singh's pet a sympathetic shake. "If you could only talk."

Ladadog became hysterical when he saw Singh being carried past. I didn't much like Singh's pet, but I was feeling sorry for him.

"Everything's going to be all right. Your master's going to get well."

It was almost as if Ladadog understood me, because he struggled even harder to get away from Dad's grip. "Whoa, there. Whoa." Dad straightened up, dragging Ladadog inside the com room and almost dropped the urya when he saw what Singh's pet had done. "That damn monster has trashed the com unit."

Shandi wrapped her arms protectively around the urya. "Poor thing; he must have been upset at being locked up."

Dad inspected the torn wires and smashed meters. "It's at least two hours' work to fix this."

I sniffed the panel. "Or more. I think he urinated on it too. Could be shorted out."

"Well, he can't do any more damage in here. Let's leave him." Dad dragged the yelping animal away from Shandi and motioned us outside while he locked him back up.

As Dad repaired the pen, we rounded up the animals. It wasn't nearly as hard as the first time. For one thing, it was nearly feeding time so it was easy to draw the various animals back into the pen, once Dad had it fixed. And with Shandi's help and the trank guns, it was easy to catch the stubborn few who didn't come in.

Shandi took off the rag that she had been using as a sweat-band. "Maybe next time you can put beepers on their collars."

Dad looked up from his inventory list. "I thought of that, but it's expensive and not very aesthetic."

"I would think your time was worth more." Shandi used her hand to fan herself. "Is it always hot like this?"

I crouched in the shade of a rock. "This is our winter season."

Dad slapped the stylus into the holder. "There's only one animal that's missing."

"Who's AWOL this time?" Shandi asked.

"Godzilla." Dad was looking grim.

"But he wouldn't hurt anyone," Shandi said.

"Even so, we'd better warn people." Dad motioned to the button on Shandi's collar. "Will that thing reach the mainland?"

"No, but I might be able to raise my ship." Shandi tried a few times, but she finally had to give up. "It's only got a short range, and I think they're beyond it."

"And the slider's com is out too." Dad glanced at me as if it were still my fault.

"We could wait till your floater comes back," I suggested. It was supposed to return for Shandi after it dropped off Singh. "That will give us more time to look for Godzilla first. I can just see Shadbell calling out the HDF and having them shoot anything with green scales."

It was fear plus years of frustration that made Dad's voice rise loudly. "That's why you should think of these things first before you let yourself be careless. You should have checked the field's wiring. If the pen was intact, we'd know it wasn't any of the animals."

"But I did look at it, Dad," I protested. "I can't help it if the equipment is so old it's ready to fall apart. You can't expect me to keep patching it for forever."

Sam was becoming increasingly upset by the scene between us. She began nipping first at my hand and then at Dad's until Dad pointed a finger at her. "I've had enough of you," he said. Reluctantly she lay down on her belly, and then it was my turn again. "Why is it always the fault of someone or something else? Why isn't it ever your fault?"

I knew where Dad was heading. I knew what he was probably going to say. And I didn't want Shandi to hear. I was getting to like her. Even more important, I think she was getting to like me. And I didn't want to change that. So I shoved Dad—shoved him back hard. "Shut up. Just shut up. Maybe you just expect the impossible."

Dad went a funny shade of purple and his hands balled into fists. "You lazy, irresponsible—" His fist drew back. I knew I couldn't win a fight with him any more than I could have with Singh. But I preferred getting beaten up to having Shandi find out the truth.

But Shandi calmly stepped in between Dad and me as if she were cutting in for a dance. "Don't you think," she inquired politely, "that we should find Godzilla before he can be blamed for any more trouble—or before he can do any more damage? We could take your slider out and look for him. He might be floating on another board. If he is, I bet the current is taking him to the same spot where I found him." But she was staring at Dad as if she was daring him to try anything.

Dad pivoted, but I knew he'd only be storing away his criticisms for a later session. "Why don't you two go? I've got research to do." He tapped the vest pocket into which he had put the samples.

I shifted my weight from one foot to another. No matter what he had said to me, I couldn't help being worried about him. "And leave you alone on the island with whatever got Singh?"

Dad seemed surprised and a little ashamed that I was still

concerned about him. "I'll be armed to the teeth. So will you."

"Neither one of us takes chances, right?" I asked.

"Right," Dad promised.

Inside Pandemonium, Dad opened the gun case and took out three switchers. They were lethal little automatics that shot off charged electrical pellets that should stun most any target. "Just remember, Piper. We can't afford any more mistakes."

I took the gun from Dad. "You're telling me not to screw up again."

He handed the other gun to Shandi. "I'm trying to be as polite as I can in front of company."

Shandi waited until we were about five kilometers from the island. "Why don't you stand up to your father?"

I didn't want her to go too far with that question, so I pretended to check the heading she had given me. "He's under a lot of pressure."

She sat on the starboard side with one foot propped against a railing. "And he's put you under even more. I can't think of anyone else who would go out on a cart. When I saw that, I said to myself that here was someone who was crazier than me."

I rested my hands lightly on the helm wheel. "That's not necessarily a virtue."

"True." Her foot thumped against the deck. "But why don't you try liking yourself for a change? Your dad's run you down so much, you believe him."

"I went on the cart because I was worried about Godzilla."

"You can get attached to some pretty ugly things." She picked up the switcher.

"I guess that's why I'm an apprentice monster maker."

"There are all sorts of monsters you can make—including yourself." She expertly slipped the clip out of the switcher. "You and I are a lot alike."

An excited Sam was ricocheting all over the slider. I tapped the recall signal, and she padded over reluctantly. "You can't be talking anatomically or financially."

She sighted over the barrel of her switcher. "Do you"—her

words came slowly, like someone moving uncertainly through a marsh, "do you ever feel like you're outside looking in?"

"Sometimes," I had to admit. In fact, it was often.

She lowered the gun. "I can buy anything I want, but I've never belonged to anyone or anything."

While Sam lay curled at my feet, I wriggled my shoulders, trying to get the kinks out. "There's your father."

"You've seen him." Shandi slapped the clip back into the switcher. "I'm more like a trusted business aide."

I stopped moving my shoulders. "And your mom?"

Shandi looked at me with a quick twist of her head—like some shy animal that had already exposed too much of itself. "I see her every few years, but mostly she's too busy spending her money."

Sam laid her head on my lap. "And you really don't have any friends of your own?"

Shandi leaned back in the seat and tried to find a comfortable position, but that was impossible on those old springs. "We've never been in one spot long enough." She gave me a conspiratorial smile. "Any one world can only stand so much of us."

Maybe she was right; maybe we were more alike than I had thought. "Well, as one outsider to another, welcome to the club." I held out my hand to her.

She took my hand and shook it solemnly. "That's it? Not even a secret handshake?"

"A committee is working on it." I grinned at her.

She propped an elbow on the side. "Well, tell them to get cracking. I don't know how long before my dad goes trotting off to some other part of the galaxy."

I had all these things that I suddenly wanted to say to her—feelings I never thought I could share with anyone—but before I could even begin, the engine sputtered and conked out. I tried to start the engine a dozen times, but the stupid thing wouldn't turn over. "You pile of junk." I hit it angrily.

Shandi tilted her head to one side. "Feel better?"

I rubbed my sore hand. "No." The mood for talking and sharing was gone as quickly as it had come. There wouldn't be any searching for Godzilla now.

"I'd be even more worried about you if you did." She began to scan the distant shoreline. "It's about five kilometers to shore. I guess we could swim."

"We'll be safer in these." I went to the locker where the diving gear was stowed.

When I flung one diving suit out, Shandi picked it up and fingered it. "These are pretty heavy suits."

I took out a pair of flippers that would attach to the feet. "They're really combat space suits that we've adapted to our own uses."

Shandi examined the suit more closely. "They look like they'll stand up to a lot of pressure."

"They were designed for deep space." I finally reached the helmets and dug out two of them. I also got out a pair of breather packs that would recycle their charges of air and adjust the mixture for whatever depth we were at.

It took us a few moments to check out the equipment and then put it on. Shandi transferred her knife to her suit belt. In the meantime, Sam, who knew what the ritual meant, had already gone over the side and was waiting for us.

We hadn't gone more than a hundred meters when a school of striped convict fish swam by, their mournful faces turning away from us. Immediately Sam shot forward like a furry missile. Trust Sam to pick the worst moment to do something useful. I tapped the side of my helmet in the signal for her to come back.

Wrong? Shandi signed to me.

Pleased, I signed back to her: *You know hand talk.*

She hovered in the water with winglike motions of her arms. *Useful. Many situations.*

Since it seemed safe, I couldn't see using the limited hand talk so I switched over to the com. "There's really nothing wrong. We've been trying to teach her how to herd fish." I watched as Sam headed off the fish and turned them.

"She's doing a pretty good job of it," Shandi said.

"It's more a game to her." I tapped the recall signal a second time, but Sam, still ignoring me, headed off the fish once again so that in desperation they headed straight for us. I floated resignedly in the water. "She likes to play it for only a few seconds. It's never long enough to trap fish in a pen."

Shandi turned on her back and swam that way for a while. "Daddy made his first fortune finding uses for things that everyone thought were worthless. He always says that there's more than one way to get what you want."

Suddenly dozens of panicked fish were wriggling past us. It was like being slapped by outraged midgets. And then the convict fish had swarmed past us. Shandi turned over on her stomach and rubbed a sore spot on her arm. "Ow. That hurt."

"She's always doing that." I supposed Shandi would be less forgiving of Sam now. She swam triumphantly back to me, but I folded my arms in an elaborate show. "NO!" I said loudly. I knew she could hear my voice faintly through my helmet. "That wasn't good."

Sam did a kind of flip that was her equivalent of a shrug at the fickleness of humans and then wriggled on.

"You're very attached to her." Shandi swam alongside me with slow, easy strokes and kicks.

"She's a nuisance," I said, "but she was my mom's. I guess that makes me a regular momma's boy, doesn't it?"

"There's nothing wrong with missing someone you love." Shandi shrugged clumsily. "At least you knew yours. I hardly know mine."

Ahead of us lay the Sentinel. Eons ago, during an ice age, the sea had shrunk so that the shoreline had extended much farther out, exposing a ridgeline. Rain and streams had carved caves and tunnels within the ridge and its highest peak. Later, when the ice age had ended and the sea had returned, the mountain had been covered with coral. From a distance, it seemed almost like a cone-shaped head covered with rainbow patches of flesh.

I told Shandi a little about it. "My mother used to take me here a lot. We like to explore the caves."

"So your childhood wasn't all work and no play," Shandi said.

"Even when Dad and she were at their busiest, she always made time to take me out."

"What else did she do?" There was a wistfulness—even a kind of distance—in Shandi's voice. It was as if she were shut out from something by a pane of glass. I remembered what she had said about her own busy mother. My own boyhood must seem normal compared to hers.

"This is one thing we used to do." I took us lower where the feathery sea pens covered the slope to the edge of visible light. It was almost as if the slope were covered with a fine, delicate fur. "I bet this is one sight you haven't seen." I swam still lower so I just brushed the tops of the sea pens, and each sea pen I touched burst into fiery life.

"How lovely," Shandi said and glided down beside me. As we moved along the slope, we left trails of soft, ghostly light burning behind us. Sam was a blur, darting and swerving in bursts of light through the sea pens.

I did a flip so that I was swimming on my back. I stared up at the surface of the water above us. It shimmered like a curtain of fire overhead. "If we had longer, you could write your name."

Shandi was quick to pick up on the implications. "Or draw pictures." She swam over me so she could look into my visor. She seemed genuinely touched that I was showing her this. "You're sweet; don't let anyone tell you differently."

That was when I saw several divers swimming down toward us. They were about the height of a human but they looked bulkier. I'd say the lightest was at least 120 kilos, but despite all their strength they moved very slowly, wasting most of their power with their clumsy strokes. I didn't think they were used to the sea.

"Who are they?" Shandi asked.

I had to shake my head elaborately to show that I didn't know who they were. Shandi started to raise her hand in greeting when one of the divers raised a long tube. There was a loud hum, and a streamer of bubbles around the tube.

Something made me grab Shandi's arm and pull her down. A small dark globe whooshed by and exploded beneath us, sending up a shower of mud and sea pens.

We both watched the top of the coral topple over. More divers were raising their tubes. Sam darted away before I could do anything. Well, she could take care of herself. It was us they wanted. I signed to Shandi: *Down!*

I didn't have to urge her to swim fast toward the protective darkness.

·10·

A moment later there was a bright light in the distance, as if a small sun were being born. I looked up just as the sound of the explosion came to us. It seemed louder in the water. A piece of the slider went tumbling past us. More parts fell in a shower of metal confetti.

The so-and-so's had blown up our slider. Then a strange diamond-shaped hull slid overhead ominously. There would be no way of outdistancing that.

"Friends of your father?" I asked. I thought it might be another of those assassination attempts she had told me about.

"Who knows." Shandi took out her switcher and tried to shoot, but nothing happened.

I tapped her gun. "These are useless in the water. We won't be able to use them again until they've been repaired."

She holstered the gun. "What do we do? We can't outswim that." Shandi had seen the hull too.

I shook my head inside my helmet. "I've really gotten us into a mess now."

I felt her calming hand on my shoulder, and when she spoke it was with a warm, secretive tone to her voice, as if we were in a conspiracy together. "We can't beat them outright. We have to work with what they're giving us." Those golden eyes regarded me urgently. "Help me think of something."

She made me feel as if we were a pair of Outsiders who could only depend on one another.

I forced myself to think. The switchers were useless in the water, and the trank gun might or might not puncture one of their suits. Anyway, I didn't like the odds of having to fight all those divers. So we couldn't run. We couldn't fight. All we could do was hide.

And then I remembered something that Mom had said when I'd been grousing about how much I hated this place. "This is your world, Piper. Don't fight it. Use what it gives you."

That's just what we'd do. "Come on." I angled downward toward an opening I knew about. From the utility belt, I took a shiner and strapped it to my left wrist.

Shandi shaped her hands like scoops so that she could move through the water with powerful sweeps of her arms. Behind us there was a chorus of hums. Little fiery flowers blossomed below us in the dark. Trying to swim and shoot at the same time was throwing off their aim.

There were a lot of ways into the Sentinel, and in that maze of tunnels I hoped to lose them—though I hadn't been back here since my mom had died. I took us through an opening covered with orange brain coral that looked like the wrinkled flesh of a pair of lips; the stalactites and stalagmites—formed when the cave had been above the sea—looked like fangs to me now.

Little purple crabs scuttled into crevices away from the light. I dimly recalled this cave. Mom had called it the Taxman. I swung the beam around the tall stone pillars. Mussels hung in gasping patches on the walls, and fringed worms hung down like unkempt wigs.

There! I signed and stabbed the light toward an opening. At this distance, it looked no bigger than an egg.

Even as we wove our way through the rocky cones, I tried to keep the light on the hole. We were about five meters away when I heard a *clonk* at the mouth of the cave. I suppose one of our attackers had brushed his breather pack against the stone. I grabbed Shandi by the wrist and pressed the shiner's button switch against my chest so that it would go off.

We floated in the water for a moment, our eyes adjusting to the dim light given off by the faintly glowing coral. The opening was like a blurred shadow in the dim light.

Still towing Shandi, I went through the opening. With my free hand tracing the wall, I swam on slowly for some twenty meters before a bend took us out of sight of the cave. Only then did I turn on the shiner. The tunnel narrowed ahead of us so that we would have to go single file.

Letting go of Shandi's hand, I led the way. We hadn't gone on for more than fifty meters when there was rasping sound like a file scraping rock and a huge arrow-shaped head thrust itself from its hole. As the wide lips opened, Shandi jerked back on my ankle just in time; the needle-sharp teeth clashed together in the water.

The rock worm gave a frustrated shake of its head and twisted to stare at us. Someone once called a rock worm a mobile stomach. Its jaws are tough enough to crush through an armored diving suit, and it is too mean or too stupid to back away from a fight. This one must have moved in since the last time Mom and I had been here.

I took out the trank gun, sighted, and fired, but the dart simply bounced off its bony skull. I needed to hit the softer skin behind the head, but the rock worm kept its body hidden in the hole. The only thing I had managed to do was waste a dart and rile up the rock worm even more.

We couldn't go back. We had to go forward. *I lead bad-bad trap,* I signed miserably. Since I used my right hand to sign, my left hand helped to balance me. *Wait!* Shandi grabbed my wrist to which the shiner was strapped. As she moved it, the rock worm's head twisted with the motion of the light.

I have idea. She slid the shiner off my wrist. The beady little eyes followed it in fascination. Reloading the trank gun, I tried to draw it out of the hole, but though its eyes hung on the shiner's every motion, the rock worm refused to present more than its head.

From the clinking and banging behind us, I knew that our pursuers must have finally entered the tunnel. Maybe it was better to leave Mr. Congeniality awake and alert behind us.

So instead I reholstered the trank gun and motioned for Shandi to take off her shiner. *Idea. Copy me.*

Bracing my feet against the floor of the tunnel, I flipped the lantern up. The beady eyes still followed it, and suddenly the rock worm's head shot forward.

I kicked off right then. The light flashed crazily on the roof of the tunnel and then stopped as the huge jaws caught it. I was so close I could see the bumps that the little parasites made, burrowing in the worm's skin, and then I was kicking on past. The jaws crushed the lantern and there was only blackness ahead.

Crazy. Shandi gestured from behind me. *We be in dark.*

Only way. You trust. You not trust. Up to you. Awkwardly I got a length of rope from my belt and cut off a few meters.

I tied the bit of rope to my belt and trailed it behind me as I swam on about three meters. Up ahead, it was going to be a tight squeeze. I didn't remember the tunnel's being this bad. Cave-ins must have narrowed it. And what if the tunnel was now a dead end?

Light suddenly splashed in the tunnel as Shandi threw her shiner into it. I heard the familiar rasping sound and the crunch of metal. In the darkness, there wasn't any way I could see if she'd made it.

I couldn't help using the com. "Shandi?"

"Here," she panted. "But it was close."

I sighed with relief. The gamble had paid off. "Feel around on the floor of the tunnel. You should find a rope there."

There was a moment of silence and then Shandi said. "Right."

"Tie it to your belt." I explored the tunnel with my hands. It seemed to go straight.

"OK. Ready to climb the mountain." Shandi tugged at the line.

I began to swim on—and banged my helmet against the rock

after just five meters. I'd have to take it slower, going on blindly, feeling the rock as I went.

Suddenly we heard a shrill scream behind us. A cloud of bubbles rolled up and around us as if a diver's breather pack and suit had ripped open.

"I think they met our friend," Shandi said.

There were several sharp explosions. "And he met them," I said as I went on.

My hands could feel a trembling in the walls of the tunnels. "What is it?" Shandi demanded in a panicky voice.

"The Sentinel isn't all that stable. I think they loosened some of the rocks." I dragged my hands over some mussels, pulling myself forward.

I wanted to tear at the rocks and kick my legs so we could hurry out of there, but the last thing we needed was an accident. I forced myself to stay calm. At one point I had to wriggle and squirm through an especially narrow opening. It seemed like a near thing.

Finally came the moment I dreaded: my breather pack clanked against the tunnel. I felt carefully around the surface. It was too narrow for me and the pack.

"What is it now?" Shandi sounded worried.

"We'll have to take off our breathers." It was hard work getting my pack off in the tight confines, but I managed it. Then I shoved it in front of me and squeezed on through.

I lost track of time and space. It could have been an hour or a day; we could have gone a hundred meters or a thousand. But we were almost out of the tunnel before I realized it.

Suddenly, I was looking up at the glittering surface of the water about thirty meters overhead. I pulled myself out of the opening and, dragging my pack along, swam upward into the blessed openness of the sea. Shandi followed a moment later, sweeping her breather pack through the now-empty water.

When we had helped each other shrug into our breather packs, I pointed toward the surface where the strange, diamond-shaped craft now floated like a black axhead. I looked around for our big buddies and just made out the excited knot of divers below us in the distance. They were gathered around the mouth of the tunnel. I suppose they were trying to free their trapped comrades.

Shandi tapped my shoulder and I turned. She was grinning through her faceplate as she pulled out her knife. She wanted to take their ship. I know it wasn't very heroic, but I hesitated. They had some kind of gun, after all. We were decompressing in our suits. Any tear could bring on a painful if not fatal case of the bends. I just wanted to get to New Benua and safety, but a little voice inside my head told me we would never get there unless we took the craft.

There didn't seem to be any choice. Gulping, I nodded my head and pulled out my trank gun.

With a kick of her legs, Shandi was already rising. Our suits began to swell as the breather packs began to compensate. Shandi went on kicking determinedly, her eyes focused on the craft.

When she was a full body length away from me, she signed for me to go toward the starboard side. At the same time, she headed for the port side. I was barely in position before she rose out of the water, her body disappearing above the surface. Dimly I could hear shouting through her helmet.

That was my cue. There wasn't time to hesitate or even think about what I was doing. Gripping the side of the craft, I hauled myself out of the water into the noontime sun. In the diving suit, I felt as big and awkward as a walrus. There was just one guard. He had his back to me as he raised his gun. I had to do something fast if Shandi wasn't going to wind up in the cemetery.

In all the holos, the hero leaps onto the deck and starts shooting. I tried my best, but despite all my scrambling, I only managed to drape myself over the side with my legs kicking over the open sea and my hands waving over the deck. In the process of trying to right myself, I even managed to lose my gun.

The guard turned, but he just stared instead of shooting me right away. He probably couldn't believe that any attacker would provide such an easy target. Suddenly he gave a grunt and there was the hiss of gas escaping from his suit. He whirled around. I could see Shandi's knife sticking out from his shoulder. He was swinging his gun back up to take a shot at her.

I tried to draw my suit knife out as I threw myself at him, only I slipped on the wet deck and I rolled into his legs instead. I could hear his angry yelp as his legs buckled and he fell on top of me. He was so large it was impossible to throw him off me. I tried to bring my knife up, but he brought the barrel of his gun down hard on my wrist so that I dropped the knife too.

Desperately I grasped the gun barrel in my good hand and tried to yank it away from him, but even with an injured shoulder, he was stronger. We pulled in opposite directions for a moment. In the middle of the struggle, our faceplates almost came together, and through the filtered faceplate of his helmet, I thought I saw a familiar bulldog-like face.

I should know it. I'd seen it often enough in history holos. It was a Rell—like the kind who had attacked this world decades ago. I was so startled I forgot to hold tight to the gun. The next thing I knew, the determined guard had brought the barrel of the gun down on my helmet. It actually didn't hurt through the metal, but suddenly I knew what it was like to be the clapper inside a giant bell. And the moment after that the guard had the hexagonal muzzle of his gun pointed right at my heart. The Rell definitely had a good knowledge of human physiology.

Shandi had clambered over the side of the craft like a modern pirate. She stood there on the deck when she saw the gun was on me.

The guard got up slowly. His gun pointed unwaveringly at my heart. There was a button on the side near his thumb. He motioned Shandi over toward me.

And suddenly this furry brown torpedo shot up from the water in a fountain of spray. Sam had found us. I take back whatever mean things I ever said about the little pest. The gun went flying over the side while the guard staggered across the deck. Sam clung to his shoulders with her forepaws while her teeth and hind claws ripped at his suit.

Shandi dove and picked up my knife, rolling to all fours in one smooth motion. She rose as the guard stumbled toward her. Stepping in, she hesitated only because she didn't seem sure what was a vital area. Then, with a frantic shove, she plunged the knife in.

She must have picked a good spot, because the guard stiffened and pulled away from the blade. His legs hit the side as he fell overboard. Sam jumped off at the last moment, spitting and making faces as if the suit material had left a bad taste in her mouth.

The ship was kind of like a slider, though its compartment was also diamond-shaped like its hull, with about a dozen saddles mounted on posts. I guess the Rell's masters kept them mean by keeping them uncomfortable.

Shandi sheathed the bloody knife and straddled a seat near the control panel. It really wasn't built for a human body so her legs perched awkwardly on either side. She leaned forward intently to study the controls. Instead of a wheel there were handles, and under rows of buttons were symbols in some strange clawlike cuneiform symbols. I heard that now-familiar humming noise and squatted down as a blue globe went whizzing by. Peeking over the port side, I could just make out a half-dozen helmeted divers rising toward us.

"Let's get out of here," I urged. "I think those fellows are still mad about something."

I could hear her barely mumble over her helmet com: ". . . said-this-one-is-it." With a shrug, Shandi pushed a button. The engine roared into life. "Piece of cake," she gloated, and then she wrapped her gloved hand around a handle and jerked.

I was knocked forward as the craft began to slide backward through the water. Globes hissed through the air. I suppose the divers figured that they didn't have anything to lose now if they shot up the slider.

"Oops, sorry." The engine suddenly idled and we drifted backward. "Don't worry. I'll get the hang of this yet."

"I just hope you do it before those clowns get the range," I said.

The next moment, a globe dropped on the control board to Shandi's right and exploded. Sparks flew into the air. Shielding her helmet with one hand, Shandi stabbed the button again and pushed the handle toward the control board. "This has got to be forward," she declared, and we began to roar forward.

Part of the starboard side exploded. Then we were jetting away. The frustrated Rell kept firing long after we were out of range.

·11·

Pulling at another handle, Shandi swung the strange craft away in a wide circle, leaving a broad white wake. It only took her a few minutes of experimentation before she had the ship bouncing and hopping over the waves.

"You see?" she said over her helmet com. "I knew you had it in you, Piper."

I fetched the trank gun. "I led us straight into a trap."

"How could you know they'd be there?" She waved a hand back toward the Rell. "And you managed to outfox them."

"It was more luck than anything else. Wasn't it, girl?" Sam just rubbed her slick head against my suit.

Shandi turned awkwardly around in the seat. Through her helmet visor, I could see the same peeved expression on her face that Sam had when I hit her on the nose. "Some people make their own luck."

I straddled the seat next to Shandi. Sam, after a brief exploration of the alien slider, had lain down in the sunshine by my feet and proceeded to fall asleep. Every now and then, she gave off little snorts. "Maybe, but some folk just stumble in and out of messes—and I'm one of them."

Shandi forgot for a moment that she was still decompressing in her suit. She brought her hand up to try to scratch her forehead but found the helmet obstructing her hand. "Why can't you take a compliment?"

Our suits had puffed out as we decompressed so they felt a little stiff. It made it clumsy even to shrug. "When I do something to earn it."

She poked an annoyed finger at the swollen chest of my suit. "Sometime you're going to have to face the fact that your father is wrong about you."

I didn't like the direction the conversation was heading. I just wanted to change the subject. "I'm more interested in getting help."

She pointed to the blackened half of the board where one beam had caught us. "Unfortunately, I think that the com was there. And our suit coms don't have the range."

The HDF was geared to stop an invasion force, not a commando unit. There were plenty of holes in our radar screen where a single Xylk ship could come through to drop off a team of Rell. I reloaded the trank gun and holstered it. "Maybe the Rell attacked Singh."

Shandi wrestled the craft toward our island. "And maybe they're behind your other troubles, too—including the breakdown of the pen fences."

I thought of what had happened to Singh and then of what might happen to Dad all alone on the island. "We've got to get back to Dad fast."

"I'm already giving it all the slider's got." Shandi tapped the control handles. "But up until today it was more like they were trying to close you down. Not destroy you."

I didn't like feeling so helpless. I wanted weapons, lots of them. I took the clip from the switcher so I could begin to strip and check it. "There's nothing strategic about our island. And we're not sitting on anything valuable. No treasure. No minerals."

She raised one leg, but the suit was so swollen that the motion was awkward. "What about your livestock?"

I pulled back on the catch and slid off the switcher's barrel.

"It's nothing that any other genetic engineer couldn't make with the proper facilities."

Shandi slipped one fin off her foot. "Well, whatever it is, they almost killed Singh for it, and they nearly got us."

I thumbed the lever that opened the bottom of the gun. I knew what we were both thinking. They might also have killed Dad for it too. I stopped for a moment to look at the sea. It gleamed and sparkled under the twin suns. It was the kind of scene tourists snap holos of and coo about how lovely it is. They didn't know how deadly it was—and now the sea was hiding the Rell. I detested this world so much that for a moment I forgot myself. "I hate this place." The words slipped out. "I'm leaving as soon as I can."

She hung the fin from her belt and started to raise her other foot. "How come?"

The switcher was useless, just like I thought. The replacement chips were cheap enough but I didn't have any on me. "Forget it."

Shandi was like an urya worrying a bone. She just wouldn't let go. "Something's eating at you. It's been eating at you for years."

I reassembled the switcher and put it away. "You just can't take anything for granted here. The only livable areas are in the high latitudes, and even then you broil in the summers. And with the water so hot at the equator, it makes for killer winds and currents like express trains. One minute it can be like this and the next minute you're in the middle of a storm. And storm winds here average some two hundred kilometers per hour—plus the tidal waves. What would be a disastrous typhoon on Earth is just a normal storm here."

Shandi tugged off her second fin and added it to the first. "I'd want three feet of concrete between me and a storm like that." She got out her own switcher and handed it to me to check.

I took it from her. "That's what mainlanders try to do. They build those massive fortresses or burrow into the rock, but it's a toss-up if they survive. It's safer under the water." I concentrated on stripping the gun. "Surface buildings like our com room are built cheap because you have to replace them." Suddenly the barrel fell out of my gloved hand and started to roll across the deck.

Shandi trapped the barrel neatly under her foot. "And the animals?"

I opened up her switcher. "They go into a special pen inside Pandemonium. My mom gave that name to the lab after one storm."

Too late, I realized I'd laid myself open. The question came that I'd hoped she'd never ask. "What happened to your mom?" Shandi said.

Part of me was afraid to tell Shandi anything, and yet the other part had to talk—as if there was all this steam whirling around inside me, ready to burst out. "She got caught in a storm. She went to the mainland for supplies. We thought she was going to stay there, but she came rushing back. We heard later that she wanted to save some of her plantings."

Shandi rose from her chair. "Didn't she send a message?"

Her switcher was just as useless as mine. "She did, and it shouldn't have been any problem—except that I didn't set up the relay to Pandemonium from the com room."

Shandi took her hand from the controls long enough to squat down and get the barrel. "You probably were busy with all your other chores."

"It was the one thing I should have remembered." I took the barrel from her. "While Pandemonium was sinking, I thought I heard a banging on the sides like someone hitting it."

She sat back down and took the controls again. "It was probably the wind."

"That's what I thought at the time." I put her switcher back together again. "Now I'm not so sure."

As I returned the switcher to her, her hand trapped mine. "It's not your fault, Piper." Through her helmet visor, I could see that her face had softened, and even over the suit radio I could hear a tenderness in her voice.

It had been missing from my life for so many years I didn't know quite what to do. Suddenly I felt like I was suffocating. It was worse than being trapped inside the suit. "You weren't there. What would you know about it?" I yanked my gloved hand free and snapped off my com so I couldn't hear her.

Even so, she leaned her helmet against mine. It was as if my confession had made some kind of compact between us, whether I recognized it or not. By shouting, she could make herself heard inside my own helmet even though her words sounded strained. "I know about pain," she said. "And I know how it can shut you off from the rest of the world."

"Quit feeling sorry for me," I snapped and got up so she couldn't talk to me anymore.

I didn't say anything until we were almost to the island. Then I checked my chronometer and turned on my com once again. "I think we're finished decompressing."

Shandi ran her finger along the neck of her suit and unsealed the helmet. Her inflated suit sagged with a hiss about her, like a fat snake collapsing. If I thought the delay in the conversation would make her ease up a bit, I was wrong. The words just came tumbling out of her as if she'd already rehearsed them. "You know, you can't go on blaming yourself for the rest of your life."

If I wanted to get out of my suit—and I did—there was no escaping her words. I unsealed my own helmet. "But I told you: it was my fault."

As she jerked off her helmet, she spoke with a special urgency. "Even if it was your fault, you're only expected to pay for it for so long."

I leaned forward to pull off my helmet. "It's not like a bank loan."

She shook her head so that her sweaty hair spread out to dry, but she was looking at me with a strange intensity. I felt like the first patient of someone who has just taken a first-aid class. All the coolness, all the shyness, was gone; there was only a clumsy eagerness to help. "This is the last thing your mother would have wanted."

I breathed in the fresh sea air. "You can't know that."

She wanted—even needed—to help. I couldn't know for sure, but I suspected this was the first time she felt she had more than money to give. "I can make a pretty good guess." She eased out of her breather pack.

I took off my gloves so I could wipe my face. It felt good to feel my own skin again. "You just don't understand."

She started to strip off her suit. Her words were chosen with care as if she'd finally realized that she was overdoing it. "I understand that you're tormenting yourself—needlessly."

I shrugged off my own breather pack and let it drop with a clunk to the deck. "You can't decide for me." Sam roused leisurely and yawned, exposing her sharp little teeth for all the world to see.

Shandi finished taking off her suit. "Just remember. There are all sorts of monsters you can make—including yourself."

I was glad of an excuse to occupy our minds with other things. "There's the island." I pointed to a dark scab on the side of the ocean.

Shandi immediately cut back on the engine. "We don't know what's waiting up there." She turned the ship slowly and approached the island cautiously, but there weren't any shots. I tried to raise Dad on the helmet com, but there wasn't any answer. That wasn't exactly ominous since he might not be monitoring the com.

Shandi let the slider drift into the dock. By that time I'd gotten out of my suit so it was easy to jump out and tie up our stolen ship.

Leaping onto the wooden planks, Sam charged forward clumsily. She skidded once on the rock as she halted and then cut into the com room. The door burst open under her weight, and she shot into the room.

A loud yelp came from the urya, and there were the sounds of two very angry animals fighting. I made my tired legs pound on the rock. "Come one. We've got to stop them before they destroy the com room."

We found Sam and Ladadog rolling around in a ball on the floor. "Get Sam," I told Shandi while I grabbed at Ladadog's collar.

The moment Ladadog felt me take his collar, he twisted around and tried to bite me angrily. "Hey!" I stood up, jerking the urya into the air by his collar. He felt like a lot of dead weight and gave a strangled bark.

Shandi, in the meantime, was crouching on the floor with an armful of very indignant Sam. "Usually uryas are so docile."

"Even dumb." I'd had just about enough of Ladadog. I wanted to try to respect Singh's pet for the sake of his memory, but this was just too much. I still had the trank gun holstered on my belt. I yanked it out with my free hand.

"Piper!" Shandi exclaimed in shock even as the trank gun hissed.

Ladadog gave a startled yipe. His legs twitched once and then he went limp. His weight almost dragged me down as he collapsed. "It was either this or strangle him," I said defensively to Shandi.

Shandi hugged the still quivering Sam. "I'd hate to see what you do when you babysit."

I holstered the gun. "Think I waste good trank juice on kids? I just tie them up and throw them in the closet."

Shandi tried to wrestle an angry Sam toward the door. "I wonder where your dad is?"

I pulled the dart from the urya and put it on the com console. "Probably in Pandemonium."

Shandi didn't make any progress toward the doorway. "You'd better put the urya away someplace. He's still upsetting Sam."

I nodded to the door of a supply closet. "Open the door."

Holding Sam by her collar, Shandi leaned over to the closet and opened it. "What's this?" With her free hand, she took out a small sack of blue netting.

"I've never seen that before," I said as I dragged the unconscious urya over.

Shandi opened the flap on a small blue sack. Inside were small blocks of white cheeselike material. "It looks like someone's lunch." She took out a handful of small thin metal sticks. "And what are these?"

I deposited the urya inside and slammed the door shut. "I don't know, but then Dad has a lot of gear that I don't know about."

Shandi deposited it on a chair. "I'll leave it here then."

I thought for sure that Dad would be inside Pandemonium, but though the equipment was on, Dad wasn't around at any level. I went to the gun case. Everything was gone: guns, ammo, even replacement chips for the switchers.

Shandi put her hand on the analyzer. "It's hot. I bet it's been on all this time."

I snapped off the machine and, going to the doorway, cupped my hands like a megaphone around my mouth. "Dad!"

Shandi took her cue from me. "Dr. Kincaid!" she shouted.

"You take one side of the island," I said. "I'll take the other."

Nodding her head, Shandi strolled off with Sam.

The wind whistled over the barren rock. The late-afternoon sun raised little ghostly ribbons of steam from crevices where spray and dew had collected. Everywhere I looked there was only the empty, restless sea or the lifeless slabs of rock. I might as well have been on a moon—except for the occasional distant shout from Shandi.

When I passed by the pen, I paused. I could see the other animals, but Godzilla's favorite perch was still empty. I had a worse feeling than ever before in my stomach. Shandi looked worried when we rendezvoused by the com room.

"No sign of him?" she asked.

I shook my head and looked at the jagged landscape. "I hope he didn't fall in some crevice. If he's unconscious, we could pass right by him."

"Could he have left a note back in his lab?" Shandi's eyes surveyed the territory.

I shrugged. "I didn't really look at the machine."

"We still probably have enough time to check." Shandi stepped over a rock and joined me with quick, long strides.

Back in Pandemonium, we found a stack of slides on the console of the analyzer. Next to the slides was his notebook with a cryptic note scrawled onto the page.

Shandi squinted as she stared at it. "How do you ever read his handwriting?"

I snapped on the analyzer before I looked at the page. "It's usually not this bad. He must have been in a hurry."

Shandi glanced at me. "To leave a clue for us?"

I studied the scrawl more intently. It was some number with eight digits.

The screen illuminated Shandi's face as it warmed into life. "Is it one of these?" she asked as she leaned forward intently.

I searched through the slides but none of them had numbers— as if Dad had just made them up. I punched in the number itself, but the computer told me there was no such slide number in its data banks. "Maybe it's one of the new ones." I fed a slide into the slot. It took a moment for the data to appear on the screen. I watched as the data continued to roll on past.

"What a mess," Shandi declared.

"Right." My fingers danced over the keys to tell the computer to try to separate the data into discrete entries. The first group was some kind of tissue sample. A second later it announced that the sample was from a human.

The next group was even more complicated. Shandi frowned as the analysis rolled on past. "What's that?"

"Let's let the computer make an educated guess." I pressed some keys. The computer hummed and whirled to itself and then told us that its best estimate was that we were looking at soap.

There were about a dozen other odd items ranging from polyester fibers to some inorganic items I couldn't identify. On a hunch, I had the computer look for more organic groups.

The first was from a Carefree kelp species known as a sea boa, but the next made me sit up; the screen flashed SPECIES UNKNOWN.

"How large are the data banks?" Shandi wondered.

"They have most of the major known species." I punched in a

congruity study. "This should find the closest cousin if there is one."

The screen flashed back some species name in Latin.

I tilted back my chair. "That can't be."

Shandi nudged me. "Translate it."

I thought I'd double-check. I called up some data from storage. Two ribbons of DNA turned in their slow dance across the screen. Red dots indicated mismatches.

Shandi peered at the screen. "What does it mean?"

I tapped the ribbon on the left. "This sample was just taken from Singh's urya." I tapped the ribbon on the right. "This is a real urya. They're kin, but they're not the same species."

Shandi picked up another slide. "How close?"

"They're close enough to be cousins. Like human beings are to chimps." I rubbed my chin. It was beginning to make a crazy kind of sense.

Shandi was quick to tumble to what that might mean. She looked at me in horror. "You mean Ladadog may be a ringer?"

"I don't know." I snapped off the console and rose from the chair. "But I'm going to get another sample and find out." I glanced at my chronometer. "Is it an hour already? We'd better hurry. Singh's pet should be waking up—whoever or whatever it is."

We were about ten meters from the com room when we suddenly heard a thump. Sam's head shot up and she gave a snarl. Shandi gave an exasperated click of her tongue. "I think we're too late."

"I'll take care of it." I started to pull out the trank gun, but Shandi stopped me.

"Leave this to me," she said grimly. "We probably don't have the time to wait around for it to wake up again."

But Sam had ideas of her own. Head low, she loped over the rocks back toward the com room.

·*12*·

*F*rom inside the com room, Sam gave an angry squeal that suddenly rose to a high, painful yelp.

We clumsy humans stumbled up a moment later to find that Ladadog had woken up and come out of the closet. An angry Sam darted her head this way and that as she tried to rear up and take a chunk out of him. There was the smell of burnt fur in the air. The funny thing was that Ladadog was crouching on just his hind paws while he held a glowing red stick in one forepaw and was using it to hold off Sam. The other held a flat blue board to which a metal loop was attached perpendicularly.

"Well, well, well." Shandi folded her arms.

The creature looked up at us and automatically started to hunch as if he were going to get on all fours. But a sudden dart from Sam made him yelp. He straightened fully. On all fours, he was waist-high but standing up he came to my shoulders. He reared erect once more. "To get this thing away from me," he ordered angrily.

I blinked my eyes. "You can talk."

"To speak more dialects than you," Fake Ladadog tried to announce proudly but a lunge from Sam made him back up hastily. "To get this seagoing vermin away before I take out its eyes."

Shandi leaned against the doorway. "Want to bet our little girl takes off your paw before you can do that?"

"To battle by the Code," Fake Ladadog protested.

"Does your code include murder and sabotage?" Shandi inquired with mock innocence.

"Everything is proper against invaders!" Fake Ladadog insisted.

"As I recall, there was only lichen and lizards here originally when we humans settled it."

Fake Ladadog spread out a paw in a grand arc. "To not waste time on details. To own all stars. To fight you giants." He gave a little yelp as Sam nipped one leg. "To not let you push us around."

I studied the alien. Standing up straight, he looked like a different creature altogether. "Are you an urya?"

Shandi slipped out her knife. "I'm willing to bet he isn't, and I'm willing to bet your lab could prove it."

"He's a genetic construct?" I looked at him in horror. It's so ingrained in our culture not to tamper radically with the genes of our own species that it's easy to forget that another species may not have the same taboos.

"To do anything you giants can," Fake Ladadog declared. He smashed the board suddenly against the wall so that it broke into a dozen pieces. Then he picked up a small globe from the desk. It had a handle that fit naturally in his paw. A hexagonal barrel protruded from one end, so that it seemed like a smaller brother to the guns the Rell had used.

Shandi edged into the com room. "I'm willing to bet that we are looking at a disguised member of the Xylk."

I stared down at the pseudo-urya. "This is supposed to be the master of those massive Rell?"

He drew himself up so that he was chest-high, and suddenly it didn't seem like such a humorous notion after all. It was a mistake to think that, because he was small, he was harmless. A gun doesn't have height requirements. All that matters is the digit on the trigger. A person can be shot dead just as easily by someone one meter high as by someone who is a full two meters.

"We are the Empire!" he proclaimed fiercely. "Not to answer to the labels of giants." He might have been small, but every gram of his body spoke of a fanatical sense of mission. I tried to think of

any human I knew who would have imitated a pet, and I couldn't
think of any. No, it would be a mistake to underestimate the Xylk
just because of their size.

Shandi joined me. "So your people have been planning this
invasion for a long time?"

"To defend our territory," Fake Ladadog insisted. "To create the
plan ever since you giants came here." He drew his lips back
from his teeth in what must have been the equivalent of a human
smile. No urya would have done that. More than anything, it
convinced me he must be a Xylk. "To be fools, you giants."

You would have thought that Sam and Shandi had been hunting together for a lifetime by the smooth way they worked together. Each approached from the opposite side so that it was
impossible for the pseudo-urya to watch them both at the same
time. He looked like he wanted to shoot, but he knew he couldn't
get us all.

"That would be some fifty years ago." Shandi was crouched,
leaning forward on the balls of her feet. "Long enough to notice
our pets."

Even with twisting his head and making his eye stalks do
acrobatics, he couldn't keep an eye on the both of them. "To think
they are slaves, then to realize only animals."

Shandi circled warily. "Like we are to chimps."

I was feeling stupid standing by the doorway so I picked up a
piece of wood. "It's probably more likely parallel developments on
different worlds—only his ancestors went on to become intelligent."

"Oh, I love you brainy types." Shandi darted in. Her knife
flicked down at Fake Ladadog's wrist, and he dropped his gun
with a squawl. The next moment Sam had bitten the wrist with
the glowing stick and pulled the pseudo-urya to the floor. Then
Shandi was yanking the stick from his paw.

"To not get anything from me," Fake Ladadog growled defiantly as Sam hovered over him.

Shandi kicked both the gun and the stick across the floor
toward me. "Here. Take charge of this."

I got the gun first. The globe fit awkwardly over my larger

hand, but I could reach the trigger button. However, I used a rag to pick up the stick. It felt warm and, as I squeezed it, it seemed to glow. A burn mark appeared on the rag. I held up the gun. "I know what this is." I nodded to the stick. "But is this a weapon too?"

A block of that white cheeselike material had been taken from the sack. It lay on the floor now and Shandi picked it up. "More like some kind of detonator for this." She looked down at Fake Ladadog. "This is an explosive, right?"

"To never tell," Fake Ladadog declared defiantly.

"Not to split infinitives"—Shandi nodded to Sam—"or let Sam eat you for lunch." She added, "Starting with the eye stalks."

"Even if rip off eye stalks." And he named another half-dozen ways of torture that I would never have even imagined and would have been disgusted if I had. If this one was typical, I could see how the Xylk kept their hold over their Rell soldiers.

Shandi nodded toward the sack. "I doubt if this is all your lunch. Shall we stuff some of this into your mouth and then put the detonator in?"

His eye stalks waved. "No, no, no. To blow this island to bits."

Shandi nudged him with her foot. "Where's Dr. Kincaid?"

"To not hurt him." Fake Ladadog glared.

"If you did anything to Dad—" I started forward.

"No, no, no. To have taken him prisoner."

"Why?" I demanded. I pointed the detonator toward him.

"To . . . to learn secrets," Fake Ladadog snarled.

That made me a little suspicious. "And why were you trying to take us?"

"To make your father cooperate," Fake Ladadog said quickly.

But his answer was a little too quick for me. "And where's Godzilla? Did you take him too?"

"To discover he . . . he just escaped," Fake Ladadog said.

"He can't swim, so the only way he could get off this island was if he found another board—or was taken."

Shandi suddenly snatched one of the eye stalks. "It wasn't to learn Dr. Kincaid's secrets, was it?"

I looked at Shandi. "What are you getting at?"

Shandi kept her eyes on Fake Ladadog. "Don't you see? There's a regular pattern here—all the glitches and mistakes that you told me about—including the last time Godzilla got loose. The Xylk wanted this place closed down."

"But we were nearly broke anyway," I said. "Why bother?"

Shandi began to search through the sack. "Maybe it wasn't you. Maybe it was your equipment. Who else has a gene analyzer on this world?"

I scratched my head. "The nearest would be at the university on Baugh."

"Which is ten light-years from here. You're the only one on the frontier with equipment sophisticated enough to detect false urya." Shandi straddled Fake Ladadog's chest.

I leaned against the com. So a lot of the past mistakes really weren't my fault. "But the gene analyzer would have been sold."

"Even so, your failure would have proved that a company here wasn't practical. It probably would have been sold to some company in the core." She nodded to the sack. "Or if you did sell it to some local company, there would have been one spectacular accident." Shandi nudged the broken board. "What was this? A com unit?"

"Not to have to answer," Fake Ladadog said nervously.

Shandi picked up some of the fragments and inspected them. "I'm willing to bet it is. That's how you got your buddies on us so soon."

"And why did you attack Singh?" I demanded. "Did he catch you sabotaging the pen?"

Shandi threw down the fragments and dusted her hands. "Or maybe he caught you making a report about me. It would have messed up your original plans if my father had put cash back into this place."

I glared down at Fake Ladadog. His eye stalks were beginning to wave in alarm as if Shandi was making too many correct guesses. "Sure, and that would have changed things. His bosses decided that the risk of discovery was too great."

Shandi gave a warning tug at the eye stalk. "So he abandoned his original plan and decided just to destroy the equipment."

I knelt down beside Fake Ladadog. "But what has Godzilla got to do with this?"

"Answer him," Shandi ordered the Xylk.

"N-n-not to know," Fake Ladadog stuttered.

I nudged Shandi. "I don't believe him. Do you?"

"Shut up. I'm trying to think like him." Shandi plucked at her lower lip thoughtfully.

"Don't get to be too much like him," I warned. "He gives me the creeps."

Shandi ignored me and poked the Xylk. "I think you snatched Godzilla. You were going to kill all three of us and put the blame on Godzilla. And, in the process, you were going to blow up the lab."

"Is that it?" I was so mad that my hand tightened on the detonator and began to glow red.

Fake Ladadog opened his mouth as if he were about to speak, but suddenly his face began to twitch. It was the weirdest sight, with his face muscles going this way and that like the surface of a bubbling pot. At the same time his mouth stretched open, half shut, and then opened again. It was like different parts of his brain were fighting for control of his face.

Sam leaped off him with a snarl as he started to shake. Suddenly his teeth clenched. He rolled his eye stalks toward us desperately and then collasped.

"What's wrong?" I knelt beside Fake Ladadog and felt under the fur for a pulse, but there wasn't any.

"He must have been under some hypnotic command to die when certain questions are raised. You'll probably find a poison capsule in his tooth or near some vital organ where a nerve impulse can trigger it." She started to drag the dead alien toward the closet.

I set the detonator down carefully and grabbed the corpse's hind paws. "More industrial spy tricks?"

"And assassins." She said this matter-of-factly as we dumped the alien into the closet.

I shut the door. "We've got to figure out where Dad is."

"Let's try the computer again." She picked up the sack of explosives.

"Hey! That stuff's dangerous."

"You never know when it might come in handy." She retrieved the detonator and fingered it critically. "I bet you squeeze this to a certain temperature and then stick it in. That would set off a chemical reaction resulting in an explosion."

Suddenly Sam began to bump my leg. "What do you hear, girl?" I wondered. But then we could hear it too. It was the hiss of a craft.

When we went outside, we could just make out a little speck on the horizon. Running to the dock, I got my helmet from the slider and put it on. Once I'd slipped down the farsight visor, I saw that it was another of the Rell's diamond-shaped craft.

We had just run out of time.

·13·

Shandi had come down anxiously to the dock. "Is it my floater?"

"No, the Rell." I took off the helmet.

Shandi looked back in the direction of Pandemonium. "We can't let them blow up your equipment. This world is going to need it to catch those fake urya."

"What can we do?" I held out the Xylk's gun. "We just have this and the trank gun."

She pointed toward the dock. "Do you think you could keep them pinned down in their slider?"

A bunch of rocks might give me enough cover. "Not for long."

"It doesn't have to be for long." Shandi was walking toward the slider.

I started to load my trank gun. "Where are you going?"

"I'm going to blow up their slider." She said it as simply as if she were going to pull up some weeds.

"Hey," I demanded incredulously, "we could still make a run for it. Who made us world-savers?"

That was when I learned something else about Ms. Shandi Tyr. It wasn't money that made her who she was. It was Shandi.

"Someone has to do it." She could have tried to shame me, but she didn't. "You beat the Rell the last time, remember?"

"I didn't have any choice." I threw the helmet back into our stolen slider. "I just want to find Dad and get to somewhere safe."

She pivoted when she felt her feet touch the dock. "Listen to me, Piper. You measure people by their dreams."

That stung. "You've got to be alive to dream."

She frowned. "You either do things or you hide for the rest of your life."

That stung even more. "Maybe."

"You know I'm right."

Unfortunately, I did. "You're impossible."

She sat down on the dock. "Thank you."

"Go with her, girl," I whispered to Sam, and when Sam looked at me uncertainly, I gave a grunt and slapped her rump. "Not you, too. I've had enough back talk for one day."

With an indignant chirp, Sam loped after Shandi. Shandi smiled over her shoulder at Sam and then splashed into the water. There wasn't time for her to get into a suit. She'd just have to hold her breath and hide somewhere—probably under the dock. "Come on, girl," she called, and Sam went right to her.

The slider was now scooting over the water like a bug. I set the Xylk's gun down on a little flat rock in front of me and then ranged the trank darts so I could get them quickly. I'd filled the darts so full of juice they should knock out even a Rell.

I peeked over the rocks, but I couldn't see Shandi or Sam. The slider was a lot closer now. I'm afraid it did cross my mind that I could still get away. Only I didn't want to be in with the majority of people who played it safe all the time.

The Rell slowed at a hundred meters and came in cautiously. It was hot sitting on the rocks—like waiting inside an oven. Part of me just wanted to get it over, but I made myself wait.

I put a hand on the blistering rock and wished I had a suit glove. Then I raised the Xylk gun. I told myself, Don't think about the pain. Just about what you have to do.

The slider bumped the dock. One of the Rell got up. I lowered my head, squinting with one eye. I tracked him as he put one foot on the dock. A rock projection was going to block me, so I started to rise.

The Rell finally saw me at about the same time that I pressed the trigger button and the gun started to hum. The first Rell fell backward into the boat as the globe hissed by him. Then all his friends were firing. Their globes blasted at the rock, sending chips and fragments flying up in showers.

I tried to shoot back, but nothing happened. Either the Xylk's gun had malfunctioned or the ammunition was exhausted. I threw it away and picked up the trank gun, wondering just how much time Shandi would need. A Rell hopped onto the dock. I snapped off a shot and saw him stiffen and look down at the dart sticking out of his leg. So the darts could penetrate their suits. Then he collapsed back into the boat.

I ducked back just as a shot blasted the rock where my head had been. Reloading the gun, I peeked between the rocks and saw another Rell leap onto the dock even while they were drawing his friend back into the slider.

I rolled over and got off another shot, but the Rell threw himself down and the dart missed. Taking cover behind the rocks again, I loaded my last charge. More and more rock chips were falling down on me, and the vibrations of the explosions were stronger—as if there was far less rock between me and their shots now.

I poked my head up to risk another shot and saw that the Rell was kneeling five meters away and waiting, with his gun already aimed as calmly at me as if he were in a shooting gallery. His finger had begun to push the trigger button when the slider behind him suddenly erupted in the water. The shock wave threw me flat on my back, and I lay there dazed for a moment. I heard Sam's angry squeal and staggered to my feet behind the half-melted rocks. Sam was charging toward the fallen alien.

"No, wait, we want to take him prisoner," Shandi called from the water.

The Rell realized it at the same time as Sam. He rolled over on top of his gun. There was the now familiar hum and his body shook once; at the same time, I heard a muffled explosion. Sam skidded to a halt and gave a sniff of distaste.

"Sorry," I said.

"Well, we don't know how much he knew anyway." Shandi pulled herself onto the rocks and set the sack beside herself. She glanced behind her at the still burning wreck. "Not bad for an educated guess about the explosive."

"Yes, you only blew up half the dock." I holstered the trank gun. Our slider was floating away.

Shandi turned the alien over with her foot. "I'll get the hang of it. It's tricky stuff to use."

I went down to the water's edge and tried to reach the drifting cable that was still bound to part of a piling. Same came over and sniffed at my fingers. "Get the cable, girl." Contrary as ever, she simply rolled over onto her back and paddled parallel to shore.

"You're going about it the wrong way. You can't order her to do something." Shandi picked up a scrap of rope and began to play with it near the surface. When Sam edged in and tried to snatch it, Shandi held the rope aloft. After a few more tries, Sam headed for the nearest rope, which was the slider cable.

The cable became almost alive between her paws, moving and twitching as if it were a water snake. Her play brought the cable in close enough for me to grab it.

"See?" Shandi discarded the rope.

"OK. You made your point." I shook the cable as Sam clung to it. "Let go."

Shandi got the Rell's gun. "We'd better get ready for another attack. The Rell can't be too far off, or they couldn't have intercepted us so quickly."

I began to pull at the cable as an indignant Sam came ashore. "We could sink the lab like we do during a storm. That should hide the gene analyzer long enough until your ship comes back." I blinked as Sam deliberately shook the water from her coat so that it got all over me.

Shandi slung the gun over her shoulder. "We could even use your animals to set up some traps."

Then it hit me all of a sudden. My stomach tightened. "When they don't get a report from this bunch, their masters might decide to shift their base and cover their tracks. They might kill Dad."

Shandi joined me and started to help haul in the slider. "We don't even know where their base is."

I kicked away some of the loops of cable that were piling up by my feet. "I think my dad found something." Sam began to pounce and entangle herself in the extra cable.

Shandi adjusted the strap of the gun so it wouldn't bang against her hip while she helped pull in the cable. "He's not here, though."

I wrapped the cable around a rock and tied a quick knot. "Dad's always a stickler for taking notes. That number has to mean something."

Back in Pandemonium, I sat down at the console and turned it on while Shandi rustled up a quick meal in the kitchen. "Maybe the Xylk agent interrupted him."

The screen flashed back into life, and I slipped in the first slide. "And then took Godzilla from wherever he was hidden—probably in that spot where he had his equipment cached."

Shandi came in a moment later with some quick-thaw dinners. "And then sent your dad and Godzilla away."

I tapped the screen. "I'm willing to bet that one of these inorganic groups is Singh's cologne and assorted other toiletry items. He was really out to impress you."

"It's a little late for that now." She set a quick-thaw dinner down in front of me and pressed the tab. Moisture began to bead on the top as the dinner heated inside. "What about the organic groups?"

I studied the listings on the computer and then shook my head. "Just the ones we saw before." I set the slide down and took the fork Shandi handed me.

She must have already activated her dinner, because she was peeling back its top. "Try another one."

But while we ate our meals, we saw the same groupings as before, more or less. It was that way with the other eight slides.

Shandi put down her finished dinner. "The human scrapings are probably Singh's—maybe from scratching himself."

I finished up my dinner. "But where did the sea boa come from?"

"Maybe it was in the alien's fur," Shandi suggested.

"Hmm, that might help." I chewed on my lip and then began to punch keys on the keyboard. "The sea boas from each area have their own identifying gene pattern—like families." I told the computer to do a search and set my own dinner down. "We'll see if it's in the data banks."

It took a moment for the computer to come up with five possibilities. Shandi's face screwed up intently as she studied the screen. Then she picked up the notebook. "These aren't numbers for a slide. They're longitude and latitude."

I glanced from the page to the screen. "That's it!" Jumping up, I gave her a quick kiss on the cheek.

Shandi didn't seem any too pleased. At first, I thought it was because of the kiss. I didn't realize it was something else until she said, "Fighting a squad of Rell is one thing. Attacking their base is something else."

I snapped off the console. "I couldn't live with myself if I let him die too. You know what was the hardest thing after my mother died?" I didn't wait for her to answer. "The mornings."

Shandi set the notebook down. "Why?"

I arranged everything the way Dad had had it before. "Because I'd wake up with a jolt and realize it wasn't a dream at all. My mother really was dead. And I'd tell myself no, it couldn't have actually happened. But I'd know it had. And it cut at me like a knife. It still does. I'm not about to double the pain."

Shandi put a hand on my shoulder to keep me in front of the console. "No one expects the impossible—not even your dad."

"You said you measure people by their dreams. Well, you can measure me by my nightmares." I lifted her hand away, gently but firmly. "It's not for him. It's for me. I've got to try to find him."

Shandi followed me over to the cabinet where the trank

charges were kept. "And what will your death accomplish?"

I dragged the drawer out. It was full of charges—one thing Fake Ladadog had overlooked. "Thank you for that vote of confidence."

"You know what I mean."

I rummaged around in the lab until I found a pouch. "Look. I'm not out to get myself killed. I'll scout around, and if there's a chance I'll go in."

She glanced at the drawer as if she wished she could use a dart on me. "No, it's too risky. Wait here with me. My crew should be back soon. Then we can all go looking for your dad. And we can radio the colony what's going on."

Hastily I began to dump darts into the pouch. "You can stay here if you like. I'm going."

Shandi picked up one that had fallen on the floor. "Will you get it into your head? It's not your mother all over again."

"Maybe. Maybe not." I took it from her and added it to the others. "You said I should stick up for myself."

She looked at me sternly over the drawer. "I didn't mean to do it with me."

I shoved the drawer shut. "Why are you exempt?"

She set one fist on a hip. "Well, it's inconvenient, for one thing."

I tapped the recall signal to Sam and she came trotting over. "Look. I know I might not be able to do anything. But at least I can try."

Shandi stopped and hugged Sam. "I wanted to build up your self-confidence. I didn't intend to create a monster."

"Maybe I'm through hiding." I got another shiner for myself.

Shandi kept arguing with me while we got Pandemonium ready for sinking. The task that took the longest was unhooking the power cables that linked Pandemonium's generator to the island. That was because we had to take our time. But all in all, it took about five minutes to run through the routine. It would have taken only a few more minutes to put the animals inside the globe; but of course we were leaving them topside.

Shandi was surprised when I said we were ready. She stopped objecting long enough to ask, "That's it?"

"We don't get much notice when a storm comes in. The drill can go even faster when you have people who know what they're doing." Everything was sealed tight, so I opened the front panel and threw the switch. Closing the panel, I stepped back. The sinking was already programmed.

Shandi glanced at me. "Thinking about your mom?"

"And my dad." I watched the water bubble around Pandemonium as the ballast tanks began to expel their air. "Can I have the sack of explosives? I might need them."

She waved a hand toward the dock. "I left it down there."

"Thanks."

"You know I can't go with you," she said softly. "I have to wait here for my crew. Someone has to get word to the colony about the invasion."

I had been half hoping that Shandi would have been worried enough to go along. But I'd just have to do what Shandi had told me at the Sentinel: use my knowledge and brains to get what I wanted. "I still have to go."

Slowly, majestically, like some dinosaur, Pandemonium began to sink into the water. Too late, Shandi jumped back from the spray. "Will you forget about what I told you? Stop being the little rooster. I don't want you to get hurt."

I just stayed put even though I got soaked. "I'll be careful."

"You don't understand. I don't want you to go." She was still assuming that we had some secret compact between us.

The large globe of Pandemonium had sunk so low in the water it seemed to have shrunk. "Friendship only goes so far."

Shandi stood there, the salt water beading her face, her long curly hair now hanging in wet strings. "Maybe this goes farther."

Sam was nervous seeing the globe sinking because she usually associated it with storms. I squatted down to put an arm around her. Dad had made Sam especially for Mom. I tried to soothe her with my hand, but I was feeling far from calm myself. "This isn't the right time for that."

Her face was as impassive as a helmet visor, but the eyes were those of a frightened child. It was as if the more scared and younger and fragile she felt, the more stonelike she had to make her face. She almost stammered the words as if she had to yank them out of her mouth. "I think I love you. I'm not about to lose you."

There it was. I took a long deep breath and then let it out slowly. The globe was just a small circle now. I couldn't help wondering if that was what Mom had seen before she died. "It's too soon."

But Shandi wasn't used to being refused, let alone rejected. The girl who could buy anyone or anything just stared at me in disbelief. "I never thought I'd tell that to anyone."

The globe disappeared. It would sink to ten fathoms now. I felt like my own soul had sunk to that distance inside my body. "And I never thought I'd hear anyone say that to me." I rose and started for the slider.

Sam came up on one side and Shandi came up on the other. "Then how can you just walk away?"

The pouch of trank darts bumped against my hip. "Because I'm not free yet."

Shandi stepped in front of me, blocking my way. There was a strange look in her eyes—almost of panic—as if she were about to fall and was reaching out to me. "I thought we understood one another."

I was hoping that she would recognize how torn I was between her and Dad. I looked silently to her eyes, pleading with her not to make me decide. "We can. We will." I tried to step around her.

Shandi put her hand on my shoulder. it was a strangely awkward motion from a person who was usually so graceful, but it was the kind of awkwardness that comes with lack of practice. "No, it has to be now."

It was far easier to outwit and outfight the Rell than it was to deal with Shandi. I shied away from her touch. "Don't make me choose."

Her eyes took on a withdrawn, distant look—as if she were falling away from me, as if she blamed me for the fall, but she had really done that to herself. It didn't matter, though. There was an air of finality about her words. "I don't let out my real feelings often, but when I do I don't expect someone to trample all over them."

"No," I said quietly. "I'm sure you don't. You wear too much armor for that. Just like me."

"Even if you do come back," she warned, "don't expect to pick up where you left off."

The hardest thing I ever did in my life was to walk on.

But I did.

·14·

*T*he island's slope rose from the dimness. Though Carefree doesn't have moons, it does have twin suns that give it some tidal action. Then, with the huge thermal differences between bodies of water that set up some mean convection currents and the simple physics of an oceanic mass moving in the giant bowl between the continents, you get enough wave action to bruise, trap, or even drown a creature as puny as a human being. And there was certainly enough to make for turbulence around the mouth of the lagoon.

Approaching cautiously, I motioned Sam forward and she swam on ahead into the lagoon. I spent several anxious minutes until she reappeared, nibbling at a crab she had found. Trust her to think of lunch.

Behind me the slider lay anchored to a tall spire of rock that thrust out of the water. I kicked forward more slowly. It took most of my nerve before I went into the dirty brown cloud at the mouth of the lagoon. Every moment I kept waiting for someone or something to grab me, but there were only the currents pulling me this way and that. And then I saw shadowy shapes in front of me. Raising the trank gun, I forced myself forward against the strong pull of the water.

Something whipped toward me and I shot it. It lay still and I moved toward it only to discover that I had just tranquilized a sea boa. The current had moved it toward me. So much for my big words to Shandi about going it alone. I really wished she was with me right now.

Loading up the gun again with darts I'd transferred to my suit pockets, I swam forward. The sack of explosives dangled below me as I swam through the sea boas. Their trunks were wrinkled, reddish-brown columns about the thickness of my thigh. Long, spearlike leaves grew from the sides, wriggling like the legs of a giant millipede. All around me, sea boas drifted like trees in a breeze.

Sam and I made our way through them, but while she managed to add considerably to her lunch, I didn't see one alien. I climbed up the stone face and pulled myself up on a ledge above the surf line. Since I'd only been swimming a few meters below the surface, I took off my helmet. It felt more like being at a picnic site than a secret invasion base. Sam was nosing all around the rocks without giving any sign that a Xylk had been there.

I inspected the foot of the cliffs with her and then took a path that circled around the entire lagoon to the ridgetop itself. Together, Sam and I searched that entire island, poking and probing for secret doors or tapping for hollow rooms, but about the only good I did was to help the tan on my face.

By the time we swam back to the slider, I was feeling pretty frustrated. It didn't help my mood any that, though I'd taken off my flippers, I'd kept on my suit. It had been pretty hot inside it as I stumped along.

The boa from Singh's attacker had to come from the sea boas here. But this might have only been a rendezvous point. So it was back to Square One. I told myself it wasn't my fault. It might not be too late yet. I wasn't letting Dad down. But I kept getting this feeling that I had. Worse, I'd thrown away whatever chance I had with Shandi. I forced myself to stop thinking about it. I had to concentrate on the task at hand.

While I consulted some charts that I'd brought along, Sam took it as an excuse to find some snacks. With the charts spread out over the deck, I figured that I would crisscross back and forth over a circle that was some fifty kilometers in diameter.

I tapped the side of the slider with one hand, but when I didn't get any reaction, I took a choco-bar from an outside pocket. Breaking it in half, I put one half back into my pocket. Then I gave the recall signal again with one hand while I dangled the candy with the other. Sam came right back to the slider. Then I pushed the button that hauled up the anchor.

We had only gone some three kilometers when the sea suddenly turned pale all around us and began to bubble. I gripped the handle with one hand while my other hand groped for the trank gun. I thought it was the Xylk, but then a slim silver body leaped into the air and hovered for a moment so we could see the streamlined missile-shaped body with the blue tail and fins.

I was caught in a school of convict fish. The first one splashed back into the sea again with a loud slapping sound. A second and then a third and even a fourth leaped into the air. But this wasn't any little school like we had seen at first. The afternoon became full of flashing bodies and loud slapping sounds. This particular school spread for several square kilometers.

Fish began to thud against the sides of the slider. I was almost breathless in the sudden turbulence these leaping fish created. It was like being surrounded by wet silver confetti. They could fill the horizon in the fishing grounds. But this was way beyond the headlands where they liked to feed. Upwelling currents brought up the rich sea floor and convict fish liked to feed off the phytoplankton that grew in the rich waters. Every now and then, a school wandered out of their regular feeding area, but never on this scale.

I gripped Sam, who was eager to dash over the side and begin a free feast. But then a fish smacked against the windshield and flipped over onto the deck. I pulled my foot out of the way as Sam pounced. I didn't want her getting the wrong snack.

Hurriedly, I got out the charts again. My rough estimate put us right over an undersea canyon that stretched almost to the continental shelf on one side and a major oceanic trench on the other.

There definitely weren't the right conditions for a normal upwell here. It was possible that some volcano had created a heat source, but geologically this was a fairly quiet area. That left one other possibility—an undersea colony. Maybe even a base.

I moved the slider two kilometers to the east, away from the fish, and lowered the anchor, not because there was anything into which it could hook but because it might slow down the slider's drifting. Then I checked everything from explosives to trank gun to Sam. We'd see if I could live up to my last speech to Shandi.

This close to sunset, the light failed at only ten meters. I snapped on the shiner, orienting myself by the stream of my own air bubbles. I reached the top of the canyon after only another ten meters. The charts had said the canyon itself was only fifty meters deep here.

I shone my light around the rocks, looking for some telltale signs, when Sam suddenly began to corkscrew through the water. I looked all around but couldn't see anything. Then I heard the loud hissing of jets.

Sam and I had time to take cover behind some rocks. I turned off my shiner and watched as a subber of some strange design approached. It was shaped like a crescent and there were mechanical arms on either side. With the headlights shining from the bow, it looked like some huge monster sliding by.

I ducked down and held onto Sam's collar so she wouldn't poke her head up out of curiosity. It hovered in the water, its beams probing the rocks all around me. Had they found the slider up above?

I was still trying to figure out what to do when a sea sled soared out of the canyon. Red lights gleamed on its sides like bleeding wounds, and its searchlight lanced through the water. As if it had only been waiting to point me out to the sea sled, the subber sank deeper into the canyon.

As the sea sled curved around for a shot, I hooked a hand into Sam's collar and slapped her rump. With a startled kick, she tried to shoot upward. She was carrying my dead weight so that we only went up a few meters, but that was enough to bring me level with the sled.

The rider was about the size of Fake Ladadog, and he wore an oval-shaped helmet with two transparent cylinders rising from the top—perfect for eye stalks. I was sure I was looking at a Xylk. I took out my trank gun as he swept past. The side of his sled just brushed my hand so that the trank gun went tumbling into the canyon.

While he was trying to turn his sled so he could bring his gun to bear, I plunged toward him. It wasn't heroics. It was just sheer desperation. My right arm curled around his helmet, and my momentum knocked him off his sled. I yanked at one of the hoses leading from his breather pack into his helmet, and the next moment we were surrounded by a cloud of silvery bubbles. Even so, he was an ornery, wriggling creature. I had to fight to keep him away from my own hoses for a moment, and then he lay still in the water.

I kicked out of the cloud of bubbles. The breather pack had run out of its charge of air so the cloud itself was dissipating, leaving just a motionless body floating in the water, his arms and legs outstretched like some broken toy. I swam over and claimed his sled, though it only supported half my body.

Snapping on my own shiner, I watched the body slowly sink— the arms and legs still spread outward. It was the first time I had ever killed anyone, and it shook me. For all I knew, the Xylk might have a better claim to this world than we did. I didn't feel very heroic. Just dirty. But I was surviving. And surviving on my efforts. That was something.

Sam swam back to scold me for the unjustified spank. Maybe it sounded cold-blooded, but it reminded me that remorse was a luxury at this moment. I had to rescue Dad first. There would be time for guilt later on, when we were all safe on the mainland. I gave her an apologetic pat on her head while I tried to think of what to do next. Suddenly a rock beneath me exploded in a brilliant burst of light. Reinforcements were arriving. I heard the roar even as the sled and I went tumbling through the water. I held onto the sides until the sled slowed its cartwheeling. I was inside the canyon now. Quickly I looked around for Sam.

She was floating about ten meters to my right. Though she was shaking her head in a daze, she seemed all right otherwise. I rapped the recall code on the sled, and she automatically swam toward me. A globe went bubbling by, and I stared in the direction from which it had come.

A trio of sleds angled toward me from below. They looked like playing cards that had been flung upward. It was like running a hurdles race where the hurdles keep getting higher and higher. At any moment, it seemed I was going to trip. Shandi had doubted that I could finish, but I'd just have to try.

I looked at the sled's control panel. There was a pair of handles in front of me, above a board full of buttons. An antenna waved from the side so there must have been a com, but I didn't see anything that would let me try different frequencies. Besides, a com on a sled this small would have the same short range as my suit, so I wouldn't be able to reach the mainland. I couldn't even tell what controlled the sled's gun. Sam gave a yelp as a portside rock suddenly blew up into a hundred fragments. I would be lucky to learn how to make the sled go forward, let alone outmaneuver and outfight them.

Sam piled into me, clinging tightly to the sled's frame as more globes slid by. I punched a button and the sled shot backward before I could even shout "Whoa." One rocky side of the canyon seemed to leap up at me. Sam nipped at my wrist in alarm and I pushed another button. The sled shuddered and there was the screeching of metal; for a moment I thought I had broken the machine. Then the sled suddenly lurched forward. I pushed the handle toward the bow, and the sled slowly picked up speed.

I figured that the button to the left of the original button probably turned the sled toward port. I punched it experimentally and the sled began to curve slowly in that direction. I stabbed the button to the right of the original button and the sled began to curve toward starboard. Three buttons down. Only a dozen more to go. The only thing I didn't want to do was push the stop button.

I glanced behind me. The guards' sleds with their lighter riders were gaining on me. I looked above me. The sunlight shone on the water as it always did. In the distance, I could see the dot that was the cloud of convict fish. This was my home. I had explored all around this area. It didn't seem possible that I was now running for my life—and losing. Not here. Not now.

I looked at the canyon walls, wondering if I could lose them there, but the walls were mostly smooth, without tunnels or crannies where I could hide. That left me exposed in the open sea. Or did it? I looked again at that distant school of fish.

I glanced behind me to estimate the distance between myself and the guards. At the rate they were closing, it would be a tossup whether I could make it to the fish. Still, I didn't think I had much choice.

I leaned down low on the sled. The windshield had been designed for a far smaller rider so that part of my breather pack protruded above it. I could feel the water pulling at me, trying to rip me off the sled as we jetted through the water. Beside me, Sam's claws scraped against the metal as she tried to cling to the frame.

When an explosion tumbled the sled toward starboard, I knew my pursuers were within range. I wouldn't be able to go flat outright toward the convict fish. I began to push the buttons so that we zigzagged, knowing that the manuevers helped narrow the distance even more.

The big school of convict fish, though, swelled from a dot to a large cloud. Shots that missed me were exploding within the school itself. Blackened bodies tumbled out of the cloud, and the survivors darted this way and that so the cloud seemed to swirl fearfully. My fingers practically danced over the buttons as I worked the sled toward the school.

Suddenly a globe exploded just above the sled. The jet gave a screech as it disintegrated and a panicked Sam dug her sharp claws into my arm, puncturing through the layers of the suit. Our forward momentum had carried us among the fish. It was far more frantic and painful than when Shandi and I had been caught among convict fish. Frightened fish slapped and thumped against us. The surrounding sea was a swirl of silver bodies.

With a kick, I rose from the sled. Sam was still hooked onto me. It was hard to swim with all the fish around us—like trying to run a gauntlet of hard slapping hands—but I forced us farther into the school. Behind us I could hear the loud hiss of jets as the sleds tried to plunge after us.

I tried to go on swimming, but my body was just giving out from the beating. The hiss of the jets grew louder. Small explosions flashed nearby and there was the sound of sizzling, dying fish. In a matter of seconds, I'd find out whether my hunch had been a bad one or not. Maybe Dad had been right and Shandi had been wrong about me: I just couldn't do anything right.

There was a series of loud coughs, followed almost by sighs, and then the jets went dead. I looped around to swim back toward where I thought the guards might be. Now that their sleds could no longer move faster than the convict fish, the fish had managed to draw away, clearing a space.

It was almost like a silver curtain rising, revealing three guards still struggling to clear all the dead fish from their jet intakes. Now that she had a target for all her anger and fear, Sam let go of me and, with a snarl, dove for the nearest one.

My suit began sealing itself with a hiss from Sam's puncture marks. The scratches she had left in my arm were going to take a little longer to heal. But I was feeling just as mean and angry as Sam. Drawing the trank gun, I swam as fast as I could toward the second guard.

Sam fell on the first guard, her forepaws and teeth biting into his shoulders. He lurched against the belt holding him to the sled. I thought I could hear his frightened, pained shout through the water. His hands tried to release the belt buckle, but it was already too late for him as her hind paws began to slice up his sides. Then a cloud of red bubbles hid them.

The second guard looked over at his partner and began to draw a handgun. He never even saw me shoot. He gave a jerk when he felt the tranquilizing dart and twisted around to see me. Then he collapsed on top of his sled, the gun falling from his weakened fingers.

I charged over him toward the third guard. He had just enough time to get off one humming shot with his handgun before I was on top of him. I brought the empty trank gun down hard on his wrist and his gun went falling through the water. But he managed to get his hands on the hoses of my breather pack. I let go of the trank gun and it dropped after his as I grabbed his wrists.

Though he was smaller than I, it was surprising how strong the Xylk was. We kept wrestling as his sled slowly floated downward. It didn't help me any that he kept butting his helmet up against mine.

Then Sam leaped upon my opponent, and he let go of me to try to deal with her fangs and claws. Maybe killing is something you get used to; maybe I was just too mad to think. At any rate, I had my knife out the next second and reached over Sam to get at his air hose. He tried to grab my wrist, but my blade was already severing the heavy plastic tube. Sam sprang away as the air began roaring upward like a genie suddenly released from a lamp.

So we'd won. I became aware of how my body was aching from the beating it had taken from the convict fish. I started to reach for Sam to inspect her wounds, but she snarled and I didn't complete the contact. She was still caught up in that killing madness.

So, instead, I swam down toward the nearest sled and got the unconscious guard's gun. I cut his air hose too. Maybe it wasn't fair to kill someone who couldn't fight back, but the odds I was facing didn't seem very fair either. Then I rolled him off the sled.

In the distance, I could see a dozen sleds rising. The sled was still falling slowly. I frantically tore the fish out of the intakes. A calmer Sam came down to see what I was doing, nibbling at a piece of fish that floated by. I got as much of the fish out of the way as I could and then got on top of the sled.

A burst of light exploded below. I was grateful to see that we were still out of range. I jammed my thumb against the button. The jet sucked in water, gave a cough, and went dead. I punched the button again. Again, it started but this time it gave a belching sound and halted. I hit that button ten times or more with the same result. A globe burst about five meters to starboard. They were finally in range and I was a sitting duck. I was going to have to abandon the sled. Angry at all the time I'd wasted, I slammed my fist down in exasperation.

This time the jet gave a kind of sigh, and the sled lurched forward. A globe flashed in the spot where I had been. The sled rocked in the water. "Steady, baby, steady," I murmured to the sled. Sam settled in beside me once again.

Slowly I pushed the handle forward. The jet gave a funny series of coughs as if clearing its throat. We moved forward in spasms. My fingers began to play with the buttons, and we started zigzagging. Suddenly, the jet roared into life and we began rushing through the water.

Once they saw I was mobile again, they gave up their pursuit. I guess the other Xylk had radioed the situation back to their base. The dozen just circled protectively as if their mission was to keep me at a distance. Their headlight beams glowed like the eyes of insects.

I took the opportunity to test the other buttons on the panel. I pushed one button and the lights came on. Sam pushed another button before I could stop her and the jets went dead. I slapped her paw and got the jets started again. The gun was controlled by a button jury-rigged to the panel near the direction buttons. I suppose the Xylk had adapted some ordinary sea equipment for this invasion attempt.

Suddenly, the guards widened their protective circle as a column of a dozen sleds rose through the center. From the way they were moving at full throttle, they seemed pretty confident that they could take me now. I snapped down the farsight hood on my visor. There didn't seem to be anything very special about the sleds; then, in the light cast by their headlights, I thought I saw something covering the jet intakes. When I squinted, I could just make out that it was some kind of wire mesh. They could follow me right among the convict fish now.

·15·

They had taken away my one real weapon—the convict fish. Or had they? Mom had said to use what this world gave me. I snapped up the farsight hood and stared through the visor at Sam. She pressed her homely muzzle against the helmet. "If there was ever a better time to remember your training," I said, "now's the time."

But Sam just twitched her long elegant eyebrows at me. She was like the superstar who never quite lives up to her billing. Even if I signed the commands to her to begin rounding up the fish, I didn't have much faith that she would follow my directions.

So there I was: stuck. We were the biggest pair of genetic flops in this star sector. Only a little voice kept nagging at me, and I remembered how Shandi had gotten Sam to bring in the cable by making the activity into a game. It was just like Shandi had said: There had to be more than one way to get what I wanted.

Suddenly things began to click together. Dad had laid down how the training was supposed to go, and it might have worked fine for Terran dolphins, but not necessarily for other species. Shandi had told me to work with what Sam gave me rather than trying to dominate her.

A shot exploded below. They'd be in range soon. Sam patted a button on the control panel. Fortunately, it was the one that turned on the lights. I pushed her paw away. "No," I said in-stinctively and shut off the lights once again.

She looked at me indignantly and then, arching her back, swam over my head to the other side and began trying to test the buttons there. In some ways, she was more like a little sister than a pet. It was as if she thought that anything I could do, she could do just as well. Suddenly I had an idea, but first I had to make sure that my sled would work.

Hurriedly I pulled out the sack of web netting and stowed the explosives in my pockets and the cranny beneath the sled's control panel. Sam swam this way and that, trying to see what I was doing. If they could cover their intakes, so could I. Sliding out my knife, I hurriedly cut through the strands. They were a lot tougher than I'd thought, and a couple of times I had to saw the blade through.

The sled rocked from an explosion below. I needed more time. Lying down on the sled once again, I set the jets on low and angled the bow upward so that I moved along slowly. Sam easily kept pace while I finished cutting the sack in two. After I had sheathed the knife, I straddled the sled and tied the netting over the jet intakes by looping the strands around bolts and every spare protuberance there was. I didn't know how long it would last, but I hoped that the mesh would help keep the intakes clear for a while.

An explosion sent the sled flipping through the water. The glittering surface above and the darkness below changed posi-tions for a moment, and then I righted the sled again, by shifting my weight around. The Xylk were within range. I pushed the one handle forward, opening the throttle, and the sled began to race ahead.

The next second, Sam's streamlined body was darting through the water alongside me once again. Overhead, the convict fish were a huge silver disk that, as we neared, separated into moving, wriggling dots.

I signed to her to begin rounding up the fish. With a kick, she tried to pull ahead, but she was already swimming at her top speed. I opened the throttle all the way and raced away from her.

As before, the nearer fish parted to either side, but the sled was going too fast for the fish at the center of the school to get out of the way fast enough. Once again, startled silver bodies thudded against the prow and windshield. The jets gave an odd gasping sound—like a giant taking in a large breath. I risked a glance over my shoulder and saw that the mesh over the intakes was still intact. Bodies were hitting it and sliding away. It might just hold up long enough for what I needed.

I cut back on the throttle because Sam had to see me herding. I glanced over my shoulder to see a very annoyed Sam swimming upward through a mob of startled fish. I kept going just fast enough to maintain that distance until my suit began to puff out. When we were ten meters, I could see the fish like dark, darting ovals against the well-lit surface.

I looked below and saw a glow of light from underneath. There was another distant bubble of light. The panicked fish began surging in new directions below. This group of Xylk was trying to stand off and shoot at me first. Fine. Let the Xylk stir up the school even more.

Punching a button, I began to tilt to port. Fish darted away above and below me. At least, I thought it was above and below, but it was easy to lose direction in the middle of that school. I leveled off and went on for about another hundred meters until the fish began to thin out and then I began to angle downward.

I glanced behind me. Sam was still following me. I signed for her to turn to starboard and begin herding the fish. Then I gently began to curve the sled toward port. Sam hesitated as the distance increased between us, and for a moment I thought she was going to go into one of her sulks.

But suddenly with a flip of her tail, she twisted around and began darting along to starboard. How long she would keep that up was anyone's guess. I could only hope. The Xylk were still firing from below, but it couldn't be much longer before they realized that cutting a path through all those fish was impossible. They'd have to try out their intake covers soon and come after me.

As I finished my arc of the circle, I strained my eyes for a sight of Sam. Just by moving through the school, I'd formed a corridor of several meters between the upper level of fish and the lower. I thought that if we both cut a spiral of ever-narrowing circles, we could separate a large group of fish from the main school.

Only I didn't see Sam. We didn't have much time. Behind me, the jets were gasping like twin asthmatics, but the mesh was holding up. I tried to figure out if I could risk moving full throttle. If I could, I might be able to separate a smaller group of fish by doing the same maneuver on my own, but I wasn't sure if the mass of fish would be large enough. I was just about to start turning in when the fish gave a panicked flurry in front of me, their tails twitching explosively as they rammed one another. And there, swimming playfully along on her back, was Sam.

I signed for her to begin tightening the circle. She gave me a curious look as if she were wondering what I was up to next, so I opened up the throttle and began to speed up. She hovered for a nerve-racking moment and then, with a backflip, she began to meet the challenge and match me.

Sam, being more maneuverable than the sled, could cut tighter circles than I could—which was fine. My wide circles kept me on the periphery, where I could keep stragglers from moving back to the main school. At the same time that I was herding, I tried to put as much of the explosive in my other pockets as I could. The detonators, of course, were slipped carefully through my belt.

Then the globes began to explode higher up within the school. Time had run out for us. The Xylk were finally coming into the fish. I gave the signal to Sam, but she just went on with the circle until I took the sled down in a tight spiral. Sam, too, began to twist and writhe her body in a tighter, more frantic downward spiral than mine.

The fish nearest us panicked and began to surge toward the

left. Careful not to hit Sam, I fired off a few shots from the sled and headed them off. They tried to surge in the opposite direction, but a few shots turned them back once again.

With only one real direction in which to go, the fish turned downward. Fish in a school are funny creatures. They trust to numbers, figuring that a hungry predator will snap up their neighbor instead of them. If a few fish start moving in one direction, the other fish are likely to switch around and swim in that new direction. It's an instinctive maneuver that probably helps carry them away from a predator.

But Sam was a sight terrorizing all those poor fish. She was practically a furry streak now, trying to hurry their exit. I made a note to tell Dad. Set up some kind of competition between her and a herder, or even a robot, and Sam would come through like a blue-ribbon champ.

I knew she couldn't hear me, but I couldn't help shouting encouragement. "That's it, girl!" I just wished that Shandi could have seen Sam's triumph.

The panic spread through our group of fish, and they all began to swim downward faster. And as all those desperate bodies churned through the water, they made a sound like a storm, but a storm of fleshy, slapping sounds. And the sound just seemed to swell until it was a rumble like thunder, and the fish dropped down like a silver boulder gathering momentum.

I could see dozens of bright, bubbly explosions as the Xylk fired frantically, but it was too late. The fish at the front might try to stop, but the ones behind them were intent on driving downward still, and they carried along the vanguard. Pushing at the direction handle, I nosed the sled downward after Sam.

Suddenly the lights stopped and there was a series of sickening thumps and the screeching of torn metal. I didn't even see any wreckage as I passed by. It must have been carried along among the panicked convict fish. I'd had no idea that a biomass that big could be so destructive.

By that time, the fish were intent on moving downward on their own so Sam leisurely arched away. I angled the sled toward

her and she came over a little smugly. I gave her the best hug
that I could considering that I was on a sled speeding downward.
She just yawned as if it were an average morning's exercise.

The fish took out most of the second group of Xylk before they
slowed their descent. On our way down, we could see the debris
of some of the sleds on ledges of the canyon, as if they had tried to
get out of the way. And then the rumbling faded into silence as
the fish finally slowed and then stopped. Convict fish have short
memories; if there's a little distance between them and danger,
they think they're all right.

So, even more quickly than it had formed, my "weapon" just
dissolved into thousands of individual fish swimming harmlessly
back to the surface. For a moment, trying to see through all the
fish streaming upward was like trying to see through a curtain of
silver ribbons.

I was so busy congratulating myself and Sam that, like a fool, I
just paraded down the center of the canyon in a straight line. The
first hint that all the Xylk weren't dead was when a globe flashed
by and shattered a rock. I blinked my eyes, almost blinded by the
light. Grabbing Sam by the scruff of her neck, I dumped her on
the sled next to me and then arched away. A second globe missed,
showering us instead with dead fish.

There wasn't any time to stampede the fish again. I swung the
sled around and snapped off a shot in the direction from which
the shots had come, but I knew I was outclassed. I could see the
Xylk expertly looping their sleds over to bring their guns to bear
on me again. I could barely guide my sled along, let alone handle
it in a dogfight.

The only thing that really saved me was that they had to move
slowly because of the fish. We looped and banked and maneu-
vered through the fish. The only damage that my shots did was to
scar the canyon and blast more fish, but the Xylk guards had
several near misses. It wouldn't be long before all the fish were
gone, and they could begin moving at full speed. I had to do
something and do it quick.

When a Xylk slid by on his sled, I stabbed at the button, but nothing happened. I couldn't say whether the gun was exhausted or jammed. Either way, it left me a sitting duck. The two surviving Xylk must have realized something was wrong, because they rose in a straight line, firing as they went.

I banked the sled and began to corkscrew upward out of the canyon. Sam was clinging to the frame and protesting my wild steering. It was one thing for her to swim that way and another for her to be a passenger having to go through the same motion.

Then I remembered the explosives. I dug one out of the little cranny under the control panel. Taking a detonator from where I had stuck it in my belt, I squeezed it as hard as I could in my gloved hand and thrust it into the block before I dropped it.

Shandi had been right when she had said that using the things was a little tricky. The explosion went off too soon. One moment the sled was jetting along. The next moment it was three meters higher and bucking like a wild horse.

The canyon itself spun toward us crazily. I grabbed hold of the direction handle and jammed it forward, trying by sheer strength to send us downward, but the sled carried us in a deadly arc against the wall. There was the screech of protesting metal and then we were curling away, leaving one of our jets behind. It slowly slid down the rocky slope.

In the meantime, the two Xylk were racing downward as they tried to get to cover. Shutting off the remaining jet, I took out another chunk of explosive and gave a kind of medium-hard squeeze to the detonator. Sticking it into the explosive, I dropped it after them.

The explosion only helped rearrange the canyon's walls rather than get the Xylk. Reaching for the last detonator, I gave it a light squeeze and thrust it into another explosive brick and chucked it over the side. I lost sight of it quickly enough.

For a long while, there were just the two Xylk scooting away like a pair of water bugs. The next moment, a bright red and yellow flower had blossomed beneath them in the canyon. A light bright as day illuminated the canyon floor.

And then the flower swelled and rose, catching up the two Xylk on its petals, and then the Xylk were lost within the explosion. I twisted on the sled to look at Sam. "Not bad for a pair of failures," I said.

Sam simply groomed one forepaw with the other. To her it was all in a day's work—or, rather, play.

·16·

I cut on the remaining jet again and discovered that no matter how hard I pressed the button, I could not go straight ahead. All I could do was move in a slow downward spiral.

The crippled sled wheezed and chugged along like an aging bellboy. For a while, it seemed as if we were drifting down to the end of the world. The headlights only exposed patch after patch of barren, lifeless rock so I was surprised when I saw a spot of color at the bottom of the canyon.

I swung the sled around in a wide curve. I could see a thin, flat spot as if someone had spilled pink paint. I wished I had one of those fancy helmets with all the instruments and the display that can be projected against the helmet visor. All I could do was assume that the canyon bottom was abnormally warm.

The sea is full of creatures that want to live, from big bruisers with fangs as long as my arm to the smallest phytoplankton, which are like microscopic plants. In fact, some phytoplankton need only heat, rather than light, to trigger photosynthesis. And where you find that humble, determined phytoplankton, you find plankton that eat the phytoplankton, and then the plankton that feed on those plankton, and on up the food chain until you find coral that suck the plankton from the water. I was willing to bet that was what the pink patch represented.

It was maddening to have only one jet. I couldn't move in a straight line down along the canyon floor. I had to do a slow spiral upward and then one downward. Eventually, Sam got impatient with me. She would dart ahead and then come back to see why I was such a slowpoke. Finally, she disappeared altogether.

If I thought I could have controlled her, I would have kept her close to me because I knew the Xylk base had to be nearby. That second group of Xylk had taken only a short time to adapt their sleds and come after me. But I knew from experience that you could only give so many orders to Sam.

As it was, I just waited anxiously on the sled. Chances are that they wouldn't shoot her even if they saw the collar. However, I was another matter. I didn't have any weapons except for the blocks of explosives, and I didn't have any detonators left for those. The most I could do was make faces and try to scare them to death.

As I counted more patches of coral, a voice in the back of my head kept telling me to leave and get help, but another voice said that it might take days on a crippled sled—assuming I had enough fuel, and I wasn't even sure of that. And that secret voice said I had done all right so far. I could at least see if there was anything more I could do. Funny, but that second voice sounded a lot like Shandi.

Suddenly I heard the faint scrabbling of claws from up ahead. I'd make faster time swimming on my own. Snapping on my shiner, I shut off the sled's jet and let it drop to the canyon floor. Then I began thrashing for all I was worth. I made a great target with my shiner on, but I needed to see where I was going.

By that time, the canyon was a mess of pinks and greens and purples like a paint store had crashed here. I was sure I was getting near the source of heat. Sam was at the end of a canyon before a circular door some thirty meters in diameter. She was rubbing her nose and testing the opening with a hind paw. There wasn't any sign of the subber so I supposed that it had gone on.

As I came up, she gave me an annoyed head butt as if to ask where I had been. "Sorry," I apologized. "I was enjoying the scenery."

I didn't see any guards by the opening so I swam forward

cautiously to examine it. The tunnel didn't look natural. The sides were smooth, as if someone had used some beam tool. In the distance, some several hundred meters, I saw a small pinprick of light at the other end of the tunnel. Shapes bulked dimly within, though I couldn't tell what they were. I was willing to bet that somewhere at the end of that tunnel was Dad.

I extended a gloved hand and Sam waited expectantly. It was like pushing at an invisible wall. There seemed to be some kind of force field guarding the tunnel. Unfortunately, I didn't happen to have any missiles in my back pocket so I didn't see how I was going to crack it open. But having made it this far, I wasn't about to give up. Shandi definitely deserved an *A* for her tutoring.

Beside me, Sam had begun clawing at the rock again. I turned my head carefully so that I could examine as much of the tunnel as I could. I didn't see any force-field mechanism in the tunnel. Something had to be running it. I tried to rest my helmet against the force field so I could examine the opening itself. Even though the angle was awkward, I managed to see that the rock at the opening projected downward from the roof of the tunnel. Maybe the mechanism had been mounted there and slabs of rock set up all around it. That was the weak point.

I stepped back. My suit pockets were bulging with explosives. If I had a detonator, I could probably get at the mechanism. I wished I hadn't used all the detonators back in the canyon.

Then something clicked inside my head. Maybe I could pack the sled with explosives and ram the rock above the opening. I might just be able to get at the mechanism itself. The only problem would be trying to aim my crippled sled.

I swam back the way I'd come, and Sam followed me at her own pace, stopping every now and then to examine some patch of coral. But once I started to fuss over the sled, she darted in to investigate. I tugged and pushed at the jet to try to aim as straight as I could. Even so, there would be a slight tilt to port. I'd have to ride the sled as close as I dared to the opening.

Well, no one said the hero business was going to be easy. I began packing explosives into the space beneath the control panel. But when I was down to the last brick, I decided to save it. Sometimes it's not important what you can do, it's what people *think* you can do. The sled antenna was a collapsible type, so I twisted and pulled at the top portion until I had broken it off. In dim light, I might be able to convince someone it was a detonator. I just shouldn't step in front of any spotlights. Carefully, I stowed the antenna top in my belt.

Sam was looking at me as if I were getting stranger and stranger, so it really wasn't any surprise when she ignored my signed command to stay put. As I opened up the jet and rose in the water, she kept pace right along beside me. I tried to sign for her to go back, but she did a saucy back flip over the prow. Short of knocking her out and tying her up, I had no choice. "OK," I said. "We started out together, so we might as well finish together."

I motioned her onto the sled beside me and she snuggled right in as we climbed in a slow spiral up above the opening some two hundred meters. I adjusted the height with some difficulty until I thought the sled would move in a gradual curve to that spot just above the opening. But it was going to be tricky. Then, using my weight, I tilted the sled gradually on its side. Sam looked annoyed as she slipped out and had to swim back in.

I took a couple of deep breaths, aware of how loud they sounded in the suit. My body inside the suit was drenched in sweat now, and I could smell how tired and afraid I was. Finally, I opened the throttle wide. The jet wheezed into a coughing hiss, and we began to slice through the water along a path that curved like a scimitar.

We swept by the rim of the canyon and then down. The opening seemed to stretch outward like a mouth as we jetted toward it. I fought to control the sled's path as much as I could, hoping that my guess had been right. I rode that sled as long as I could, but finally I put an arm around Sam and let the sled slide away underneath me.

Then I swam for all I was worth back toward a boulder I had

sighted earlier. I wanted it between us and the blast. Sam easily shot ahead of me, and though I tried, there was no way I could keep up with her. More and more, I felt like I was in glue instead of water. No matter how hard I kicked with my legs and pulled with my arms, I only seemed to move centimeters toward the boulder.

Sam was waiting patiently by the rock to see what new craziness I might suggest. I swept one hand out and snagged Sam while my other reached out to the rock. With one desperate pull, we lurched behind the boulder. A moment later, I heard a crumpling of metal, cut short by a loud rumbling like a giant with indigestion.

Light flashed, followed by a loud roar, and then rocks were shaking down the walls of the canyon. With a kick, I rose up again and slipped around the boulder. Sam wriggled in protest and I let go of her. If I'd swum fast before, I tried to swim even faster as I dodged over the rocks toward the opening.

Gravel and rocks were piled before the mouth of the tunnel, sparks were flying from exposed wires, and there was twisted and burnt metal. Sam shot ahead of me into that pesky opening—and bounced right out. The force field was still on. If I ever need a fortress, I'm going to ask a Xylk to build it.

Recklessly, I grabbed a handful of wires and yanked. Sparks flew every which way, and when I extended an arm and it went through where the force field had been, I didn't see any guards there either. Sam blinked her eyes while she took that in, and I took the opportunity to grab her collar.

She wriggled and squirmed and nipped at my gloved hand in irritation, but I kept hold of her as I swam forward. Now that I was in the tunnel itself, I could see spy eyes embedded in the walls, but the blast had shattered them.

I swam on through a tunnel that seemed to stretch on forever, though it was probably only some five hundred meters long. I found myself swimming over some kind of motor pool with more sleds and even a slider sealed in some kind of viscous plastic.

Every meter I expected to hear the hum of Xylk guns and see globes come whizzing toward me. But the pinprick of light grew to a small window in a large door, and still nothing happened. I peered through the window to see another windowed door. I had to be facing some kind of airlock. It was huge, about twenty meters on each side and about five meters high—large enough to handle large machinery and vehicles.

It took me a moment to find the knobs. They wouldn't move up or down in any direction that I could see so I just tried squeezing them hard. There was an answering hum and the lock began to fill with water. Whatever else the Xylk were, I had to admire their engineering, because as big as the airlock was, it didn't take very long to become full.

When the outer door opened, Sam and I swam in. I let myself float cautiously toward the inner door and peered through the window.

I was looking into a huge natural cavern a square kilometer in area and about a hundred and fifty meters high. Lights were set all around the perimeter to shine on a large three-story dome. Surrounding the dome were all sorts of computers and communication gear. This wasn't some summer camp that had been knocked together hastily. This was a forward command post. The Xylk must have been preparing for this just as long as they had with the pseudo-urya.

I checked the immediate area on the other side of the door. Crates filled the space to my left. A machine shop stood to my right. It looked like the perfect place for an ambush because they could bring more guns to bear than in the tunnel.

I didn't see any Xylk, but that didn't mean they weren't there. This was going to take more subtlety than smashing someone with a school of fish or blowing up a front door. But again, it was as Shandi had said: there was more than one way to get what I wanted.

Sam pawed at the second door, anxious to explore this new territory. There was a knob beside that door. I took hold of Sam with one hand and the knob with the other and squeezed. There was a hum and the outer door slid shut, and a pump began to chuckle as it took out the water.

That was all I needed to know. No matter how different the Xylk might be, their airlocks would have to function just like ours. One door would not open unless the other one was shut. There was probably some device that was tripped as a door shut to signal that it was OK to begin the cycle.

I squeezed the knob again, and the water level rose once more before the first door slid back open. I swam over to it and checked the doorframe. The trigger was just a button on the inside of the track. The closing door would push it, signaling that it was all right for the water to be pumped out and the air in.

I had to shove against it until I thought my thumbs were turning blue. That meant that Sam couldn't do it. I got my knife and wedged it between the door and the doorframe. Then I went back to the inner door and motioned Sam over to me.

I squeezed at the knob once more. The outer door tried to slide shut again but couldn't because of the knife jammed into the doorframe. Of course, Sam started to copy me, and I encouraged her with a few friendly pats. Then, before she could get distracted, I swam over to the outer door and shoved at the button.

Instantly air hissed and bubbled into the room. After a few minutes, though, it shut off and nothing else happened.

It took me a moment to realize what an idiot I was. There had to be some sort of sensor that wouldn't open the inner door unless the room was pressurized with air. Otherwise, there could be a nasty accident for the people in their base.

I found another spy eye. This one was intact so I smashed it with my fist. Then I searched the walls and ceiling until I found the device. It was really a simple little thing over in the corner with a hole that led into some kind of diaphragm. Leaving Sam to poke around the room, I went back out to the canyon and got a breather pack from one of the Xylk corpses.

When I had lugged it back to the airlock, I found Sam still nosing around and tapping at the glass as she tried to get into the cavern, but she took time out to inspect the pack that I dumped near the sensor. Then I fed one of the hoses into the hole itself. It was a loose fit, but if I left it on full force, it just might fool the sensor.

Unfortunately, Sam had now lost interest in squeezing the knob. She shook her head while I went on doing it, as if she already knew it was useless. But I was finally learning how to handle Sam. I'd just have to try some other trick.

While I searched my pockets, Sam circled me, knowing that something was up. When I pulled out the choco-bar, she glided toward me, but I'd had experience dealing with her so I twisted away. The sea this far down was pretty cold, but I hoped that maybe some of my body heat had leaked through the suit to keep it warm. I even rubbed my gloves together, hoping that the friction would help. I couldn't feel whether it was soft or not. I could only hope.

During all this time, Sam hovered around me like a large, hungry fly. When I finally squatted down near the knob, she darted in. I had to keep one hand free to shove her away while my other hand smeared the choco-bar over the knob. When the bar had just about disintegrated in my hand, I stepped back and Sam dove for the knob. Eagerly, she licked and bit at the top of the knob.

While she seemed intent on doing that, I turned on the spare breather pack. Air began to cycle into the hole, though little chains of silver air bubbles escaped all around the opening. I didn't have much time before the air charge in the pack would exhaust itself. Swimming over to the doorframe, I jammed my finger against the button.

Once again, air flushed into the room. One minute went by. Then a second. The air bubbles around the sensor were only straggling up now. The breather pack was exhausting itself. I just hoped it was enough. Suddenly, the inner door slid back in its frame.

Before I could say or do anything, a giant invisible hand seemed to snatch up Sam and me and fling us into the cavern on a torrent of water.

·17·

I remember seeing a startled Xylk looking up at me from behind a crate—and then the water had shot us past him. I'd managed to spoil his little ambush, but I wound up getting draped over a long tall crate. While I lay there on my bruised stomach, wondering if I'd broken any ribs, I could dimly hear frightened shouts mixing with thuds and crashes.

I shoved myself up, aching in every muscle, and checked for Sam, but I didn't see her. Water was spreading over the cavern floor, and sparks and smoke were rising from the computers and com equipment. Sam and I were pretty good at sabotage when we set our minds to it—and even when we didn't.

But the suitless Xylk weren't worried about their equipment. They were staring in horror at the water that flowed into the cavern. One of them frantically began slogging through the water toward the airlock while the others made for the suits and breather packs that were hanging on one wall to the side.

I lunged forward off the crate and just managed to catch his ankle. He gave a cry as he toppled backward. I tried to wrench the gun from him, but he held on to it as if it were glued to his hands. So I forced him over into the sheet of water. He kicked and spluttered as I used my free hand to force him under. He struggled for a moment more and a globe shot from his gun to blow up a crate of what looked like toilet paper. I pulled at the gun, and just as he was straining to yank it in the opposite direction, I let him, guiding the gun butt so that it caught him in the chin. His fingers went limp as he slumped backward; I lifted the gun away.

There were four Xylk with guns and maybe another three of them who had lost theirs but were coming with sticks or pipes. I fired a globe that exploded over their heads and made them stop. "Do you want to live?" I shouted through my helmet, but they couldn't hear me at that distance.

I wound up pointing at the suits that they would need to survive and then at my own gun. Eventually, they got the idea that I could keep them from their suits. One by one, their weapons splashed into the water.

I let them get into their suits and then had them put the unconscious Xylk into a suit. I pantomimed for each of them to tie up the others. After checking the knots, I tied up the seventh Xylk and then the unconscious Xylk. They weren't as hairy as Fake Ladadog, and there were some slight differences in the shape of the skulls, but I was willing to bet that it hadn't taken too much to convert Xylk into pseudo-urya.

By that time, Sam had woken up and come over to investigate. Though she seemed sore, she was still game. I felt certain that someone would have come storming out of the dome by now, but the remaining Xylk were playing it safe. So I hung up my prisoners from the former suit hooks. Then I opened up a pouch in my suit and took out some of the darts that I'd filled when I'd left our island. One by one, I stabbed the Xylk and put them out.

As I went to look for my knife, I told myself that Shandi's pep talk had done me some good after all. And I decided then and there that I wasn't going to let her walk out of my life without a fight on my part—no matter how angry she had looked or what she had said when I left her on the island. I went into the airlock and found I was in luck. The knife was still there in the airlock doorframe.

I wrecked two of the guns and, slinging one over my shoulder, I held onto the last. By the time I slogged over toward the dome door, I felt like a regular walking arsenal. Unlike the airlock, this was designed just for Xylk bodies so it was only a little over a meter and a third high. There didn't seem to be any lock on it. I don't think any of the Xylk expected an invader to get this far.

I squeezed the knob and then jumped to one side as the door slid open. But the cavalry didn't come charging out. That really wasn't the Xylk style. Well, it wasn't mine either. Of course, a curious Sam is another thing. She wanted to go plunging right into the dome, but I managed to snag her collar.

With Sam snarling and biting at my gloved hand, I peeked around the doorway to look at a corridor about a meter and two thirds high and some thirty meters long. Dark doorways stood to either side and large crates on the floor. If the Xylk ran true to form, there was bound to be an ambush there.

So, sticking the guns into my belt with the others, I tried to pick up a pipe from the floor of the cavern, but Sam was fighting to get free and explore so I had a hard time.

"Cut it out. Your medical insurance isn't paid up." She was still struggling when I flung the pipe inside. It clinked nicely on the floor and then started to roll.

Instantly, Xylk popped up from behind crates and from out of doorways and began shooting. I counted five of them, all told.

Sam immediately grew still as the smoke rolled out of the corridor. Thinking she had learned her lesson, I let go of her and got out the last brick of explosive. Then I slipped the antenna from my belt and stuck it into the center of the brick.

"Well, here's hoping our luck still holds up," I muttered to Sam and chucked the brick into the corridor so that it hit the floor and slid. For a moment I thought the antenna was going to fall out. The firing instantly stopped. A second later, three Xylk were stampeding for the opposite end of the corridor. The other two slammed their doors shut.

Sam instantly went on the attack and scrambled into the corridor. Picking up one gun in my right hand and sliding out my knife in my left, I ducked under the doorway and ran after her. I had to bend forward because the corridor was built for Xylk heights. With a snarl, Sam leaped gracefully on the ground and bounded on top of the nearest Xylk. He twisted around in the corridor, flailing with his gun.

His cry made the others turn around. By then, I had caught up with Sam. I didn't have time to think about what I was doing. My knife disposed of him as I shot at the next Xylk. He was only three meters away so I could hardly miss. The Xylk guns were certainly deadly against regular flesh. I was going to snap off another shot but luckily I caught sight of Sam from the corner of my eye. She darted right into what would have been my line of fire.

I dove to the floor as the Xylk fired. Sam instantly ducked behind a crate. Rolling onto my back, I got off a series of wild shots. The first exploded against the base of a wall, but the next caught another Xylk and sent him spinning dead against a wall.

I kicked open a door to my right. It was a room filled with machinery. Suddenly a Xylk rose from behind a machine where he had been hiding. He was almost in front of me, about chest-high, so neither one of us could miss. Fortunately, I was faster.

I heard a door open behind me, but even before I could turn, Sam chattered angrily, and her claws scratched the metal floor as she leaped. I whirled around to see the last Xylk firing wildly, his shots knocking holes in the wall.

I couldn't fire because of Sam again so I had to step in and finish him off with my knife. Sam jumped off with a snarl of distaste. After I sheathed my knife, I picked up the last brick of explosive. Then I chucked the antenna away and stowed the explosive back in my pocket.

All that was left now was the dome itself. It looked awfully big now that we were inside it.

I quickly checked the remaining rooms on the corridor. The last one seemed to be a locker room with suits and breather packs. I recognized Dad's old patched yellow one, and then I saw a red one that I'd seen on Shandi. I checked it more carefully. Yes, there was the orange patch on the elbow. It was definitely the one Shandi had been using. Something must have delayed her crew, and the Xylk had caught her; maybe it was the crew from the subber.

Doubly determined now, I went over to the door at the end of the corridor and shoved one of the buttons. The doors slid back to reveal a large shaft with two poles, a white one and a red one. Holding onto the doorframe, I looked up and then down. A hum echoed faintly in my helmet when I did so. The poles seemed to run through the entire ship. It must be some Xylk equivalent of an elevator.

Behind us, I heard a frantic whispering—like an hysterical insect. It was coming from the belt com of a dead Xylk. I guess the bridge was getting frantic to know what had happened. They'd probably shut off the juice to the shaft in another moment. I tapped a recall signal.

Sam poked her head out of a room she'd been investigating. I held an arm out hopefully, and everything was strange enough that Sam gave up being coy. She came loping into the corridor, her claws clicking along the slick floor, and leaped into my outstretched arm.

I settled her around my shoulders and then jumped over to the red pole. She gave a protesting chirrup as if this wasn't quite what she'd had in mind, but it was already too late. I caught the pole in my right hand, but I didn't need to worry. It was if I were standing on some invisible platform. As I slowly began to descend, some martial synthesizer music kicked in and a Xylk voice started to yip in a monotone voice. I guessed that the voice was part of the "elevator" mechanism that requested the floor, but since I didn't know Xylk I rode it all the way to the bottom.

The bottom was littered with little shells as if the Xylk were better snack eaters than they were housekeepers. They crunched underfoot as I went to the door and touched it. It opened instantly on a long curving corridor, and I stepped out. The shaft stopped humming even as I did so. The captain had finally pulled the plug, but I was still one step ahead of him.

Stripes at the top of the walls gave off a dim, diffuse light. Panels had been taken from the walls in different places to reveal wiring and pipes; and here and there would be some tool. Some were recognizable, like wrenches, but others were long tubes on which rested balls with spikes. Everything had the look and feel of someone's basement, right down to the dirty, oily rags.

Sam did not wait for an invitation but sprang away from my shoulders. She gave me one nasty look as if to tell me that I left a lot to be desired as a tour guide and then started down the corridor, every now and then sniffing the air to examine all the numerous and interesting scents.

She went straight to a room filled with crates that had been set up to hide a corner. Some Xylk had made himself comfortable there with an old pallet down on the floor and a couple of what looked like Xylk porn magazines. There were also ashes all around and a small, slender strawlike pipe with a small bowl.

I pulled Sam away from the pipe. "Come on. You're too young to smoke." And we went back out into the corridor.

Suddenly she gave a chirrup and began to scamper along the floor. "Hey, don't get ahead of me," I shouted, but my voice was probably too faint through my helmet, even assuming that she would have obeyed me anyway. So I was left to plod along at my clumsy human pace as she skidded around the curving corridor and was lost to view.

Suddenly a loud familiar *fwee-eep* echoed down the corridor. I picked up speed. When I found Sam, she was busy scratching at a metal door behind which I could hear plaintive *fwee-eeps*.

I put my hand on the door. "Here I am, boy." But because of the helmet and the thick metal door, Godzilla couldn't hear me so I squeezed the doorknob. Sam oozed inside the moment the door was open a crack.

Godzilla was chained to the rear wall of a storage room, but otherwise the Xylk hadn't taken any extra precautions. He probably could have used his fire to get out, but he hadn't been riled or frightened enough to stoke up his furnace. In fact, he seemed happy enough picking around the lower shelves of a storage room. There were broken boxes and jars all around him as if he'd been sampling the Xylk stores. When he saw me, he let out a cheep of protest.

"It's me, boy." I squatted down so Godzilla could see my face through the helmet.

He blinked his eyes then, and if he was capable of smiling, I think he would have done it right then. Instead, all he could do was rattle his chain. *Fwee-eep.*

"Right. Coming right off." I motioned Sam back and blasted the chain from the collar around his neck.

Godzilla clawed at the collar and I could see where it chafed through his scales. I patted his paw. "Don't do that. You'll make it bleed."

Fwee-eep. He sounded annoyed.

"Well, I can't do anything about the collar until we get out of here." I examined him quickly, but outside of the scrapes on his neck, Godzilla was in a lot better shape than I was. "All right. One down and two to go."

I herded my little menagerie back out into the corridor and began to search again. I had hoped that Dad and Shandi might be down here too, but after we had made a circuit of the main corridor and had gone down every cross corridor, Sam and Godzilla hadn't caught any familiar scents.

I didn't want to chance the elevator any more, but I figured that there had to be a maintenance stairway alongside the elevator, so I headed back there. We found a ladder set into a much narrower shaft that could be reached through a square panel. Sam was game, but Godzilla balked at the ladder. He promptly hunkered down. "Just pretend you're back at the resort," I told him in exasperation. "You were scampering all around when you were there."

But Godzilla sat square on his haunches as if he had been poked, prodded, and carried far enough.

"All right then. Suit yourself." I began to climb the ladder.

Godzilla waited until I was two meters above him, when he forgot his dignity and got up again. With an annoyed peep, he began to climb after me.

The next deck had a large hydroponics room with some pretty exotic-looking plants and fungi of all shapes, sizes, colors, and creeds. Next we found a messroom that would only have seated some ten Xylk. I suppose they ate in shifts.

When I heard a clink from the next room, I took out my gun and moved past the small tables and stools. Stooping under the doorway, I entered what must have been the galley. It looked like a small, efficient place. Pots bubbled on the stove; a Xylk was busy crumbling bits of dried purple fungus into what looked like a purple stew. From the other things I saw in the pot, I couldn't say much for Xylk cuisine, but there was a slab of fresh red meat sitting on a cutting board beside a big cleaver.

The cook turned around in annoyance when he heard us enter, but his irate expression faded away when he saw us. His mouth just stayed open as he looked from me to Sam and Godzilla. He took a stop toward the cleaver but stopped when I waved my gun at him.

If anyone knew where Dad and Shandi were, it would probably be the person who had to feed them.

"Tell me where the other humans are," I shouted through my helmet.

He just slowly raised his paws and shook his head as if he didn't understand. So I tried pointing toward myself and then holding up two fingers. I thought I saw a flicker of comprehension behind his eyes, but he was still playing dumb.

"I ought to make you eat your own cooking," I grumbled. I did the pantomime again and started to get the same result when an impatient Godzilla started for him. Immediately, he began to nod his head and gestured for me to follow him. Sometimes it pays to travel with the right company.

He led us to the elevator and gave an exasperated click when he found it was shut off. I'd left the panel off the maintenance stair and the cook went right into it. I followed the cook, and Sam and Godzilla came after me. He led us up to the next level and then out into a well-lit corridor. As we passed some of the open doors, I could see bunks inside. We were apparently in the living quarters.

He led us confidently to one room with a massive box on the wall next to the doorway. He tapped out a code and the door slid back. He almost bumped into me when he jumped back in alarm.

The room would have been a tight squeeze for four Xylk, let alone two Xylk and two humans. The cook seemed especially frightened of a small Xylk in a long brocaded cape, who sat on a stool tilted back on two legs so his head could rest against the wall. Next to him was a mean-looking Xylk. He had a large hexagonal pipe thrust through several globes that rested on his shoulders. It was aimed at Dad, who was sitting on the floor. Shandi was sitting next to him.

To say the least, Dad looked shocked—as if I'd just managed to change rocks into gold. Shandi seemed almost as surprised. But this wasn't the time to take a bow.

The Xylk in the cape—I assume he was the captain—held up something that looked like a jeweled fly whisk. "To call of your pets."

"Sam. Godzilla" I motioned them away and they drifted sullenly back.

"Now to drop your weapons," the captain casually instructed. "Or to order funerals for friends and family."

"Don't do it, son. We're dead anyway—" Dad began, and then the guard brought his gun down viciously across Dad so that he fell across Shandi's lap.

"Not to interrupt," the captain observed, and flicked his fingers for Dad to sit upright again.

From the bruises on Dad's face and legs, I was willing to bet this was not the first time the captain had instructed him in the finer points of Xylk etiquette. There were a few cuts and bruises on Shandi too. Even if I'd been willing to trust the captain, this sample of his hospitality would have been enough to change my mind.

"No, captain. I think you're the one who's going to drop his weapons." I took out the brick of explosive from a suit pocket.

The captain drew his teeth back in that gruesome Xylk smile. "Please. Not to insult my intelligence. No detonators or would have used by now."

I held up the gun and aimed it at the brick. "But I have this. I'm willing to bet an explosion will generate enough heat to set this off."

The captain sat upright on the stool, the legs going bang on the deck. "To point out, you would blow up too."

I shrugged. "As Dad said, we're dead anyway. I don't have anything to lose and a lot to gain by blowing us all up."

The captain slowly lowered the whisk to his lap. "Not to be hasty. To talk this over. To be reasonable."

"I wouldn't take too long." I flexed my index finger. "Maybe Dad didn't tell you. Our family has this terrible affliction that makes our trigger fingers twitch."

Dad gave me a broad grin and then turned around so the captain could see his fingers. "He's serious, you know." He wriggled his fingers for the captain.

The captain twisted one eye stalk to look at Dad and the other at me—a useful trick. "It is useless to try to escape." He pressed his lips tightly together as if he had said too much. Abruptly he flailed his fly whisk toward the guard and said something in Xylk. The guard's gun clattered to the floor.

I jerked my head at the guards. "Now untie them."

The captain barked something over his shoulder, and the guard and the cook both went over to Dad and Shandi. There was really so much that I wanted to say to her, but all I could manage to do was be flip. "We can both eat that eight-course meal of crow later."

Shandi's face was an interesting study in emotions. Surprise mixed with happiness at seeing me, but there was also a kind of—well, wariness. She was eyeing me the way a small animal might examine a trap. "I wouldn't be so sure of that. Your father and I were having such a nice chat before you barged in. It was all about your misguided youth."

Dad twisted around so one Xylk could get to his hands, which had been tied behind his back. "I assured her that none of your flaws came from either your mother or me."

Not knowing what to say to Shandi, I looked over at Dad. "You're not off the hook yet. If it's not heredity, then it has to be environment, and guess who's responsible for that?"

I caught a movement from the corner of my eye. The captain was raising his fly whisk so that the bottom of the handle was pointed toward me. I threw myself to the side even as the captain squeezed the handle. A beam of light splashed against the wall. Sam sprang at the captain, but the captain tilted back on his stool and crashed against the deck and Sam went sailing over him.

In the meantime, the other two Xylk were scrambling to get to the gun. I rolled onto my stomach and shot the guard. Sam wrapped herself around the head of the cook, and Godzilla sat down heavily on his stomach. In the meantime, though, the captain had scrambled to his feet. Sam leaped at him but only managed to sink her teeth into the hem of his cape.

The captain dragged Sam across the floor for a moment before he undid his collar and Sam was left with just a mouthful of cape. I snapped off another shot but only managed to blow up part of the doorframe as the captain tumbled through. By the time I'd gotten to the door, the captain was long gone.

I got out my knife and went back into the room. Shandi rose to her knees and twisted around so I could reach her wrists. "Some of their divers caught me by surprise." There was an edge to her voice as if she were still controlling some of the hurt and the anger at my leaving her.

"I saw the subber. You must have been inside." I knelt beside her. "It's a good thing I didn't stay with you, don't you think?"

"I'll admit it worked out for the best—but," she said quickly as I started to grin,"I still haven't forgotten what you said."

I'd overlooked the fact that Shandi was a real person with real defenses, a lot of defenses, defenses that kicked in the instant she felt threatened. The smile froze on my face. "I just saved your life."

"And I'm grateful. But do you think I'm so simple that I'll forget everything because of gratitude?" The golden eyes were as cool and distant as when we had first met at Xanadu. She had withdrawn behind a wall again, a wall I knew I'd helped build.

"If I'd listened to you, we'd either all be captives or dead." I started to cut through the cords.

She sat down and extended her legs. "I've tried and tried to tell myself that. I wish it were as easy as that." Exasperation edged her voice. Maybe she was as frustrated by that inner mental wall as me.

As I reached for her ankles, I felt as if I were trying to break the wall down with my head. "But I'm here now."

She parted her ankles the moment the cords broke. "I'm . . . not ready to risk being hurt a second time."

I sat back on my heels. "There wasn't any choice."

She drew her knees up so she could massage the blood back into her feet. "That's the sad part about it." She sounded almost fatalistic.

Shandi only respected proud, independent people like herself. At the same time, they made her feel insecure. That was the maddening catch. "You can't build your whole life around not getting hurt."

"I shouldn't, but I do." Shandi folded herself protectively into a ball. "I don't like hurting you, you know."

I wasn't about to give up—not after what I'd gone through in the last few days. "I warn you. I'm persistent."

She began to rock back and forth. "So am I, I'm afraid."

I was glad of the excuse to turn to Dad. He was obviously curious, but he didn't ask any questions. I guess it was a measure of some new respect for me. "We'd better get out of here before he throws another welcoming party."

Dad looked at me over his shoulder while I cut his bonds. Aside from a few scratches on his cheeks and having the wind knocked out of him, he was in good shape. "The rest of the rescue party should be able to handle him."

I sheathed the knife. "I'm it, Dad."

Dad bent to untie his legs. "This is no time for jokes, son."

Shandi was rubbing the circulation back into her ankles. "Why, don't you think your son could get in here on his own?" At least she was willing to give the devil his due.

"The guards and everything else." Dad looked up with the cords in his hand.

Shandi got shakily to her feet but had to crouch because of the low ceiling. "He got here, didn't he?"

"I had a little help from my friends." I nodded to Sam and Godzilla.

Dad slowly drew the cords back and forth through his fingers. "It's hard to believe."

"That he has it in him?" Shandi appropriated the guard's gun. "He just never had a chance before. You know, you really ought to get to know your son. I think you've been underestimating him." She spoke proudly but with a strange distance, as if she were talking about some second cousin she had raised. Shandi definitely didn't trust me.

I felt like I was dying bit by bit inside, but I concentrated on the tasks at hand. I put the cook out with a trank dart and glanced back at Dad. I might as well enjoy some of my moment, at least. "Still want to say I didn't inherit anything from you?"

Dad leaned on a bunk and tried to shove himself to his feet, but he sank back down. Apparently, his bruises didn't stop with just the ones that I could see. "Do you?" he finally asked.

I got a hand under one arm. "I think the basic gene stock is pretty good."

·18·

Crouching, we ran down the low-ceilinged corridor. I was glad to see that Dad moved quicker once he'd warmed up—even though I'd given him half my arsenal. On the way, he told me about what he had overheard. Some of it confirmed what Fake Ladadog had told us about the time scale for the invasion. This base had been built stealthily over the decades, with equipment brought in by a scout ship entering through the holes in our radar umbrella.

"They plan ahead." I motioned them down the maintenance ladder.

Dad got down on his knees stiffly. "They're a long-lived species. When you live two hundred years, you plan differently from the way our species does." He went through the opening. "You also need more living space."

Shandi waited for Godzilla to follow him. "But you just put the classic monkey wrench into their schemes. When the Xylk couldn't find you, they decided to move up the time for the invasion."

I watched Sam go after Godzilla. "How soon? Next month?"

"Today." Shandi squeezed through the opening next.

I took one last look around the corridor and then plunged through the opening. "I did a little damage coming in. Maybe they've changed their minds."

Dad's voice echoed up the shaft. "The Xylk here are only the headquarters staff. They planted pseudo-urya with important people—rich civic leaders, military personnel, government officials."

Shandi was concentrating on the rungs. "And at the signal, their agents will carry out assassinations and acts of sabotage."

"What's the signal?" I asked.

Dad was picking up speed on the ladder. "We don't know, but the captain seemed to think that their agents will leave Carefree confused and ripe for the taking."

"And the Xylk will have all the colonists as hostages when the Union Navy comes to counterattack." Shandi hurried after Dad. "But at least we have a fighting chance now."

I told Dad to stop since he was by the airlock level. They stared at the corpses as I guided them into the strange room.

Dad glanced at me. "It's funny. You think you know someone because you've raised him, and then you find that you really don't."

"I didn't really know I could do it either." I took down Dad's suit and handed it him. "Here. Better get into this now. They had a little problem with their plumbing."

While Dad and Shandi got into their suits, I went out into the corridor, because in that tiny room there was space only for two. Godzilla and Sam were prowling the corridor. "Don't wander, kids."

I kept an eye on the corridor until Dad and Shandi came waddling out in their suits and flippers. Under his arm Dad had a Xylk breather pack. Motioning Godzilla over to him, he slid it over the reluctant animal's shoulders and adjusted the straps. I felt a little guilty that I hadn't even thought about him.

"Will he keep the mouthpiece in?" I wondered.

"I'll carry him if I have to." Dad shortened the straps for Godzilla's slighter shoulders. "I'm not leaving anything for the Xylk."

"Dad?" I asked as a new thought occurred to me. "What about the pressure?"

Cradling Godzilla in his arms, Dad fit the mouthpiece into Godzilla's mouth. "I've run through the design. I built him well."

That's what Dad had thought about Godzilla's voice too, but I tactfully didn't say anything about that.

Sam and I were the first ones out the door, but for a change there weren't any surprises in the cavern—just burnt and burning equipment. Keeping a careful watch, I beckoned them after me.

Once we were outside the dome, Dad straightened in relief. "I thought I was going to get a permanent stoop from being in that ship." Then he caught sight of the wreckage in the cavern. "Good grief. This is more than a 'little' damage."

Dan and I were never good at talking about these kinds of things. I was just as embarrassed as he was. "Let's get going before they try to give us the bill." I started for the airlock.

But Dad clapped his hand on my arm and stopped me. "It's been one disaster after another since we came here, and I've been blaming you."

"I had a little talk with him too," Shandi said quietly. Apparently she was still willing to be a friend.

I studied Dad through the helmet visor. He looked a lot older than I remembered. Part of it was that I was growing up, but I think all his problems were also aging him faster.

Dad glanced away from me for a moment while he tried to find the right words. "I'm better at dealing with ideas than with people."

"I know, Dad," I said softly.

Dad gave a grunt. "You really have grown."

I had to laugh. "And if we want to grow any older, we'd better get out of here."

It's foolish, I guess, but I did feel taller as we went to the airlock. But I shrank right back down to normal size when I found that the captain had shut the inner door and tried to lock it. Since there was a manual override on this side of the airlock, the captain must have known he couldn't keep us shut up inside the cavern. He only wanted to delay us, and that worried me because there was still the subber out there somewhere.

The only bad moment came when the airlock began to fill with water and Godzilla began to struggle, but we all patted and stroked him and he calmed down once he realized he could breathe.

When we were inside the tunnel, I gave them a quick lesson in the sled controls. Dad fiddled with what he thought was the com. "It seems to be preset to one frequency. I wouldn't count on our using them unless you want to talk the captain." Giving up, he made Godzilla sit in front of him.

"Personally, he's not my type." I swam over to another sled.

Shandi kicked her jets and took her sled up as if she had been piloting one all her life. "In fact, we should use hand talk from now on."

We jetted slowly through the tunnel until we were near the mouth. I could see the canyon floor beyond us. *Hold,* I signed to Shandi. I motioned Sam to swim on and then cut my jets.

Shandi gave me a questioning look but reached out a hand to hold onto the frame while I dropped away.

As Dad passed by, I put a finger to about where my mouth was behind the faceplate. He just nodded as he followed Shandi into the canyon.

I waited until they were clear of the tunnel before I took out the brick of explosive once again and set it over the tunnel. I figured that the tunnel opening was already half closed by rubble from my first efforts. I might as well finish the job. It wouldn't stop the Xylk forever, but I was willing to bet the nuisance would turn the captain purple—if Xylk get purple when to go into a rage.

Dad and Shandi were floating some twenty meters away with the sleds. As I climbed on, I asked Shandi, *Can hit?*

She gave me the OK sign, and while she did a loop so she could face the tunnel again, I made Sam take hold of my sled. Then Dad and I got on either side of her sled and grabbed hold. Just as Shandi fired, Dad and I each opened up the throttles on our sleds. We lurched forward as we held onto Shandi's sled.

The explosion erupted like a giant moth spreading its wings, and then the roar and the shock wave caught up with us and we were tumbling about on our sleds. When we had righted ourselves, I signed that there might be a slider up there. But both Dad and Shandi thought it would be too dangerous. Even if it was there—and we couldn't be sure if divers from the subber had claimed it—the slider might be watched and booby-trapped.

We jetted along the line of the canyon, because it aimed toward the mainland. As the rock slid by under our headlights, I kept thinking about the captain's slip. He had said that escape was impossible.

I slid up beside Shandi and stretched over to touch my helmet against hers. "Did the captain say anything funny to you?" I shouted. "It's like he figured he had an extra ace up his sleeve."

"The captain was just plain funny," came her muffled reply, and when I told her about my worries she just shrugged clumsily in her suit. "He probably was thinking about the subber."

It certainly seemed likely enough, but I kept thinking about it as we went on. For a while, I even forgot to be hungry. About noon by my watch, Dad called a rest, and we watched enviously as Sam came back with a fish. Godzilla squirmed on the sled, looking accusingly at each of us in turn.

"Don't look at me," I said through my helmet. "I'm just as hungry as you."

Shandi touched her helmet against mine. "Is that Godzilla or my stomach growling?"

"Probably both." I motioned Sam over and set her down on the sled. "Come on. The sooner we get to the mainland, the sooner we can eat." I glared at Sam. "And don't look so smug."

For the last five kilometers the canyon narrowed, and its floor rose as we neared its end. By then, we could hear the mainland long before we saw it. When I heard a distant roar, I angled my sled up.

Shandi copied me. *What that?* she signed.

The explanation would have taken too long, so I matched speed with her. I had to stretch because Sam was lounging on the sled in front of me, but I managed to touch helmets with her again. "The sand falls. The longshore currents shove the sand down from the beach and over a cliff."

Dad signed to me. *Three kilometers?*

I held up two fingers because that's how many I thought it was. I was just wondering if we could swing by the sand falls for a look when two huge golden eyes suddenly winked at us from the darkness above.

The light flooded the canyon as we stared up at a flat black ovular shape some five meters wide. A growl filled the canyon like a giant clearing its throat and the eyes suddenly rose. I threw my weight to the starboard and felt the sled tilt in that direction, almost losing Sam in the process.

At the same time, Shandi banked sharply to port. The globe caught the bottom of her sled. Fortunately she kicked away from it. The sled shielded her from most of the blast. As pipes and torn chunks of metal went flying, she fell away.

"Yipe!" she shouted.

"I'll distract them." Dad curved in like a crazy sparrow. His shot went wild. Dad was a fine scientist but a lousy gunner. And then I lost sight of his antics as I took the sled up in a loop. The whole sea rotated crazily around me and then I was leveling off and heading back down the canyon. Shandi was waiting with outstretched arms.

"It's the subber," Dad radioed to us.

"Shandi was right. This is the captain's surprise. He must have known it was around." I cut back on the throttle and drifted past her.

She grabbed hold of the frame. "He's the life of the party, all right."

I opened the throttle again and sped up one wall of the canyon. "They must use it to smuggle in supplies."

Shandi had taken out her gun and was struggling to aim it one-handed. "Including party hats and favors." She gave a yelp as I sent the sled corkscrewing back up through the water away from a globe. Shandi was flung outward and then back against the sled, and I was continually having to adjust for the shift in weight. As the globe exploded underneath us, she demanded, "Who taught you how to steer?" She'd lost or dropped her gun and was holding onto the frame with both hands.

"The mad bomber behind us." I nodded to Dad, who was buzzing around the subber.

The bottom of the sled banged against one side of the canyon and our flippers were dragging over the stone. I cut back on the throttle and our momentum carried us downward as another globe went whizzing overhead.

Shandi dug an elbow into my side. "Better let the first team take over."

We switched positions and then she opened the throttle again and rose through the water in time to see one of Dad's shots hit the subber squarely. It simply scorched the side.

She paralleled the lip of the canyon. "The sides are armored." In the last moment, she had to duck down behind a line of rocks to avoid another shot from the subber.

Dad slipped along beside us. "Let's get out of here."

Shandi kept pace right next to him. The subber rose above the canyon, and the beam of a searchlight slashed across the sea floor.

We were heading toward a kind of plain where the mud lay in curving, ripplelike ridges like sand dunes. Dad took us along one narrow channel and cut off his light. Shandi did the same, following him by the sound of his jet.

Another globe sizzled through the water right over our heads. "They must have sonar," Dad said. Since it didn't matter whether we ran dark or not, he snapped on his lights and again Shandi copied him.

This far down on the ocean floor, we could see the odd markings of the few scattered animals who lived here. Little clusters of dots from crablike creatures or long curving lines by some giant worm. The tracks could have been there for a day or for a century. Wreckage had a way of lasting forever this far down where the cold and darkness discouraged even bacteria. I didn't intend to add our bones to this place.

"Dad," I radioed, "if we're near the sand falls, we must be near that big forest of sea boas."

"We should split up and head for different parts of the forest," Shandi said.

For a moment, Dad was racing alongside us. "One of us should get the news to the colony." He sounded reluctant, though.

I knew that it would increase our chances of success, and yet I felt as hesitant as he did. It was as if I were just getting to know him. "I guess we should," I admitted.

"Son, in case we don't see one another again, I'm sorry about things."

"I'm sorry too, Dad."

"No, no, you don't have anything to apologize for." We sped along, even though each second that we continued in a straight line increased our danger. "If we get out of this," he added, "I'm going to make it up to you."

I wish I could have seen his face. "No, *when* we get out of this, Dad, not *if*."

"Right." He swerved off to starboard.

Shandi banked toward port. "You'll see him again."

"Is that a promise?"

"Sure, or you can repossess my wardrobe." Shandi lay on her side to make room for me.

"I don't think it would fit me." But I was encouraged as I squeezed in beside her and on top of an irate and wriggling Sam.

Our jets made a fine hissing sound and we kept our heads low as the water swept over prow and windshield, trying to snatch us from the sled. We followed the sea floor as it gradually slanted upward, brushing the bottom every now and then and sending up a plume of mud.

Fortunately or unfortunately, the subber went after us. An explosion sent up a shower of mud behind us. "We're out of range," Shandi said.

"But not for long. They have better legs than we do." I stared down at the sea floor, trying to remember bits and snatches of what Dad had tried to teach me about the sea's flow.

Something made Shandi zig to the left and a globe boiled through the water where we had been. She zagged sharply then. "This is your world, Piper, any ideas?"

That left me free to concentrate. When I saw the deep ripples of mud, I put a hand on hers. "Take up up. There's one of those express-train currents hereabouts, and it'll carry us right into the heart of that forest."

"Up it is." She pulled back on the vertical handle and tilted the nose of the sled up into the strong, swift current, and it was like having a giant hand pick us up and push us along.

The subber shot at us, but the globe fell short. We were out of range again. "Not bad, Pipes. What's the heading?"

I tapped her suit compass to indicate to her to head due west along with the current. Right then my only real worry was that the subber would come up into the current too, but they stayed near the sea floor as they ran parallel to our course. Every now and then they would take a shot, but we were still out of range. They seemed content with just keeping us in sight. I tried to reach the colony over both my suit com and the sled's, but I couldn't raise anyone.

Finally we began to rise up the slope. The surface was a luminous gray, as if the sun had not yet risen. The rolling slope sped by dizzyingly, and then a reddish-brown wall of sea boas loomed ahead of us. It was many times larger than the one in the lagoon. The forest stretched on for kilometers. I put my helmet against hers in case the subber was monitoring our radio transmissions. "Cut the jets," I said. "We don't want to hit it full force."

Shandi nodded and cut back on the throttle so that we slid with a thump against the first trunks.

"Now we get off and push," I said. "Let their sonar try to find us in here."

Sam was ready to leap off too, but I signed for her to stay. I wasn't about to lose track of her in the forest. The broad, reddish-brown leaves brushed past my visor as we began to shove the sled along. Five meters into the forest and I could barely see Shandi next to me, and the sound of the boa trunks swaying in the current would help mask our sound patterns.

We heard the solid thud of the trunks on metal as the subber impacted, then the growling of its engines and the sudden whine of kelp winding around its propellers. Frantically, the captain of the subber cut the engines, and they died like a beast grumbling itself to sleep.

Soon it would be the mainland, a quick com call, and then a big steak dinner.

We were still shoving our sled ahead of us when the first explosion blew up some sea boas to our left. I couldn't help cringing as seared leaves and sections of trunk fell around us. "They've got us," I said, "but how—"

"Maybe they have thermal trackers too." Shandi slipped my gun from my belt. *Grab Sam*, she signed, *and get off.*

I touched helmets with her. "Now who's forgetting the magic word?" I got my fingers under Sam's collar, even though she nipped at my glove in protest, and rolled off the sled. Shandi opened the throttle and slid off to starboard. I could barely make her out through the boas. She was no longer on the sled but instead was aiming her gun. The next moment, there was a bright ball of fire billowing through the sea boas. The shock wave sent me backward so that I got all tangled up in the long green leaves like a little cabbage roll.

I didn't try to struggle like a greenhorn tourist, because that would have tangled me up even more. Instead, I gently eased first one leaf and then another off me. All this time, though, Sam was fighting to get away so I let her. Her streamlined shape was far better in these boas than mine.

"Where are you?" Shandi asked.

"Over here to your left."

By the time Shandi found me, I was finally unwrapped. She put her helmet against mine. "That should foul up their thermal trackers." She hooked her hand through my belt.

Suddenly a half-dozen boas exploded and their trunks and leaves went flying round. "The subber must have sent out divers," Shandi said, "but I don't see how can they track us now."

"I don't know, but let's not stick around to find out." I turned and headed down. Sam and Shandi followed.

More shots exploded in the boas up ahead. Divers must have been sent ahead with some of that same portable tracking gear. I knew we were cut off from the mainland. With a sickening feeling, I turned and headed us back out toward the sea.

We swam low over the slope, trying not to brush the sea pens as we went. Overhead and to our right, the hard unchanging surface of the subber appeared, like a knife-edged disk cutting through the restless ceiling of the sea. Ahead of us was open water, where we were now easy targets. To our left came the roar of the sand falls. More divers emerged from the subber even while we watched.

Shandi let go of my belt and shot ahead of me with a kick. "The sand falls. It's our only hope."

I swam after her, but though I churned through the water, there was no way I could catch up with the swift, graceful Shandi. The sun shone through the sand falls so that they stood like a thick, whirling cloud of light.

"Shandi, come back," I called, but the falls had already swallowed her up.

There was only one thing to do, and that was go after her into the sand. Sam drew up at the edge of the falls and stared at me in shock as I swam on past. The falls hit me with the force of a slider on full speed and I was carried downward. The gun was ripped from my hand. My breath was taken away by the pounding of the sand. I twisted this way and that in frustration while I searched for Shandi, but she seemed only a small, dark shadow seen through the veils ahead.

When the sand began to billow and rise in a large cloud, I knew that I was near the foot of the falls. I tried to angle out of the falls, fighting both the force of the sand and the water.

For a moment I hung at a tilt to the slope, but the cascading sand flung me down flat against the soft piles at the foot of the falls. The sand poured down about me, burying me quickly so that I could hardly even breathe as that terrible weight crushed down on my back.

·*19*·

I don't recommend being buried alive. I kept waiting for the recycling machinery in the breather packs to break down, but the filters must have kept out the sand. It seemed to take forever to reach the sea floor. Slowly and painfully I began to squirm and kick through the sand, though it was so heavy it felt as if I were trying to crawl through slowly hardening tree sap. But finally my hands broke into the lighter pressure of the water. Another moment and I had wormed my way onto the sea floor.

Overhead, I could just make out the divers re-entering the subber. I suppose they figured no one would survive that plunge.

Sam swam down and wriggled the long tufts of her eyebrows like some indignant little old duchess. In her opinion, this entire escapade was getting a bit out of hand. But I ignored Sam to glance around anxiously for Shandi. For a moment, I didn't think she had made it. And that made me ache inside almost as much as when Mom had died.

Then I saw the molelike ridge appear on the slope. Apparently, Shandi had decided to let the sand carry her out from under the falls and down the slope. I swam over and began frantically to dig at the sand. Sam came over and began to help. It seemed to take forever before Shandi's hands appeared. I guessed she'd lost her gun just like I had. Grabbing hold of her by the wrists, I pulled backward. Shandi erupted in a cloud of sand, and the two of us collapsed on the slope.

Shandi wagged her arms and legs in the sand with the sheer joy of being alive and the sand rose around her like veils. I pressed my helmet against hers. "Thank God. I thought you were dead."

She put her hands on my shoulders to keep me from hugging her. "Whoa. There's a difference between what you want and what you can get."

I tried to keep our helmets touching. "I know that. All the wishing in the world didn't bring Mom back to life."

"You can't do that with feelings either." She drew a leg up so her knee was against my belly.

I tried to read her expression through her visor but couldn't. "I didn't mean to let you down."

"There are all kinds of failure."

I sighed. "Whether I fail to save my father's life or your feelings."

"Poor Pipes," Shandi said, "you've got a lot more responsibilities than you started out with, haven't you?" Apparently I'd managed to poke a slight hole in Shandi's defensive wall; that was encouraging.

"You're the reason I've gotten this far."

"Well, you don't need me anymore. You're a self-starter now." Stopping a Xylk invasion was easier than dealing with her. "There are still a lot of design changes that are needed."

"Sorry about that." Almost guiltily, Shandi threw me off her. Then she sprang upward. When Sam wriggled over to her, Shandi grasped Sam's paws, and the two of them circled like slow dancers.

I swam up and held out my arms to try and catch both of them, but Shandi did a creditable otter imitation and wriggled free as easily as Sam. I was left grasping empty water.

Shandi pirouetted as gracefully as she could in the suit and held out a gloved hand as if to invite me for a swim. Then, with a kick, she sent herself in the direction of the shore.

I followed with Sam. Apparently everything was going to have to be worked out according to Shandi's timetable—if ever. We paralleled the slope, our suits expanding as we decompressed inside them.

As we neared the beach, the surf raised the sand like holos I'd seen of storms in the desert. There was this 'dark, rolling, opaque cloud that hissed against my helmet and suit. I lost sight of them for a moment, and then I could make out Shandi's shadowy figure. I reached out and caught her arm and then worked my way down to her gloved hand. In that murky confusion, she seemed glad of the contact because she gripped my hand tightly.

It was difficult finding footing in the sand, and the currents kept pulling me this way and that. Suddenly there was just the splashing of the surf as my helmet broke out of the water. On the distant horizon, the rising sun made a red smudge on the sea. A lone tassel bird, hidden in the twilight that still hovered over the land, screeched from somewhere above the dark beach. Sam was already out of the water, padding cautiously onto the beach and sniffing at the air.

Water rilled down the folds of my suit as I stomped up onto the beach. My breather pack seemed to weigh heavily on my back now that the water wasn't helping to support it. But there was air and dim light all around.

"We made it!" Shandi turned, kicking with her flipper so that water splashed all over me. I returned the favor, and then Sam was romping in between us.

"Hey, there. Hey!" I never thought Constable Shadbell would be a welcome sight, but he was. He was waving his arms like a windmill in front of his jeever. Maybe the captain of the subber had been afraid of being spotted. If that was the case, I owed Constable Shadbell a dinner with all the trimmings.

I started to wade toward him. "Are we glad to see you!" I shouted, but he couldn't hear us over the surf.

While we struggled up onto the beach, he strutted down toward us, his head perched on that long neck of his, and again I thought of a goose waddling. The gun holster he now wore made him look far more official. When he got near us, he bent his knees and peered through my faceplate. "Afternoon, Piper." He seemed surprised to see Shandi with me. "Miz Tyr. There's a passel of folks looking for you."

"You didn't get my message?" I asked.

"No."

Both Shandi and I started to talk loudly through our helmets at the same time and only seemed to confuse Shadbell all the more. "Hold on. Hold on. Just 'cause I got two ears don't mean I can understand two people at the same time."

I let Shandi do most of the telling since she seemed ready to explode and concentrated instead on keeping Sam distracted. "There are Xylk on this world," Shandi was saying. "We just escaped from them."

Shadbell looked from her to me and back to her again as if he were skeptical but was too wily to insult someone with her money. "Do tell."

Shandi stood on one leg to take off a flipper. "They look like urya. They have agents disguised as pets."

Shadbell ran a hand over his stubbly chin. "And I suppose some tassel birds are their air force?"

Shandi leaned on me as she took off her other flipper. "I'm serious, Constable."

Shadbell stared at her thoughtfully. "This wouldn't be no spoiled rich kid's joke? 'Cause if it is—"

She hung her flippers from her belt. "If I'm lying, I'll hop into your worst jail cell and lock the door myself."

Shadbell tilted back his head and let out his breath in a heavy sigh. "Well, if this is a hoax, you're the best actors I've ever seen."

I finished stripping off my own flippers as I nodded to the jeever squatting in the sand dunes. "In the meantime, maybe we better com the colony."

Shadbell hitched up his belt over his large stomach. "I'd like to, but the com doesn't work. That's the problem of buying war—"

"Surplus," I finished. "I know, I know." The traveling salesperson who dumped all that stuff on the colony must have been one smooth talker. I explained to Shandi. "It's over two hours back to New Benua."

Shandi started striding up the beach, her flippers banging against her hip. "Then we'd better get back there."

"Yessum, I guess we'd better." Shadbell followed in her determined track as she went right to the jeever. The sand grunted and barked underneath our feet.

The front hood of the little all-purpose hover curved downward sharply between its headlights like a butler looking down his nose at the common folk. On the side panel was painted the seven-jeweled swan of the colony. Other than the nine-gauge ripper in the large side holster, it was your standard-issue jeever.

Shandi climbed right into the driver's seat as if she owned it. Shadbell came to a halt and just dangled the keys from his fingers. "I'll do the driving, ma'am." He looked polite but firm.

Shandi looked as if she were going to argue, but I shook my head and helmet slightly so she swallowed her pride. "All right," she said stiffly and slid over into the front passenger seat. I got into the back seat and Sam, happy to have a new place to explore, climbed in.

Even though the jeever rode on a cushion of air, Shadbell kept it low to the ground to save on fuel, but that meant the jeever followed the rolling contours of the ground so that we were bounced around like balls on a roulette wheel.

Sam, of course, was the epitome of curiosity and wanted to poke her nose into everything. I made a halfhearted attempt to keep her back by giving a tug at her collar. "Hey, remember what happened to the cat."

But Sam couldn't be kept out of the front seat for very long. Eventually, she poked her nose between the front seats and sniffed at the com. Shadbell turned and snarled at me. "Keep that wet rat off of me."

I had to remind myself that he had indirectly saved our necks back on the beach. "Sorry." This time I kept a firm grip on her collar when I dragged her back.

"What's with him?" Shandi radioed to me.

"Terminal oneriness." I kept an arm firmly around Sam.

Shadbell glanced at both of us. "Don't mind me. I've been out most of the day looking for you two."

"Didn't Dr. Kincaid tell you?" Shandi asked.

Shadbell shook his head. "Tell me what?"

I gripped the back of Shadbell's seat. "He was trying to get to shore too."

Shadbell got a worried look on his face. "We started looking for you folks when I went back on Miz Tyr's floater and found it deserted."

"You've got to turn out the Home Defense Force right away," I urged.

Shadbell draped his arm over the back of his seat. "Who do you think has been looking for all you folks?" That was a plus. At least some of the HDF was mobilized.

Shandi tried to reassure me. "They could have found your dad already. We just wouldn't know because his com is out."

"Sure." Shadbell was quick to chime in. "Him and his pet are probably sitting somewhere safe and pretty."

I got that funny tickling feeling at the back of my neck again, like there wasn't something quite right. Then I realized that while we had told Shadbell about the Xylk and the pseudo-urya, we hadn't mentioned Godzilla at all.

"How did you know about Godzilla?" Shandi voiced my question.

"I just assumed the critter was with Doc Kincaid," Shadbell ad-libbed quickly. "And I heard reports about sightings."

Shandi straightened in her seat. "I thought you said the com was dead."

Shadbell barely glanced at her. "It busted right after that."

"Well, maybe it's all right now." Shandi flipped a switch and the com lighted up.

"Hey, it works," I said, leaning forward.

Shadbell had drawn his Colt Lightning and aimed it at me all in one smooth motion. "Why don't you just turn off that com, Miz Tyr."

Too late, I realized what had been bothering me. There had been meat in that stew the Xylk cook was concocting. Not fish but red meat. And that beef had looked *fresh!* Someone had to buy it for them. And a Xylk couldn't go in and plop his credits down because he would be taken for an urya. There had to be a turncoat in the colony.

I felt like the world's biggest fool as I stared at Shadbell. "You're the Xylk's ace."

"I prefer to think of myself as an agent," Shadbell said.

"Does this mean we cancel our welcome-home parade?"

"Right. Now switch off the com, ma'am, before I do something we'll both regret." As Shandi's arm went up, the gun swung toward her. "Slowly."

With elaborate caution, Shandi flipped the switch so that the com went dead. Shadbell swung the muzzle back toward me. "Now why don't you sit forward, Piper. No, by Miz Tyr." He winked. "You make such a cute couple."

"And easier targets," I said, but I leaned forward so that I was right against the back of Shandi's seat. From what Dad had told me, there were only two parts of Shadbell that hadn't grown lazy: his eyes and his trigger finger. "Have you checked with your friends lately? I think we put a little monkey wrench into their scheme."

"Oh, you might have made things difficult, but they aren't impossible." He took his hand from the wheel for a moment.

"How can you betray your own kind?" Shandi demanded angrily.

"Do you know what the life expectancy of a constable is?" He didn't wait for us to answer. "Three years. And even if you survive, the pension is so skimpy you wind up starving." The rings hummed into life when he pressed a stud. Then he flung them at me. I caught them even as he put his hand back to the wheel. "Here. Hook yourself up to the little lady."

I thought of trying to hit his hand with the metal part of the vibrocuffs, but he seemed to read my mind. "Just behave yourself, Piper."

Reluctantly, I snapped one tingling ring over my wrist. "If you
go through with this, your name is poison in the Union."

"There are a lot of places on the Rim where the only question
they ask is how much money you have." He grinned as I snapped
the other ring over Shandi's wrist. "And, young'un, after this, I'm
going to have all the answers I need."

"Why cuff us?" Shandi asked. "Why not get rid of us now?"

"Because you're my insurance." Shadbell gave a little hop in
his seat so that the spring squeaked. "Yes, ma'am. A whole lot of
insurance."

· 20 ·

We had been heading generally south for several hours before my chronometer signaled that the decompression was safe. Shadbell could hear the sound too, and he nodded to us. "All right. You can take off the helmets."

Despite the circumstances, it was still good to unseal our helmets and breathe fresh air. I took a big deep breath. "I'm glad to smell something besides me."

Shandi grinned at me. Her sweaty hair had plastered itself against her head in wet ebony curls. "Then you shouldn't be upwind of me."

We were just getting out of our breather packs when we heard the buzzing. The three of us scanned the skies, but it was Shadbell who spotted the little dot in the air. With elaborate slowness, he lowered his Lightning so that it was near his waist. "Snuggle up, you two, and keep those cuffs low."

The dot swelled until we could see it was a skitter drifting far overhead. Then it turned a hundred and eighty degrees to make a lower pass. Shadbell kept right on driving, though he lifted his left hand from the wheel to wave at the skitter for a moment before he restored his hand to the wheel.

Only the skitter just kept pace, and I could see it was Frankie. She seemed to be saying something with exaggerated motions of her bill-like mouth.

Shadbell lifted his hand from the wheel once again and, point-ing at the com, shook his head. Then he put his hand on the wheel again to control the jeever over a hummock of red soro weed.

The skitter hovered for a moment and then drifted on fifty meters ahead and set down, sending up a fine cloud of dust and the thin, spiderly soro weed. "Don't either of you say a word," Shadbell murmured over his shoulder.

Nodding, I kept a good hold of Sam because I didn't want her getting loose and maybe making trouble.

When Frankie had raised her canopy and taken off her head-set, she called out, "Hey, Shad, Pipew, is dat the missing giwl?" She was wearing the yellow HDF sash we all did when we were on maneuvers.

Shadbell halted the jeever about three meters away. "Yep, it's them, Frankie. My com don't work or I would have told you folks."

"I thought so. A lot of folks'll be glad to hear that." She stood up and flung one leg over the side so that she was straddling the cockpit. "I'll give huh a lift in. Dey say huh daddy's waising hell. Even twied to get a linuh to turn awound. Dey's a lod of folks awound New Benua wid deah eaws chewed off long-distance."

"Then I better bring her in myself." Shadbell tried to wave her off.

"Well, she oughd do dell huh people dat she's all wighd." Frankie beckoned to Shandi.

Shadbell lowered his hand to the wheel. "Later, Frankie."

Frankie gave him a funny look but shrugged. "You de con-stable." She plopped back down in the cockpit and began to punch buttons.

Shandi gave my hand a little disappointed squeeze as Shadbell started to turn the jeever to go around the skitter. "Buy you a drink in New Benua," Shadbell called.

But Frankie had her headset on and was busy talking. We hadn't gone more than a few meters when Frankie popped back up again. She looked a little awed. "Hey, hold on. Huh daddy wands do dalk to huh."

"He can talk to her later." Shadbell kept rolling slowly along.

"Do you know how much a deep-space line cosds?" Frankie asked. I did. It would have been enough to have supported a farmer for years. Frankie pointed to her headset. "I'm nod gonna be de one do dell him he's god a wong numbuh."

Shadbell tried to pick up speed. "I'm tired of playing nursemaid to these spoiled rich folk."

"He's insisding," Frankie shouted as the distance increased. "Shad, he says id's yo' job."

Shadbell obviously didn't care much about his job anymore, but it would have made Frankie suspicious if he had just ignored her. In fact, it would have made most of New Benua curious. The word was probably out already about a call that expensive.

I kept hoping that Shadbell would do something stupid, but he knew he had to do something to throw off folks' attention. He halted the jeever with a jerk about three meters in front of the skitter. Then he twisted around to stare at us meaningfully. "You two better play along. Understand?"

Shandi nodded her head. "But you better give us the right cues."

Shadbell gave a grunt and then looked beyond us toward Frankie. "Frankie. Can you keep a secret?"

Frankie covered the mike on her headset so that any listeners wouldn't hear. "Whad's up, Shad?"

Shadbell jerked a thumb at us. "I had a spot of trouble with this pair." He whispered to us. "Stand up so she can see the cuffs."

We stood up slowly, and Frankie's eyebrows raised. "I don'd think huh daddy's going to like dat."

"They didn't want to go back." Shadbell motioned for us to sit back down and we did.

Frankie's eyes had a bright look as if she were racing to all the wrong conclusions. She gave a low chuckle. "I didn' know you had id in you, Pipuh."

"So be a pal. Cover for me," Shadbell pleaded. "I don't want her talking to her daddy till she's had time to cool off."

"I'll do what I can," Frankie promised and began speaking with a smile into her headset.

We had only managed to go some fifty meters before Frankie was calling to us again. Shadbell stopped the jeever once again. "Now what?" he yelled back to Frankie.

"Id's OK," Frankie called innocently. "He says he unduh-stands. He won'd hold anyding agains' you. He just wands do dalk do his daughder."

"Tell him what you see," Shadbell said. "She's all right."

Frankie said something into her headset and then shouted to us. "He insisds on dalking do her."

"Why does she have to play fairy godmother right now?" Shad-bell muttered. He fixed his eyes on us. "All right. Go ahead and talk to your father. But I'll have a gun on your boyfriend here." Twisting the wheel around, he turned the jeever back to the skitter where Frankie went on chattering in blithe ignorance.

"Just remember," Shadbell warned. He took a disk from his belt and set it against the cuff on Shandi's wrist. The cuff fell off, clunking against the seat back.

Shandi massaged her wrist. "Just don't do anything to Piper."

Shadbell twisted one corner of his mouth up. "So maybe my story isn't a story after all."

Shandi ignored him to look at me. "And no heroics. I'll get us out of this one way or another." I think she was figuring that no matter what happened to the colony her father's money would buy our freedom. So she still did care about me in her own way.

Shadbell brought the jeever to a halt about three meters from the skitter. Shandi jumped out of the jeever and walked over with long, graceful strides. Frankie leaned down from the cockpit. "Dey's a step cut into the side of the fuselage."

Shandi had found it in the meantime. "Thanks." She did take Frankie's proffered hand and let herself be helped into the skitter.

But as soon as Frankie had the headset draped over Shandi's

head, she went over the side. "I'll led you have some pwivacy."

"No," Shandi said in alarm. "It's all right." She tried to grab Frankie, but Frankie had dropped to the ground.

"Frankie, don't—" I began, but Frankie was already trotting over the short distance to the jeever. "Don't wowwy, Pipuh. If you kids awe sewious aboud dings, we Soltjans awe champion matchmakuhs. . . ." Her words trailed off when she saw the gun in Shadbell's hand.

Shadbell swung the Colt Lightning around from me to Frankie and fired all in one smooth motion. Frankie didn't have time to scream. She was falling backward even before we heard the roar of the gun. Before I could even start getting up from the seat, Shadbell had the Lightning trained back on me. "Take off that headset," he said up to Shandi.

Shandi slowly removed the headset and draped it over the side of the cockpit. "My father will be even more upset now." Even from here, we could hear frantic buzzing over the headset.

"We'll just have to advance the timetable a little," Shadbell said. So the invasion had to be soon. "Now get down."

Shandi rose cautiously and then climbed out of the cockpit and down the side. She skirted around Frankie. "She was only trying to be friendly."

Shadbell looked with genuine regret at the body. "Why did you make me do that?"

"We didn't pull the trigger," Shandi pointed out as she climbed back into the jeever.

Shadbell cuffed her again. "Frankie had two small kids."

Shandi regarded him coldly. "You've got a funny set of ethics. What do you think will happen during an invasion?"

Shadbell jerked the jeever into the air and swung it around. "She would have been all right. Her farm's off a ways."

"And the others?" Shandi demanded.

Shadbell said nothing. He only snapped off two quick shots that penetrated the skitter's thin skin into its fuel tanks. Flame suddenly engulfed the little scoutship as Shadbell opened the jeever to full throttle. It was almost as if he were anxious to get away from the scene.

Shadbell had turned on his com and tuned it to the upper part of the band that didn't get used much. He spoke several code words and then repeated himself another time before he added, "I've been discovered. The surprise party has to be moved up. Is everything ready?"

"Yes," the unseen person said. I recognized the accent of the Xylk.

Now seemed like the most opportune moment, when he was distracted by the com. I glanced at Shandi. She nodded. With a world at stake, our own personal problems suddenly seemed petty. At least at this one moment, there was that secret compact between us again. I just hoped it wasn't our final moment.

I let go of Sam, and Shandi and I threw ourselves at Shadbell, Shandi from the front seat, me from the back. I managed to get an arm around his big neck while Shandi fell across the arm that held the Lightning.

"Get back," chocked Shadbell. "Or I'll crash this jeever." The jeever swerved from side to side crazily as if he were ready to carry out his threat.

"Go ahead. You'll miss your invasion." As hard as I tried to squeeze, I couldn't really cut off Shadbell's air. Underneath all that fat was the muscular neck of a bull.

"It's going ahead," Shadbell gasped, "whether I'm there or not."

"Then it's going to have to happen without you." Shandi tried to twist his thick wrist so she could get his gun.

Shadbell abruptly banked the jeever sharply to the left at the same time that he ducked his head in the same direction. The result was that I lost my grip on his neck and was flung toward the side. Since we were cuffed together, I pulled Shandi back as well.

Shadbell leveled off the jeever just as abruptly, so that we lay sprawled over the jeever's seats. "Do you think you're the first two prisoners to try to attack me?" He held the Colt Lightning on us steadily.

"All right," I said, struggling to sit up so I could die with some dignity. "It was stupid. So shoot me, but leave Shandi alone."

Shadbell gave a little shake of his head. "I like cheap insurance policies, and she just raised the premiums too much." But Sam had finally gotten her bearings after being tossed all around in the jeever. With an angry chirrup, she crouched on the rear seat ready to spring.

Shadbell must have caught the motion from the corner of his eye and swung his gun toward Sam. He fired at the same time that Sam launched herself into the air.

I could smell the stink of burning fur even as Sam hit Shadbell. Dad might talk about involuntary muscle responses. I like to think it was just sheer contrariness. Sam never did what anyone wanted her to do—least of all a stranger like Shadbell. She landed right on Shadbell's face, and he let out a yell that was pure pain and terror as her upper half started to bite and claw even though the lower half of her was blown away.

And the next thing I knew, we were plowing through dirt and soro weed. Shandi and I were thrown out of the jeever and on our backs so hard we just lay there, listening to the screech of crumpling metal. A second later there was a huge explosion, and when we sat up we could see the huge fireball soaring up toward the sky.

"There won't be anything left of her." I tried my best but the tears started to come anyway. "You're going to think I'm terrible—crying over an animal and not over Frankie."

"But Sam was, uh—" Shandi tried to get to her feet but had to wait until I got up as well—"Sam was almost human."

I stared at the black oily cloud that rose into the sky from the burning wreckage. "She was a pest and a nuisance. I didn't even like her all that much."

Shandi shook her head. "I don't believe that. She was your mom's after all."

I was feeling lost and empty. "I don't know," I said finally. "It's a little like having Mom die all over again."

She rapped an exasperated knuckle against the side of my head. "I just wish that you'd get it through your thick skull that it's not your fault you're alive."

"I know, I know." I squeezed out the words, though it hurt to think about Sam. "I'm not responsible for everything like . . . like Sam's death."

She caught my chin and forced me to look at her. "Congratulations, Pipes. I think you're growing up."

"Maybe we both are. But shall we continue this conversation later?" I wiped away the tears with my free hand. "Assuming that we're both alive."

Shandi's grip became a light caress on my face before she let go, and I began to feel like the walls were really falling again. "Well, let's see that a lot of other people stay alive too." She started to tug me along.

We headed east because the colony's power plant lay just a kilometer away. The land here fell away from the mountains to the coast in gentle swells of fast-growing, shallow-rooted soro. It was easy to ride over, but it was another thing walking.

For one thing, we couldn't take off our suits because we were still cuffed together, and while the suits were fine for diving, they had never been meant for a land hike. It felt like clumping along in someone else's skin. For another thing, what looked like gentle rolling ground became a series of mounds that had to be hiked up. And then again, when you tried to go down the other side, you could slip on the soro and fall, gouging out a strip of turf and getting stung by the needlelike leaves.

After six falls, my palms were stinging from a dozen cuts, and Shandi had suffered almost as many falls and wounds. "Maybe this wasn't such a good idea after all."

She helped me up. "No, there it is." She pointed with her free hand across the red soro.

Squinting, I just made out a little bead on the horizon against the bright blue streak that was the sea. A startled hopper leaped suddenly through the soro, and I started to run after it. "Come on. We made it."

Laughing with relief, Shandi let me tug her along. "You're going to be rich. All the holos are going to bid for the rights to your life."

I led us down into a little dell so that the power plant was hidden from view. "Then I'll treat you—" I had started to say, when two Rell almost literally popped up out of the ground. Their camouflage uniforms were dusty from lying in shallow holes. Strips of soro had been attached to tarps that they had thrown back when they had jumped up.

"Maybe I was a bit premature," I said.

A half-dozen more Rell poured out of a hole in the ground. They were all camouflaged like the first two and bristling with weapons and battle gear. A Xylk officer in a turtleshell-like helmet looked out of a narrow slit in the ground.

"To keep quiet, giants," the Xylk instructed sternly. He waved his hand for us to join him.

We went through the slit to find ourselves in a kind of dugout, which had been covered with a much larger tarp over which wide strips of soro had been cleverly arranged.

"To be thoughtful to wear chains." The Xylk nodded to the cuffs.

"Oh, this," I adlibbed. "It's a love bracelet."

"Yes?" The officer turned to a Rell who leaned slightly forward under the weight of a large box strapped to his back. Since the box had an antenna, I figured it was some sort of Xylk com. The officer said something in Xylk to the com operator and then looked back at us. "To have not heard from our hireling. To see the similarity between your 'love bracelet' and his imprisonment devices."

"They're cheap," I said. This Xylk officer might have only come up to my chest, but he was as different from the guards of the Xylk base as a Union Marine was from me. I never saw the paw that hit me. All I knew was that suddenly I was flat on my back again, trying to breathe and choking on the blood that came down my throat from my nose.

"You broke his nose," Shandi said in outrage. When I tried to sit up, Shandi pushed me back down. The officer directed a Rell to cut the cuffs.

"Also to see the similarity between you and two giants we are to look out for," the officer declared in a bored voice, as if smashing a prisoner's face was part of his daily routine. "The same giants the hireling caught."

And all of a sudden it hit me what the Xylk invasion plan was— probably with information so helpfully provided by the now dead Shadbell. There were only two places with grid defenses. One was the generator, of course. The other was the spaceport. Large ships—including troop transports—couldn't land there. Any invaders would have to come in smaller ships that could be attacked by the fighters of the HDF.

But the HDF depended on the sensors at the spaceport control tower to help them intercept invaders. With the com system and sensors of the spaceport, the HDF was a capable defense force. Without them, the HDF was just a disorganized mob. No doubt they would do their best, but too many of the Xylk would still get through.

The com operator, who had been fussing over his device, said something now to the officer. The officer looked down at us grimly. "Where is the constable?" When we didn't answer, he pulled a small globe out of his belt holster. There was a tube at one end which he aimed at my foot. "To answer my question. To not answer—to have an appendage blown off. To have no more limbs—to begin on the trunk of your body."

"You'd be wasting your ammo," I said.

"To have plenty to spare." The officer had a cold, efficient look. I knew he wasn't bluffing. So did Shandi.

"He crashed," she snapped.

The officer barked an order to a Rell, who grabbed us and tied our free wrists together so we were back to back.

In the meantime, the officer opened up a pouch on one pants

leg and began to sort through sheaves of paper until he came to one set. Apparently, Shadbell's death wasn't going to make them cancel the operation, only change their plans. Then he conducted a quick briefing for his squad and they all sat down. Some closed their eyes and tried to rest, others sharpened their knives, but they all had an alert, tense look to their faces and bodies.

After about an hour, the officer stood up. He spoke a few quiet words that must have been some kind of pep talk. Then, with a nod, he marched past us out of the dugout along with the rest of his grim no-nonsense squad. I didn't doubt that they were going to make trouble for someone today.

· 21 ·

When the last Rell had marched out of the dugout, I turned to Shandi. "I hate the tourist season."

Shandi started to probe and tug at the knot around my wrists.

She muttered under her breath. "I'll give those little fellows this much: They could teach scouts something about knot tying."

Suddenly the scar-faced Rell appeared on the lip of the dugout. "To lie still." He waved his gun for us to do so.

He pulled a knife from a belt sheath and jumped into the dugout. I kicked out my legs, but he nimbly hopped to the side and flipped me over onto my back. I waited for him to plunge the knife in, but he simply cut the rope arount our wrists.

"To behave yourselves," he said and climbed out of the dugout. "The lieutenant says to come."

I got to my knees and then tried to get to my feet. They were a little wobbly from lack of circulation so that I bounced against the wall of the dugout.

The Rell immediately ran around and tapped the side of my head with his gun butt. "Not to play fool."

"Ow." I managed to straighten up. "I'm not playing. Being the fool comes natural."

The Rell just feinted with his gun and snarled to show that he meant business.

"Can it, Piper." A worried Shandi had struggled to her feet.

"These critics use guns when they review bad acts."

Together we managed to stumble onto the plain. We moved slowly at first, stumping along with awkward steps. It didn't help any that the Rell guard kept prodding us with his gun and urging us to hurry. But as the blood started flowing again in our legs, we managed to pick up the pace.

From a distance, the power plant looked intact, but as we approached it I could see that the fence was shorted out and the gate was gone. There was just some twisted, burnt metal to mark where it had been. The one-lane road wound around for half a kilometer down the slight slope to the power generator. There was a large two-story building dwarfed by the large globe of the generator itself. They looked like a child's ball and toy block dumped by the seashore—except that there were shiny sequins scattered all around.

It was only when we were by the buildings that I saw that the sparkling "sequins" were really bits of broken glass. All the windows had been shot out and the doors had been blasted in. Rell now bustled around laying charges everywhere. They didn't just want to wreck the generator. They wanted to level it. The wires were being laid out to a small oval object out on the dock. I supposed that was the detonator.

"Not to dawdle." The guard poked me with his gun for the twentieth time, and that gave me an idea.

I turned, the glass crunching under my feet. "Look, Lumpy. Touch me again and you'll be eating that gun."

I was pretty sure that the foul-tempered guard would hit me. I didn't have to fake falling on my back. Shandi gave a shout when she fell next to me. Quickly I palmed a piece of glass though the sharp edges cut into my hand. Then I got ready to get up again. So far, so good. What I didn't count on was a working over.

I caught a gun butt in the stomach that knocked all the air and any quips out of me. Then the muzzle slapped my chin. When I fell over, it wasn't acting. It was for real. I lay there for a moment while he proceeded to beat me like he was tenderizing a cheap side of beef. It felt like my sides were on fire. If the ribs hadn't been broken before, I was sure they were now.

"Stop it. Stop it," Shandi said and kicked up at the guard. The guard was going to start on her next when the lieutenant came strutting over.

"No time for games now," the lieutenant scolded him.

"To get up, dwarf," the guard growled and jerked us to our feet. Then he made us walk to the dock.

Shandi leaned in close to support me as I staggered along. The stunned techs in orange coveralls were sitting down by the dock with their hands on their heads, but my eyes locked onto one prisoner who was sitting in the front row. "Dad!"

He looked up in surprise and relief. "You're still alive." There was a whine next to him, and a green snout leaned forward. So Godzilla had made it too. He was tethered to one of the pilings that supported the dock.

I half expected a scolding for getting caught, but I guess he couldn't scold me if he hadn't done any better. "Did you get a message through?"

"No." Dad dipped his head apologetically. "Sorry."

The Rell tied our wrists together so we were back to back again.

"To rest your posteriors." The Rell prodded me along. We dropped down between Godzilla and Dad. If only there was some way to get Godzilla to attack the guard, but Godzilla would turn belligerent only when he was frightened.

"Neither did we," Shandi said.

"And they beat you." Dad could not keep the outrage from his voice.

"An occupational hazard." I shifted the glass in my hands and began awkwardly sawing at the ropes. "Shadbell was their man."

"Shad?" Dad shook his head. "Was he the one who beat you?"

"No, the Xylk did. But Shad had us for a while. Sam died helping us to get away." While I went on cutting at the ropes, I waited for the scolding.

But Dad stunned me by just shrugging. "What matters is that you're still here."

"Shad's dead, though," Shandi added.

Dad gave a grunt. "Good. Then he can't do any more damage."

In the meantime, our guard had been chatting with the guard watching the other prisoners. They didn't seem particularly worried about us. "Only I walked right into their trap."

"It must be in the genes then," Dad said. "I was on the beach when another commando squad swept me up."

"I think they're trying to short out the grid defenses." It was all I could do to keep from wincing. The glass seemed to be doing more damage to my hand than to the rope. "Then there won't be any way of coordinating a defense against their invasion fleet."

Dad nodded. "That's what I figured too. And I'd be willing to bet a general power blackout will be a signal to all those fake uryas to carry out their missions."

Was it my imagination or did the ropes seem a little looser? "From assassinations and sabotage to drawing mustaches on statues—whatever the Xylk thought was important."

The next thing we knew the subber was rising in the cove. I couldn't worry about my hands anymore. I began frantically sawing at the ropes even though the Rell commandos were running down to the dock, led by their lieutenant.

The subber eased up to the dock, and a hatch in the conning tower clanged open. They made the subber fast to the dock and a gangplank rose from the side of the subber and adjusted to the height of the dock. Then some twenty of the Xylk crew marched out in battle gear from the subber onto land. The last one was our friend the captain. He'd finally dug his way out of our little surprise for him.

I pulled at my ropes. They were definitely looser this time. I tugged at them quietly, but they needed more cutting so I set to work. The captain and the commando lieutenant spoke curtly for a moment and then the officer snapped off a quick salute with a closed paw and returned to supervise his men.

In the meantime, the captain paused on the dock, his eye

sweeping down the rows of prisoners. His eyes settled on us. "Well," he said. "To find an unexpected pleasure. To observe that you left too abruptly. Never to have finished our chat."

"You seemed a little preoccupied," Shandi said.

"True, true." The captain flicked the fly whisk at the air. "Especially since you to have inconvenienced me. To have made this a"—the captain rested the fly whisk against his lips as he hunted for the right word—" a most stimulating experience."

"We tried our best," Dad said.

"To have raised many challenges. To require my extending my gratitude to you when I have more time." His lip curled up menacingly. "To thank you at a more leisurely pace."

That gave me incentive to try and free one hand, but all I managed to do was leave some of my own personal hide on the ropes.

Dad looked down at the captain. "You don't really think you can hold this planet until an invasion fleet comes, do you?"

"To hold nothing." The captain gestured toward the sky. "To know you giants can never rebuild or replace anything before the mighty Xylk fleet comes." He brought the whisk down to point at Shandi. "To request this young lady merely to make up for some of the trouble she has caused. To have good constable land two squads of Rell at the spaceport. To now serve in his place."

Shandi glared at him defiantly. "You just want to make sure you wreck the defensive screens and the com center. I'll never help you."

"Oh, to insist." The captain drew a gun from its holster and aimed it at me. "Or to have your dear friend suffer." I yanked and twisted my hands, not caring if the captain noticed, but he was too busy playing mind games with Shandi. "To rearrange his features even more. Perhaps even to be an improvement."

Suddenly, the commando lieutenant barked something to the captain. He must have seen my shoulders were twitching when he had come back to the dock. Too late, I stopped. The captain turned. "To inquire why you are wriggling?"

"I've just got this incredible itch," I said.

The captain raised one booted foot and caught me behind the neck, knocking me forward so that I sprawled on the dock with his foot on my neck. The commando lieutenant had his gun out too.

The captain increased the pressure. "To drop the glass."

The piece of glass dropped to the dock. It felt wet—probably from my blood.

"Death to escape," the commando lieutenant said.

"To agree," the captain said. "To have annoyed me once too often. To find other means of persuasion for the female."

The two Xylk looked tall when you stared at them up from under a boot. Almost like skycrapers. And suddenly I could hear Mom again. "Use what people give you." That had always been her way. Only I wasn't sure if she would have tried it with the Xylk. "Wait," I said. "I'll take you to the spaceport. They know me there too. They won't suspect a thing."

"Piper!" Shandi sounded shocked.

"You can't mean it, son," Dad said sternly.

It cut me up inside to see that look on their faces. Still, I had to play along with it to convince the captain. I frowned at Shandi. "A dead hero is worthless."

"You'll be even worse than Shadbell," Shandi warned.

I rolled my eyes toward the captain. "She's right, you know. I'm going to need the same sort of deal you were going to give Shadbell."

"Not to be in a position to bargain." The captain sniffed.

I talked as fast as I could. "The HDF is still buzzing around. You could get shot up pretty bad without someone to alibi for you."

The captain considered that for a moment. The commando lieutenant said something quick in Xylk, and the captain nodded.

"Just switch my name for Shadbell's on whatever secret bank account you were going to give him," I coaxed.

Dad's eyes narrowed. "Don't be a fool."

"I've risked my life enough times," I declared. "I know when I'm beaten."

Dad glared at me. "You're not any son of mine."

Shandi just shook her head in disbelief. "You can't really do this. I know you."

No matter how much it pained me, I had to spread it on thick for the captain's sake. "That's easy for you to say. You've got your dad's money to take you wherever you want. This may be my only ticket away from this dump."

Shandi just turned away contemptuously—as if I were beneath words.

I think it was Shandi that decided the captain more than anything I said. "To agree." He let go of my neck so I could sit up slowly. Then the commando lieutenant took out his knife from a boot sheath and cut my ropes while the captain rattled off the terms. Poor Shadbell must have been desperate to sell out for the terms he did. Basically, it was transport to the worst hellhole of a world on the Rim with an account that had a comfortable but not astronomical amount of money.

Shandi, Dad, and the other humans kept on my case all the time that it took a Xylk sailor to take off the handcuffs and wash the blood off my face and bandage my bruised ribs, torn-up palm, and scraped wrist. Some of it got pretty abusive, but I had to take it to sell my act to the Xylk.

Finally, I got up and glanced at Shandi. She still wouldn't look at me. Dad looked ready to split. A couple of the other human prisoners actually did, and some of the nonhuman techs found novel ways to show their contempt. I ignored them all. I just started to walk away with the captain and stopped in mid-stride. "Oh, and one thing more. I'll need my pet along."

The captain gave me a suspicious look. "Why?"

I just had to pray that Singh's pseudo-urya hadn't filed any reports on my habits. "He goes most places with me. People would be suspicious." I turned around to Dad. He had this startled look on his face as if he had finally realized that I had some kind of plan.

"Don't do it," he urged. He almost forgot and said "son."

That would never do. I shrugged elaborately. "I don't care what you call me. It's no use trying to get me to change my mind."

Dad got this worried, hopeless look on his face—like he was torn between what he really wanted to say and what I was asking him to say. But he picked up on his cue and called me a few choice names that I wasn't aware he knew. Shandi looked suspicious—as if she had picked up on the change in Dad's voice but wasn't sure of the reasons.

The captain just seemed eager to be away from an unpleasant family squabble. He motioned with his fly whisk, and a Xylk sailor went over to the piling and gingerly released Godzilla.

I snapped my fingers at him. "Come on, boy." Godzilla came, trailing the line behind him.

"To have a meeting with destiny," the captain boasted.

I just hoped that destiny had more than one surprise for the captain.

· 22 ·

*T*he Rell had gotten out the power plant's large flitter with a small two-passenger compartment up front and a big boxlike structure in back that could take up to four thousand kilos. A small door—hardly more than a window—provided passage between the two sections.

Two squads of Rell commandos piled into the back while the Xylk lieutenant crouched down in the front compartment with a gun on me. Godzilla squatted on the seat next to me. His line had been fastened to a handle on the door. He sniffed at the sleeve of the tech overalls that I'd put on, and I gave him a friendly pat before I buckled my seat belt.

He stamped his feet nervously on the seat a little as I lifted off from the plant and swung the flitter toward the spaceport.

"To calm this thing down," the lieutenant hissed.

I stared down at the muzzle of his gun. "In case you haven't noticed it, I happen to be the pilot. Shoot me and we crash."

"To be capable of flying this," the lieutenant said.

"Nifty." I had been hoping that the lieutenant was strictly a groundhog and that I could bluff him, but no such luck. I took one hand from the wheel and patted Godzilla. "Easy, boy, easy." Godzilla finally squatted down but he looked paler, somehow, under all those green scales.

Still, I had other things on my mind. I figured the time to make my move was when we were on the ground at the spaceport. How was I to know that Godzilla was going to get sick—and on top of the lieutenant to boot?

The lieutenant glared up at me from underneath the tarp. "To insult not just me but all of the mighty Xylk arms."

I tried my best to keep a straight face. "I don't see what you're complaining about. You were covered by the tarp."

"To not mention pet got airsick." The lieutenant was suddenly so suspicious that he slid out from underneath the tarp. "To hear you say he travels everywhere with you. To inquire why he gets sick?" He barked an order and the window slid open behind us and a Rell commando pointed another gun at me. One hole would have killed me just as dead as two.

My mind went into overdrive while I tried to think up an excuse. "Don't blame me. Blame that cheap chow you boys fed him when he was your prisoner." Godzilla had started up when he heard the window open behind us. I made myself turn around then and try to calm him down once again. "Sit down, boy."

There was a snicker from the Rell behind me as if he had understood me and agreed. The lieutenant merely grunted. Apparently, an insult to Xylk arms was one thing; an insult to Xylk cuisine was another. He grumbled something beneath his breath and slid back lower under the protection of the tarp.

I honestly think that things would have gone along a lot simpler if I'd been able to carry out my original plan and pull my stunt when we were on solid ground. But a patrol of the HDF found us when we were fifty kilometers from the power plant.

There were three of them, so low on the horizon I thought they were birds at first, but they closed fast and began to rise when they saw me.

"This is Buzzard Boy of the HDF," the com crackled. "Identify yourself. Over."

"To be careful," the lieutenant cautioned as I reached for the com mike. It was on a long cord. Even when I had it in my hand, the cord itself was brushing my foot.

Telling them my real identity would have raised more questions than I wanted so I did what came so easily. I lied through my teeth. "This is Harvey from Carefree Power and Electricity. I'm on a supply run."

"We got reports of smoke and explosions from the plant site. Over." Buzzard Boy sounded curious.

"Just a trash fire. Some fool put in a pressurized can." I watched the fools climb on an intercept course. "No real harm."

"We got orders to investigate anyway. Over," Buzzard Boy announced.

"To turn them around," the lieutenant whispered fiercely.

"It's all right," I said urgently. "You don't have to go."

"We still got orders. Over," Buzzard Boy insisted.

The large fighter roared by in front of our bow so close that I could see the Buzzard insignia painted on the side. I was still fighting to control the flitter when the two smaller scouts whizzed by. There are all sorts of folk in the HDF, from farmers who are out to be sociable with their neighbors to folks living out their fantasies. And of all the people in the HDF, I had to meet a hotshot who thought he was a flying ace. Not only did I now have to contend with a bucking flitter but a newly sick Godzilla as well—and an enraged lieutenant.

"To get them to turn around," the lieutenant ordered.

I tried desperately to obey. "Buzzard Boy, go back."

Buzzard Boy was having too much fun playing at hero. "Since when are you in command of the HDF? Over."

The lieutenant sat up abruptly and threw back the tarp. His hand went to the com dials, and for a moment he took his eyes off me to tune in. I took a chance and put my foot on the mike cord and jerked down. The cord came loose—though I couldn't be sure if it was enough to break the connection.

He set the sending frequency to a high part of the band and then grabbed the mike from my hand. "To give me that," he said.

The lieutenant began to call out the same word over and over. I think he was trying to raise the power plant, maybe to tell them to go ahead with its demolition. When the power plant didn't answer right away, I figured that the cord really was disconnected.

"What? Who's that?" Buzzard Boy demanded. "Identify yourself or we'll shoot."

Between the trigger-happy lieutenant and Buzzard Boy, I was facing a fiery crash at the least and possibly the destruction of the entire power plant and the beginning of the Xylk campaign of terror. Everyone on this planet was bent on making this into a disaster.

Well, they had left me no choice.

It was time to unleash Godzilla.

I suppose it's funny that the fate of the entire colony depended on some hokey routine for tourists. I turned to my favorite little monster. He looked pale but functioning. "Tokyo, boy. Tokyo."

Godzilla just looked at me, puzzled because there weren't any cutouts of buildings here for him to stomp.

The lieutenant stopped sending long enough to give me a suspicious look. "Toke-ee-oh? To tell me what that is."

"It's a kind of prayer." I nodded purposefully at the lieutenant.

The lieutenant jerked his gun at me. "To pray later. To not interrupt."

Tracers licked the sky in front of the flitter. A moment later, the fighter roared by, rattling the flitter again. "That was a warning shot. The next time I won't miss," Buzzard Boy warned.

As I desperately fought the controls, I dipped my head toward the lieutenant. "Tokyo, boy, Tokyo."

A gun poked me from behind again. "To hear lieutenant," the Rell commando warned. "To not speak."

At last tired, nauseated Godzilla reared up in his seat and got into his stance. He'd finally gotten the idea, or maybe he'd just decided to fix all the blame on the lieutenant for his discomfort. The real question was whether he could do it in his condition. He flailed his paws mechanically at the air.

"To ask what he is doing," the Rell commando hissed in my ear.

I just shook my head dumbly. After all, he'd warned me not to talk. In the meantime, Godzilla gave a halfhearted stomp and whipped his tail back and forth.

"To answer, or to die." Rell repartee left something to be desired.

The lieutenant was still speaking into the mike. Godzilla got that intense, constipated look.

"This is the last warning," Buzzard Boy said.

It was a small flame, pencil-thin and only about a third of a meter long, but it splashed right on the lieutenant's gun. With a cry, he let go of the hot metal. I ducked as the Rell commando fired. The plastine windshield shattered as I swept my arm up and knocked the gun to the side.

The flitter dipped crazily as cold air suddenly rushed into the cabin. There was frantic babbling both from inside the flitter as well as from the com while the flitter dove sharply. The lieutenant smacked up against the unbroken side of the windshield, thoughtfully providing a cushion for Godzilla, who landed on top of him. At the same time, all the commandos had been tumbled against the forward wall like so many melons.

I was straining at the wheel, trying to turn the flitter's nose up, but it was like trying to lift a tub of laundry while standing in the middle of it.

The farmland below looked like the pale tan and green patches on a quilt. It seemed to reach up as if to wrap itself right around us. It was hard to think that anything so soft-looking could turn the flitter into a compact heap of junk.

I don't know whether it was a sudden updraft or brute strength or sheer luck, but finally the nose of the flitter began to tilt up, and then we were roaring along over the fields. So there was room—but barely. I think we took the tops off some corn and scared a few years out of a wandering milkaroo.

I raised the flaps and put on the front hover jet. The flitter screamed in protest at having to make the kind of stop that it was never designed for. I think it even shot a couple of rivets. Then I cut everything all together, and we dropped with a tooth-rattling jar. Crisp green cornstalks snapped with crunching sounds as if a giant grasshopper were taking a snack.

I unbuckled my belt and snatched up the lieutenant's gun from the floor of the compartment. Godzilla was sitting dazedly on top of him. "Tokyo, boy. Tokyo." And I stomped my foot in illustration. This time Godzilla got the idea sooner. He began to bounce around on the lieutenant like a cheap chiropractor while the lieutenant tried to wrestle with him and keep his flame-throwing muzzle pointed away from the lieutenant's fact.

Then I twisted around in the seat. It was my turn to poke the gun through the window into the rear compartment. "Don't move. There are three ships of the HDF ready to bomb us to ashes." The Rell in the back were still so shaken up from our little dive there wasn't much fight in them. "Hand your weapons through the window." I tried to count the heavy clunks but gave up after a dozen. I'd just have to be cautious when I got them out of the flitter.

Then, while Buzzard Boy and the other scout circled low overhead, the second scout set down cautiously in the middle of the cornfield. On the side was the red tercel of Carefree. Tercel proved to be a middle-aged woman with a drawn handgun who raised the canopy.

I opened the door. "Come on. I've got some prisoners for you."

"What's going on, Harvey?" she wanted to know as she climbed out of her flier.

"The name's Piper," I told her. "Piper Kincaid." Then I called Godzilla off the lieutenant.

He felt his ribs sourly. "To think that ribs are broken."

"You're lucky you weren't barbecued." I stepped down from the driver compartment.

"We've been looking everywhere for you," Tercel said as she came up to me.

"Yeah, I know." Godzilla came rumbling over the floor of the compartment, pleased as punch with himself. I rubbed his head. "Double rations for you when I've got them." I bent my knees and made one arm into a cradle so that Godzilla could climb on it.

Tercel must have been full of a dozen questions, but they all died in her throat when she saw the Xylk lieutenant crawl out of the compartment. Well, I guess I'd be a little surprised if I walked up to a flitter and found a miniature Godzilla and what I thought was a urya in a camouflage uniform. All she could do was scratch her head with her free hand. "You starting up a circus or something?"

I took the wrist of her gun hand and trained her weapon on the lieutenant. "I don't have time to explain. This isn't a cute, cuddly urya. It's a Xylk officer, and he and I've got a flitter full of Rell killers." I motioned for the other fliers to come down.

"Why don't you use the com?" she wondered.

Broken cornstalks crunched underfoot as I went around to the back of the flitter. "Because he's got some friends who might be monitoring it." I opened the rear doors cautiously. "We're right in the middle of an invasion."

The Rell commandos eyed me from where they were sitting. I waved my gun. "Out." As they crawled or dropped out one by one, I looked at the swath of broken cornstalks that littered the field, and that gave me an idea. "You boys wanted this planet so you might as well as do a little farming." I pointed my foot toward the cornstalks. "Toss those into the back." I called to their commanding officer. "You too, lieutenant."

"To be barbaric," the lieutenant said. "To be of warrior caste."

"Do you want Godzilla to play tag with you again?" I asked.

The lieutenant continued to grumble, but he got up and began to work with the Rell. While Tercel kept an eye on him and his men, I stuck the gun in my belt and checked out the back of the flitter, but it was empty except for a sack. Picking it up, I went into the front and dumped in the guns and left the sack in front.

By that time, Buzzard Boy had landed. He turned out to be a potbellied Simcan like M'cer, which explained a lot. His farming overalls were covered in different insignia. Of course, he was even more full of questions than Tercel had been. I shut the rear doors on my mound of green cornstalks. "I don't have time to explain. Too much is at stake, including a lot of lives. I have to get back to the power plant."

"What? The power plant?" Buzzard Boy's mind was working faster than his tongue.

I jerked my head toward the aliens. "There's my proof. Don't trust them. Just keep them here. You can call for help in . . . oh"—I did some quick figuring—"about an hour and a half. You can't use your coms before then. Their pals might be monitoring. They've wired the power plant to blow up on just a sneeze." I started to climb into the flitter.

He stopped me. "But what about you?"

"I'm going to see what I can do about disconnecting the charges." I set Godzilla on the flitter seat. He let out a protesting *fwee-eep* and tried to jump back out, but I blocked him with my body and got in.

"How?" Buzzard Boy wanted to know.

I had to laugh—maybe a little louder than I should have. "Do you think any of this has really been planned? I'll come up with something on the way—or get shot trying." I rolled down the window of the door on the passenger side.

"I just hope your luck holds out." Buzzard Boy closed the door on me.

"So do I." I rolled down that window too and then motioned him back. "Remember: an hour and a half and then come gunning." I buckled myself in.

"Wait." He had to shout to make himself heard over the flitter's air jets. "Where's—" he began; but I just took the flitter up.

I had an appointment to keep.

· 23 ·

After an hour, I began to wait anxiously for the sound of an explosion, because it was long past the time when we should have hit the spaceport. But the captain was still feeling confident. Every now and then his voice would come on the com and he would ask something in Xylk, though he never spoke for very long.

Lucky for me that the power people were so messy. I took every scrap of paper from the floor of the flying compartment and twisted them into tight cylinders while I was in flight. As I was finishing, I glanced down at Godzilla. "How did you and me get into this business anyway? Huh, boy?"

Fwee-eep. I had hoped that the cold draft from the hole in the windshield would help Godzilla, but he didn't seem any better than the first time.

I laid the rolled paper on my lap where it would be handy, along with five others, and gave him a sympathetic pat. "Being a monster isn't all it's cracked up to be, is it?"

Godzilla gave another plaintive cheep.

"Well, neither is being a monster maker." I grunted and swung the flitter out to sea.

I followed the coastline, riding about five meters above the surface. I couldn't help thinking what a nice day it would have been for a picnic on some cliff's edge with the ocean roaring below. Or maybe on some beach with bright, shining sand. Instead, I had to play hero.

When I saw the last headland between me and the power plant, I held up the paper in front of Godzilla. "Tokyo, boy."

Godzilla grew still and his eyes took on an inward look, and he obligingly lit the paper. Then I lit another paper with it before I twisted in the seat and threw the first one carefully through the window into the back of the flitter. I repeated the process until all the papers had been thrown into the back. It wasn't long before a tendril of smoke curled slowly out of the window. The tendril flattened, until long snakelike streamers of smoke were slipping out the rear compartment. As I'd hoped, green cornstalks gave off a lot of smoke. I only hoped that there would be enough ventilation for us from the door windows and the hole in the windshield.

Then I plugged in the mike cord. Turning to take a whiff of smoke, I began to cough into the mike. "Help. Had an accident in the air. Terrible explosion."

The captain came on the com. "To identify yourself. To give details."

But I just hung up the com and stuck my head out of the window. The wind roared past my ears and flung a satisfying column of smoke far behind me. The captain should be able to see it even over the headland.

I swept in low. To my relief, the globe and the offices of the power plant were still standing. I tried to take in as many details as I could. The subber still rode at the dock and the prisoners were still there, with only one guard over them.

He pointed at me and started to shout as soon as he saw me. Xylk came running from the building.

I came in low, paralleling the line of prisoners on the dock. They were staying seated. Good. The astounded guard frantically waved his arms while I bore down on him in the flitter, and then he leaped over the side into the water as I roared past.

When I was at the foot of the dock, I whirled the flitter around 90 degrees, sending smoke whipping around like tentacles. Then I set her down. Smoke filled the compartment once there wasn't any wind to stop it. I grabbed Godzilla with one hand and un-buckled myself with the other. Then, cradling Godzilla, I opened the door. I'd rehearsed this dozens of times in my mind while I'd flown up here. With the sack of guns in my free hand, I stumbled out onto the dock.

"Here," I croaked to the techs and almost doubled over coughing while I set down the sack of weapons. "I've got guns in here."

What I hadn't planned on was their reaction. The techs just stared. Well, they weren't really Carefreeans. Most of them were under contract, would serve their time, and then go back to those anthills that were the core worlds. "Go to the sack. Fight," I said.

I started to run toward the detonator near the subber. One of the Xylk finally realized what was going on. His shot went to my left. I turned and yanked out my gun so I could snap off a wild shot. "Come on and fight."

That seemed to break the spell. The nearest techs scrambled for the sack, and the others followed their lead. I didn't expect them to kill any Xylk, just pin them down for a while.

I dropped to my knees and skidded to a halt, scraping off a good deal of personal skin in the process. Hurriedly I set Godzilla down and undid the screw and twisted off a wire. They couldn't blow up the plant now. I gave a sigh of relief; then for good measure I chucked the detonator over the side. It gave a satisfying splash as it fell into the water, taking the other wire with it.

The fire fight had gotten pretty crazy, with the techs on their stomachs shooting at the Xylk and the Xylk firing back as they retreated toward the plant. The only trouble was that I didn't see Dad or Shandi. Godzilla stumbled along behind me as I crawled over to the nearest tech. She was a Tumbler, with a fine red feather announcing her avian ancestry.

"Where's my father?" I asked her.

She twirled her neck a full 180 degrees and nodded toward the offices. "They took them inside for questioning." She stopped firing to watch as I banged my head a couple of times against the planks of the dock. "Why are you doing that?"

"That's what I get for making too many assumptions. I should have come in slow and made sure." I looked at the flitter. Despite holes through the rear compartment, it still looked as if it would run. I nodded toward Godzilla. "Take care of him, will you?"

"I suppose so." She eyed Godzilla doubtfully.

I got to my feet but crouched low. "Stay here, boy," I said to him, and then sprinted toward the flitter. I heard him give a mournful cheep, but a glance over my shoulder told me that the tech had grabbed his tail so he couldn't follow.

Then I was back in the flitter cab. I heard an urgent Xylk shout, and the flitter shuddered under the impact of a dozen explosions. Somehow, though, it lurched into the air. If Aerospace Ford ever wants a testimonial, they've got one from me. I did not try to raise it very high, only a meter or so. That was just enough to let me turn and send the flitter lurching clumsily toward the offices. The Xylk were so busy with me they neglected the techs—and paid for it.

The windshield melted into globs of plastine, and bits of molten metal flew in the air as the flitter floated toward the offices. When I was five meters away, I got out. I didn't open the door; there wasn't any door to open—only a metal section that had fused into the frame. I just went through the hole head first, tumbled, and then rolled as the nose of the flitter ground with a screech into the pavement.

Then it was a very undignified leap into the doorway. Pieces of burnt concrete pelted me as I went through the open door. I was up and running the next moment, checking out the offices on the lower floor. In one of them, a Xylk looked up from a desk. He was still reaching for his gun when I shot him.

I found Dad and Shandi tied up in the director's offices on the first floor. The captain was lounging in the director's big overstuffed chair. He looked like somebody's toy dog that had been set there.

"To notice that I do not take chances," the captain observed and gestured to the squad of soldiers surrounding Dad and Shandi.

Another squad of soldiers came up to the doorway through which I had just come.

"To be surrounded," the captain said. "To throw down your gun."

I stood there, sweating and thinking, knowing that Dad and Shandi were expecting me to pull another rabbit out of the hat. And I couldn't come up with any kind of solution. Not one blessed thing. My luck had just run out. So had my ideas for improvising.

I dropped the gun in disgust. "It's over, you know," I said to the captain. "Your commandos are prisoners and the HDF is coming."

The captain rocked back in his chair as if he didn't have a care in the world. "To reconnect wires." I suppose he had seen me from the office window. "To blow up plant."

"The techs have guns," I pointed out.

He simply drew his teeth back in that horrible grin of his. "To wait till their ammunition is exhausted."

Even as I listened, I could hear the firing slackening. I glanced out one of the windows and saw the techs putting up their hands to surrender again. The Xylk were ordering them forward. I suppose they had carried spare ammo for their guns. The only encouraging thing was that Godzilla stayed where he was instead of following the tech with whom I'd left him.

The captain rested his fly whisk against his shoulder. "To give up?"

"Like hell." I glanced at Dad and Shandi, but they could only shrug helplessly. Then I looked at all those gun muzzles and knew I was licked.

"To be sensible," the captain urged.

All right. So I wasn't a world-saver. But I might be able to narrow things down and focus on two people. I could still save Dad and Shandi because I still had one thing left to bargain with: my life.

I kept the gun steady on the captain. "Promise me you'll treat

Dad and Shandi like regular prisoners. No special prison sentences. And *no* torture."

He seemed amused. "To inquire why I should promise you anything?"

"Because I'll shoot you," I explained sweetly.

The captain indicated Dad and Shandi. "To know they would then die and so would you?"

"They'd still be better off," I said. "And I suspect so would I."

"To point out that I"—the captain slapped the whisk against his chest—"would not be."

"No plan is perfect." I jabbed the gun at him. "So what will it be?"

The captain hesitated. "I cannot let *you* off so lightly."

I swallowed. "Then don't. You can do what you want with me as long as you take it easy on Dad and Shandi."

"Don't be a fool!" Shandi blurted out.

I could see Shandi's disapproving frown even as the captain brandished his whisk grandly. "To feel magnanimous in my moment of triumph. To agree. To—"

Anything else he was going to say was drowned out by the noise of the jets. The ships came so low that the roar was almost like some giant invisible animal pouncing on the plant. Then they were past and the windows were rattling and even breaking and there were five thunderclaps as they went faster than sound. Outside, whirlwinds blustered and I recognized the sound of large transports hovering: a lot of them.

The captain stood up and went to the window, though his guards were disciplined enough to keep their guns on me. Tucking my hands into the pockets of my shorts, I took a chance and strolled over to the window next to him.

There were about a half-dozen large hovers settling into the powerplant yard. I recognized the New Benua ferry, and one of them had the Xanadu Arms resort symbol—whatever the HDF could commandeer. From out of the hovers jumped a hooting, whooping militia. And the loudest and fiercest was M'cer with his security guards—they'd been drafted into the operation, I guess.

Some of the HDF were in fatigues and sashes as if they had been involved in the search for Shandi, but others were in civilian clothes and without sashes. I'd swear one fellow was in a bathrobe; he hadn't wanted to miss out on the fun.

Overhead were a dozen fighters and armed scoutships, and coming in for another pass far overhead were five more. I saw the familiar red tercel on the side of one and the buzzard on the other and found myself waving at them.

As I found out later, they had sent one of the farmer's sons in by tractor to New Benua like a modern-day Paul Bunyan—make that Paul Revere—to spread the word without using coms. At any rate, when Buzzard Boy and Red Tercel set out to join me, they brought along part of the HDF. Buzzard Boy might be a stickler for the rules, but he had a head on his shoulders.

Already, the Xylk in the yard were throwing away their guns as if the metal had just caught fire. Xylk are smart—too smart to tackle long odds like that and too smart to be suicidal.

I jerked a thumb toward the window. "You boys might as well give up." I shouted to make myself heard. "It's our HDF." A guard near me craned his neck to see and then looked at the others.

Shandi held out her hand to the nearest guard. "I'll take that."

He hesitated and passed over his gun, and then it was as if the Xylk couldn't get rid of their guns fast enough. They piled them in Dad and Shandi's arms and all over the desk.

"I'd give you a hug," I said to them, "But I'm not used to embracing walking arsenals."

"If you don't mind"—she puffed—"I'd rather have a hand than a hug."

I raised my hands so she couldn't give me anything. "You were awful quick to think I was going to turn traitor."

She dumped her load onto the desk and gave me a guilty glance. "How could I know that acting was among your many talents?"

I pressed my fingertips against my chest. "Well, you should have known my sterling character."

Shandi picked up a gun. An apologetic smile flickered across her face, disappeared, and then came back again. "My dear, do you expect me to trust anyone who would be seen with me?"

Dad piled his guns on top of the rest. "I hate to interrupt this fascinating discussion, but where's the captain?"

Shandi looked around the milling Xylk. "He was here a moment ago."

I motioned for the Xylk to back up against one wall. I didn't see the captain either. "But where is he? He can't get away and he can't blow up the plant."

Shandi nodded in the direction of the power plant. "He can still turn off the power."

"But it won't do any good," I protested. "It would just be temporary. We'd turn it back long before the invasion fleet got here."

Shandi started for the doorway. "He could still set off a wave of assassinations and sabotage. He'll want to leave us a real memento to remember him by."

Dad grabbed up a gun and started after Shandi, but I stopped him. "Hey, someone's got to wait until the HDF get here."

He seemed about to argue, but then his face broke into a tired grin. "Well, I guess you've done all right so far." He gave me a shove toward the door.

I stared at Dad for a moment with a lump in my throat. I think it was the first real compliment I can remember.

"Go on," he snapped and turned to watch the prisoners. "Git."

So I went ahead and got.

· 24 ·

When Shandi heard my footsteps in the corridor, she crouched and swung around with her gun. I thrust my hands, weapon and all, into the air, "It's me. We didn't finish our conversation, remember?"

She straightened. "It won't do any good. I still don't know if I trust you, Pipes."

I risked lowering my hands. "You're a fine one to talk about trust. You thought I was a traitor."

For once, Shandi couldn't come up with a quick answer. "I'm not proud of it," she finally confessed.

I wasn't about to let her off easy now that I had her. "How come you get to make mistakes and I don't?"

She pivoted thoughtfully. "I've paid for my mistakes."

"And I haven't? Do you realize that in the past two days I have been nearly shot, drowned, maimed, blown up, and buried?" I slapped a hand against my leg in exasperation and winced as I hit a bruise. "And I'm covered with contusions, cuts, and assorted injuries."

She gave me an amused look over her shoulder. "Any fool can go to a holo and then go dancing."

I trotted after her down the corridor. "And we aren't just any fools, are we?"

Her mouth worked for a moment as she tried to hold back a low laugh—and failed. "We certainly aren't." I took her laughter as the best sign of all.

I grunted. "Are all your dates like this?"

She glanced at me from the corners of her eyes. "No, some of them are fun."

I wasn't going to let a small point like that discourage me. "This is nothing. On Saturday night, I jump into volcanoes."

She cradled the gun in her arms as we came to a corner. "That's one thing I've never tried." Her defensive wall was finally tumbling down.

"Interested?" I asked as we paused.

"Back me up first," she whispered.

I nodded my head and got ready with my gun. Shandi jumped around the corner, legs braced, feet spread apart for balance, but when there wasn't any bushwhacker lurking there, she waved me to come on. I stepped around the corner to find we were fronting a hallway of offices.

"Well, I do have to admit you grow on a girl." Shandi pointed to the right. We could both feel a silent communication between us now.

Nodding my head, I began to check the offices on the right while Shandi looked into the rooms on the left. The rooms seemed empty. The lights were still on and the cups of stim were undrunk. Papers lay scattered over the floor from the initial Xylk attack. "How do I grow on someone?" I called from one office. "Like a fungus?"

"Honestly." She shook her head elaborately as she came out of one office. "I've spent all this time on you, and you still can't take a compliment."

I lingered in a doorway long enough to point out, "And I've saved your life twice and you still don't trust me."

"I caught you at Xanadu," she said, popping into another room.

"The guards did that with a net." I gave a quick inspection to the last office on the right and then stepped out into the hallway again.

She was skidding to a halt by a door that led out of the hallway.

"But I gave them their orders. Let's give credit where credit is due."

I joined her by the doorway. "You only need a loud voice for that, not brains."

She leaned her free hand against the doorway, blocking my way. Even now, she had to feel she was in control, but there was a playful, almost Sam-ish arch to her eyebrows. "And what do you use?" she asked. "You don't have either."

"I'm stubborn. So are you, That's how we got stuck with saving a world." Impulsively, I bent forward.

Her free arm slid around me, and I felt her lips work against mine. Then she pulled her head back and sighed reluctantly. "I guess we're still not finished."

I cocked my head to the side. "That's the problem with this business. There's no way to resign. There isn't even a decent medical plan."

"I wasn't talking about being heroes. I was talking about us." She slapped me lightly on the forehead as if I were a misbehaving puppy.

I put a hand protectively over my face. "So was I."

"You'll pay for that." She poked me in the stomach. "That's on account." Then, wrenching the door open, she went through.

I backed through the door, keeping an eye on the hallway behind us for unpleasant surprises. When the door shut behind me, I turned around. Shandi motioned me to be quiet.

We were standing among a lot of pipes and banks of instruments and dials and flashing lights. The techs could have told you what was what, but I couldn't. However, I did recognize Xylk explosives when I saw them.

We both took a minute to survey the surroundings for the captain, but there wasn't any sign of him so I nudged her and she nodded. While she covered me, I began to pick up blocks of explosives. A female Dz'isu suddenly came around from behind a large computer. She wore nothing but her own scaled skin and a yellow HDF sash with the thin blue diagonal slash of a corporal. Usually the reptilian Dz'isu stayed down in the broiling temperatures down at the equator, so she was shivering as she moved along slowly. Her gun was strapped over her shoulder and she had a pile of explosives underneath one arm as if they were common bricks. She halted when she saw us. "What are you kids doing here?" she asked in a loud voice.

Shandi kept looking around. "There's a Xylk officer in here someplace."

Three techs in orange overalls followed her into our section of the plant. One of them, a man, came over with a plastic basket and immediately relieved me of my burden. "Here. Let me take that."

The corporal looked around disinterestedly as if she were looking for a stray cockroach. "The only thing I've seen has been the weirdest green lizard you ever saw."

I stooped to indicate Godzilla's height. "Is he so high?"

The corporal also dumped her load of explosives into the tech's basket. "Yeah, is he a friend of yours?"

"He's more like a little brother." I holstered my gun. "Where is he?"

She pointed toward the center of the plant. "I left him back there feeding on some rations."

Rations were usually bars of fish protein concentrate, something at which Godzilla normally turned up his nose. "He must be hungry."

The corporal lounged against the computer. "Well, your Xylk is bound to turn up. There's a whole platoon in here. Not to mention techs." That was the reason the Xylk captain hadn't come in here shooting.

My Tumbler acquaintance tech came over and brusquely gave the corporal a shove. "That's not a piece of furniture. This is the main computer, you know."

The corporal turned. "This antique? We've got newer ones in my company's warehouse."

The tech checked over the panel intently. "It's not like the power company spent a lot of money modernizing this place."

The other pair of techs had been checking a set of large pipes about a meter in diameter. They suddenly stood straight up, as if they were marionettes and a puppeteer had just pulled their strings, and backed away hastily as our friend the captain emerged from hiding. He was covered from head to toe in grease. "To thank you for that information. To be unsure before." He took us all in with a glance. "To drop your weapons."

The corporal and I dropped our weapons to the floor. Shandi was the last to do so. "You might as well give up, you know. It's useless."

"To insist on the contrary." The captain swung his gun back toward the tech with the basket. "To put that down gently on the floor."

Even as the tech carefully obeyed, Shandi started to reach for her gun, but the captain fired a warning shot at her feet. The square tiles shattered. "Not to try that again," he warned and ordered us to kick the guns into the center of the room. When we had reluctantly done so, he motioned the corporal and the techs across the room over to us.

Then, shoving the basket along with his foot, the captain warily crossed the floor toward the main computer. I kept looking for another of the HDF to appear, but apparently they hadn't heard the captain.

The captain slipped the fly whisk from his belt where he had tucked it originally and flicked it at us almost as if he were blessing us. "To be most resourceful opponents. To have fought well. To be no great shame to lose to the High Destiny of the Xylk." He turned to use the gun hidden in the fly whisk.

There was about ten meter's space between us and the captain. I stooped immediately and snagged one of the broken tiles from the floor. Like I said before, my main occupation as a kid had been skipping stones across the water. I'd have to see what I could do with the tile. With a hard flick of my wrist, I sent it spinning at the captain. The next moment I was running after it, and Shandi was right by my side.

I hoped to hit the captain's fly whisk, but either I was out of practice or the broken tile had strange ballistic characteristics because the tile hit the captain in the shin. With a yelp, he went down, but it didn't do us any good because he sat up right away. With a sinking feeling, I knew that Shandi and I would never be able to reach him before he fired.

Suddenly a familiar snout poked around one side of the main computer. It was Godzilla. He must have heard my voice and come to look for me. Crumbs of FPC dusted the corners of his mouth.

I pointed at the captain and yelled, "Tokyo, boy!"

Seen from above, Godzilla is a curiosity, but seen face to face, you can study the original's menacing features—sort of like a mashed-in ape face with green scales. It's a little disconcerting even when you're used to it like I am, but it can be downright frightening if you're a stranger like the captain. And the captain was practically snout to snout with Godzilla.

If the captain had swung his fly whisk and shot Godzilla, he might have had a chance, but instead the captain instinctively drew back with a shout. Whether he heard my command or was simply frightened, Godzilla screwed up his face into that blessed constipated look and opened his mouth. The sharp fangs showed. The captain finally twisted his fly whisk around and aimed the hidden gun at Godzilla, but it was too late.

A pencil-thin wisp of flame leaped from Godzilla's mouth. As fiery breaths went, it wasn't much, but then Godzilla didn't have much time to stoke up a showstopper. And what he did send out was good enough. The flame ignited the hairs at the end of the captain's whisk.

Fire instantly swept up the entire whisk, but I'll give the Xylk captain this much: he was a determined man. Twisting around desperately, he raised the whisk to fling it into the basket of explosives.

"No." I started to run toward him even though I knew I would be too late.

The next moment Shandi had shot him. While I was starting a noble but hopeless charge, she threw herself at one of the guns we had kicked into the center of the room, picked it up, and fired.

I walked over to her and offered her a hand. "One of these days you're going to miss."

"Then I'll get glasses." She took my hand and let me pull her to her feet.

I went over to the computer and squatted down by Godzilla. "Come on, boy," I said as I picked him up. "It's time to go home."

·25·

So that's what set up the battle of Carefree. I won't go into the details because it was on all the holo services afterward. Besides, I didn't take part in it. I was simply a spectator cheering from the sidelines while the home team kicked the pants off the visitors.

I heard the Stellar Union is now going after the Xylk hammer and tongs with official letters of protest and every five-syllable word in the dictionary. Xylkdom may never recover from the avalanche of paper.

Singh recovered and is back helping Dad. Now that Mr. Tyr is backing Dad with megacredits, Dad is making noise about sending me back to the Core worlds to go to his old alma mater for some advanced schooling, but Mr. Tyr thinks that a prospective son-in-law should go straight into his company and learn the ropes. Fortunately, *my* future is about the only thing the two of them disagree on.

Myself, I'd like to see a little of the galaxy first, so I'm inclined to adopt a false name and sign up with one of Mr. Tyr's exploring teams once the kits grow up.

Oh, I meant to tell you. Dad dug out Mom's old designs for Sam and created a pair of kits—Sam Junior and Tertius. Right now they're as cute as the devil and just as contrary, so Dad must have done something right.

At any rate, Shandi says that the kits and I are too dangerous to unleash on the rest of the galaxy, and she's threatening to go along as our keeper.

We'll see.